Cleansed:
How to Sanitize a School
Louis Edwards

Copyright © 2022 Louis Edwards

All rights reserved. No part of this book may be reproduced or transmitted in any form or by any means, electronic or mechanical, including photocopying, recording or by any information storage and retrieval system without permission in writing from the publisher.

Expecting Excellence Press—Cranfrod, NJ
ISBN: 979-8-218-04982-9
Library of Congress Control Number: pending
Title: *Cleansed: How to Sanitize a School*
Author: Louis Edwards
Digital distribution | 2022
Paperback | 2022

This is a work of fiction. The characters, names, incidents, places, and dialogue are products of the author's imagination, and are not to be construed as real.

Dedication

To all the professionals who work in schools that come to work every day to teach and nurture the children. These folks never forget that it's always "all about the kids."

Chapter One
Goodbye Mr. Peoples

It wasn't easy. I held the principal of my school, Mr. Leroy Peoples, around the neck and I was squeezing the life out of him. Peoples thrashed about. He was hard to hold. He foamed at the mouth. Peoples gasped, and he gasped until he gasped no more. It wasn't pretty.

I knew his routine. I laid in wait for him and jumped him from behind as he was leaving the school. When I had a hold of him, it seemed like one of those mechanical bull rides that you see in an old honky-tonk or perhaps in a boardwalk amusement arcade. I was a bit surprised the old geezer had that much strength left in him. It equally surprised me he was pulling me off of the ground.

It was a Friday, and I was glad that we were alone in the building. No one could hear his squeals and yelps. No one could hear us bouncing about the room against the walls and the equipment stored there. I chose this location because Peoples always walked out of my boiler room door to his car. He never changed. Probably for the past twenty years, he exited out of this same door. I knew the lay of the land. This was my home. There was no reason for me to be uncomfortable there. I never dreamed this engagement would throw us around so violently. I never dreamed it would take this long. It was almost like we were engaged in some violent, well-choreographed dance. Let me assure you, we were not dancing. He was fighting for his life and, in a way; I was also fighting for my life. No way we were both walking out of here. And I was younger and stronger. I would not lose.

The lights seemed to flash like some sort of laser light show that you might see in Disney World. I think I was getting light-headed from the fight. I could feel the life draining from Peoples. His fight was leaving him. I almost cut his tongue in half from his uncontrolled biting and gnashing of his teeth. Blood was leaking from his mouth. The blood flow seemed like a river, not some leak.

The whites of his eyes looked red and also looked as though they might soon pop from his head. I know that this could be my imagination talking, but in the heat of the moment, that is what it seemed.

As I held on to my own handmade garrote, that I made of a length of shade cord and a sawn-off broom handle, I relaxed a bit. I knew I was over the hump when I smelled the remains of his bowels and bladder, leave his body and enter his pants. It was an odd smell as it mixed with the stale air of spoiled milk and a heavy layer of dust. No matter what I did, my room always smelled of stale milk. The boiler room was next to the student cafeteria, and little kids were always spilling milk. I think that somehow, the stale milk embedded in the the tiles. No matter how much I cleaned, I could not get that smell out. And now this smell mixed with the smell of death.

That unique smell heightened my senses. I thought I could smell things that I never smelled before. I could see things that I never saw before and I could literally hear a pin drop across the room. My skin seemed to crawl. Maybe I had some sort of "spider sense," just like Spiderman. Who knows?

In the movies, it is always quick and clean. It is not. If James Bond killed Mr. Leroy Peoples, I am sure that he would sip a martini right now as he adjusted his bow tie of his tuxedo with two beauties by his side. I stopped to look at the large old school clock on the wall and the entire episode almost took ten minutes. These ten minutes felt like an eternity. I am sure for Peoples these minutes felt much longer. He suffered. It was not a pain-free way to go. Although I do not know what is a good way to go, I can tell you that strangulation is a method of death to avoid. However, dead is dead, no matter how you go.

I laid slumped in my chair panting and bruised. My arms were sore. My back hurt. The room was a mess. I saw nothing broken, but I surely saw nothing that was in its right place. I had to gather myself and figure out what to do next. I really never planned this far ahead.

As I sat there and thought, I chuckled. Mr. Peoples would ride me mercilessly about the shades in the building. He required all the shades to be at one level before I could leave the building. His fixation with the shades made him obsess. There were times he called me back into work to correct the shades after I was already home for the night. Although the school looked better with his requirement; he took it to the next level. Now, he died by the shades that, as a principal, he worried so much about. Mr. Peoples couldn't give a damn if the kids learned. He felt no need to support the teachers. The shades always had to be right.

Chapter Two
The story begins

I did not just wake up one day and decide to kill Mr. Peoples. It was a long time coming. It was not the first time that I killed someone. Although one can never perfect that skill, I got my share of practice in Vietnam. It was never funny that no one ever called it a war, but for us sent there, it was a day-to-day battle to stay alive. I did what I had to do to survive. When my squad needed a dirty job to get done, it usually fell to me. And I was OK with that. We will talk about that more a bit later. For now, let's get back to Mr. Peoples.

Peoples was a no-good SOB. For that, I am sure. I watched him long enough to humiliate both staff and students alike. After I returned from Nam, I settled into this school district as a janitor. I thought it would be a temporary job, maybe for a month or two, but it lasted a lifetime.

Mr. Leroy Peoples was a terrorist. He terrorized everyone in the school. Maybe that is how principals operated in the old days. But time had caught up with Peoples. The world just passed him by.

Chapter Three
Meet the one and only Mr. Peoples

I should probably change that heading because sadly there are many Mr. Peoples. Mr. Peoples was nothing more than a racist bigot and for him to be in a leadership position in a school was a sin. He should have been molding our kids into fine citizens. Instead, he was destroying more kids than I could count.

Peoples was a stiff old white guy who rarely, if ever, smiled. I do not know who was more afraid of him, the teachers or the kids. I think educators back in the 50s and 60s became principals because they put their time in and they were white males. Maybe he was just the last guy left in the room when the jobs were being handed out. He fit all the criteria needed to be a principal.

I worked in a white school that woke up one day and had busloads of black kids dumped into it because of forced desegregation. They prepared no one for this. All the kids, both black and white, had a hard time handling it. The teachers also had difficulty accepting this change. Although I have to say that most of them were sincerely trying to embrace this change that the world had forced upon them. I believed in my heart that most of the teachers really loved the students, no matter what color they were. You remember that for some people in this school; it was the first time that they had seen black people up close and personal. The kids accepted each other unless their parents' racism reared its ugly head, which at times, it did.

Probably the person who had the most difficulty accepting this change was Mr. Peoples. He was the oldest and whitest. I used to think about him all dressed up in his Klan costume. He would have looked good in our Halloween parade and it would not have surprised any of the parental spectators at this event, seeing him lead the parade of costumed youngsters proudly sporting his white robe and pointy hat. Instead of being outraged, they would have smiled and waved at him.

I learned early in my life how to melt into the walls. I learned this in my home and mastered it in the U.S. Army. It was a wonderful skill to possess. I heard the kids talk, and I heard the teachers talk. Some adults could not help themselves as they told racist jokes, thinking no one heard them. Most times, I was just able to let this talk run off of my back. I could not let it go when I heard the kids talk that way. I would talk to the kids about it and how it made me feel, and I think they got it. Most kids liked me very much. I especially tried to steer the black kids in the right direction. The only black person in the school was me. I could not let them down.

I would also, nightly, take down any racist cartoons pasted on the faculty lounge bulletin board. Did the people who posted it or laughed at it think I did not see it? And how could these same people to my face treat me as a friend? They just did not care.

I got through my day by "yes siring" and "no siring" Mr. Peoples. I thought many times, he wanted me to do a quick tap dance for him. He probably would have liked it. I played his game and kissed his white ass regularly. I survived, but it just made me sick. I really hurt for the teachers that were trying to make it right. The other teachers could rot in hell with Peoples.

Peoples also thought that I was his indentured servant. Maybe he just thought I was his slave back on the plantation? He regularly charged me with doing his personal errands, like picking up his cleaning, or running to the drugstore. He even charged me with doing errands at his house. I had to rake his leaves and shovel his snow. I really did not care because it was all done on school time. He especially liked it when I cleaned and polished his car.

One day, something just snapped inside my head. From now on, my mission would be to torture Peoples. I was going to have some fun with this old bastard. At night, I would think of ways to antagonize him. Making him crack up and hopefully retire was now my goal. It became my mission. I WANTED TO LIBERATE THE SCHOOL. I HAD TO LIBERATE THIS SCHOOL!

I hid his stuff. I hid his favorite pen. It was a gift to him from the board of education for 25 years of service in the district. He treated it like the Medal of Honor. I hid his stapler. I hid one of his rain boots. You name it, and the more he liked it, the more apt I was to hide it. I would let it stay missing for several days or weeks. Then, somehow, I would miraculously find it. I found this little game hilarious. I fondly remember stealing his budget preparation book prior to a big district board meeting. He got his ass chewed out by the superintendent and looked like a fool in public for his lack of preparation. I was loving every minute.

Every time I worked in his car; I did a little something to it. I let air out of a tire; I put some water in the gas tank or I hid some rotting trash under his back seat. He could never figure out what smelled. I spent more time in the car pretending I was trying to solve his problems, but in fact, each time I was adding to them. I was enjoying the laugh until one day when some lunch money went missing from a teacher's classroom.

Chapter Four
The straw that broke the camel's back

We have all heard that expression before. It fits here. I was slowly driving Peoples crazy and really was not looking to escalate my little game. I was patient. I could wait him out. He had to retire soon. Until the missing money occurred. One teacher alleged that someone stole the milk money from her pocketbook.

Peoples assembled every black boy in the school in the auditorium. Please remember that these kids were between seven and eleven years old. I stood in the back, effectively leaning on my broom. Mr. Leroy Peoples knew I was there. He nodded his head at me when he arrived. He had something to say to these kids and did not care who heard it. There were also several teachers present in the auditorium.

It did not take him long to get all worked up. I will tell you exactly what he said and I apologize for using his language. He told these youngsters that, "all you niggers ruined the school and that made him sick and tired." He continued by stating that, "this school was the best until the niggers arrived and it would never be the same." Yes, he ranted and raved. I stood there in shock. I looked at the teachers, who were also standing at attention with a horrified look on their faces. The kids just sat there wide eyed and afraid. He made each student walk up onto the stage one by one, where he emptied each kid's pockets and he patted each one down. It was humiliating. The action disgusted me, but I was more disgusted that I just stood there in disbelief. He found no money. I knew he never would. No kid stole the money. I could almost guarantee that. And let's not forget that we are not talking about a million dollars here. The amount really was nothing more than chicken feed. I could have dug into my pocket and replaced the money. But I did not. I just stood there.

I am sure you have figured out the end of the story by now. Later that day, the teacher found the money in a back pocket of her briefcase. She had merely forgotten where she placed it. It turns out that the previous night she was grading papers and reorganized her bag. She was embarrassed and sorry. If she only knew what her forgetfulness caused. I knew it was an unintentional accident but Peoples had the staff so intimidated and afraid of him. I think she worried about losing her job over these few dollars. Why didn't she just replace the cash from her own pocket? She was embarrassed and left Peoples' office crying. I was outside of his office while he berated her. It was a sin. I felt bad for her.

But who felt bad for all the boys that he had abused? No one was crying for them. For them, it was just another lesson in life of being black in America. Every black man and woman in America have experienced this type of humiliation.

For me, as I lay in bed that night, I knew what I had to do. The humiliation in this district had to stop. It was up to me to do something about it. And I did. And I did it with no regrets. Sorry, maybe my one regret was not doing this long ago.

Now Mr. Leroy Peoples was no more. However, he now laid in front of me, lifeless, eyes bulging, blood coming from his mouth and the stench of his body waste mixing with the sour milk.

Now what?

Chapter Five
Adios, you bigoted bastard

I knew I had to gather myself. The adrenaline rush in my body was leaving. It was always the same feeling for me when I had to act. The feeling was both bad and good at the same time. I know that sounds crazy, but for me that is the best way I can describe my insides after an event such as this.

He could not stay here. That was for sure.

But first, believe it or not, I was hungry. I knew no one would be in the building, but I cleaned up a bit. For the time being, I stuffed Peoples in an old garbage barrel and I mopped up the floor with the standard institutional cleaner. My room now smelled fresh as a pine forest. That institutional pine scent smelled awful. It would mask the smell of anything, but many times that pine smell was worse than what you were trying to hide. That distinct odor has never changed.

The local bar is where I went to eat and think. I really enjoyed my meal. I ate in silence by myself, but inside I was beaming with pride. One of the worst men I had ever known was gone. If he had a past life, I am sure he would have been some cruel plantation slave master. That was Peoples. He would abuse no one anymore. Not kids, white or black, and not the teachers for sure. Although his body still lay in a trash barrel in my office, his spirit evaporated.

As I sat there, I thought about how a man like that could ever become a teacher. Peoples had so much hate in his heart. He was just an angry man. He was a non-biased hater. Mr. Peoples just hated everybody and everything.

As my content feeling went away, I thought about how many other people in my school or in my district were just like him. I think they just liked the power that being a teacher brought them. Yes, power, believe it or not. These folks had to feel important and when they stood in front of a room with twenty-five kids, they could become king of the kiddies. I saw them scream and yell at the kids from the moment they arrived until they left in the afternoon. They ruled by threats and intimidation. When kids cried, their gratification skyrocketed. They were non-discriminatory bullies. They verbally and some physically just beat up on kids. I like to think in my heart that the many excellent teachers that worked hard for the kids outnumbered these teacher bullies. It is a sin that this bullying vocal minority leaves a lasting impression that far outlasts the impression left by all the excellent teachers that worked in my building.

Maybe the way to improve our school would be to get rid of all the adults and start all over. Who knows?

No doubt about it, I changed that day. I would not sit idly by again. I would really clean the school. I would really sanitize it and I meant it.

Chapter Six
Up in smoke

Murder is easy. Getting away with it is hard. I remember hearing that line one night from an old black and white movie as I lay sleepless on my bed, alone with my thoughts.

Now I had to reach back to all of those sleepless nights and come up with a manner to dispose of the body. I guess perhaps if there was no body, there could be no crime. I had the perfect solution.

Back in the day, all schools had incinerators attached to the school furnace. The school had a very tall chimney and anything that could burn would mix with the waste of the furnace and float away. We burned everything. There was no recycling and there were no rules about garbage removal.

Peoples would join that smoke that floated away on that evening. It was a nice, breezy night. Yes, he would burn here, just like his soul would burn in hell. I knew that, for sure.

There was one minor problem. He did not fit in the incinerator's door. I had visions of having to chop him up. Not a pleasant thought, but I would do it if I had to.

I was minimally concerned with being caught in the act. My car was at the building all hours of the day and night and if the police did a drive through check, they would not sense that something was off. I made sure that by double locking the doors, no one would disturb me. Although many people had the key to the bottom lock of the door, no one had the key to the old top deadbolt. I made sure that was on. Also, it is important for you to remember that this was before any video camera monitoring. No one was going to bother me.

I pushed and pulled at his body. He just would not fit. I am glad he was not fat like most principals. I twisted and turned and had to use a piece of a two by four for leverage. As I pushed and prodded him into the fire, I heard his shoulders and spine crack under the pressure of my wooden pry bar. Once I got his shoulders in, I knew I was home free.

So, Mr. Leroy Peoples on this late fall evening burned up with the wastepaper, milk cartons and any other burnable trash on that evening. I stepped outside to check on any odor. There was none. I was happy that it was a windy night. The remains of Peoples just floated away.

I waited for the embers to cool and I swept them out and put them in a large trash sack and took it to the dumpster. The trash men would come the next day before anyone was at school.

I left for the night with a good feeling until I stepped into the parking lot. There was his car sitting there. What should I do with the car? I should have thought of that. No one would miss Mr. Peoples. His wife had died years ago. He had no children and I doubt if he had any friends.

I had kept Peoples' keys, and his car key was on the key chain. I drove the car across town to my friend that owned a salvage yard. He owed me a favor or two and he was happy to get rid of the car. He told me he would crush it. Knowing my friend, I doubt that happened. He probably tore it apart to sell bits and pieces of it, or perhaps called a friend to drive it away to be altered in such a way that no one would ever be the wiser. I trusted him. I knew it was not the first time that he had disposed of an unwanted car. He drove me back to my car and asked no questions. That's what friends are for. Right?

I slept very well that night.

Chapter Seven
My story begins

It seems like only yesterday that I was starting my lifelong journey. I was always told that as the years marched on, they always seemed to march faster. Those that told me that were right. The last two decades of my life just flew by. Where did it all go?

Ever since the day that I enlisted in the Army, I always wanted to make a difference. Going straight to Vietnam was my only option, and that did not bother me. I saw that trip to Nam as an opportunity to make a difference. Did I ever make a difference? Who knows? I will let you decide that.

I am eager to tell my story. I am glad that you want to listen. I hope you will understand my actions and motivations. For whatever reason, for you to understand my actions is important to me.

And yes, I became a murderer. That is hard for me to say and perhaps even harder for me to hear. But it is true, there is no doubt about it. The day that I liberated the school from Mr. Leroy Peoples, I became a changed man. I now murdered people to make a difference. I murdered people to make the lives of other people better. Was that, OK? For me, it was. I viewed it as not only OK, but as my duty. There was no looking back, and there was no turning back. I was on a mission.

Just like everyone else, I will look back and think about all of my "should haves," "could haves," and "what ifs." I took care of my business. I have no regrets.

Like many people, my job became my life. Who I was actually was determined by my job. I never married, nor did I ever have any children (that I know of). I never had that significant other. I was a loner.

Although I considered myself a loner, I must admit that perhaps that was not really true. I married my job. My job became my significant other. My job became my family. And just like that protective mother bear as she watches over her cubs, I guarded my job and the people there with the same ferocity.

I never retired. In the confines of my school and my job, I mattered. I identified with my job and I believe my job identified me. I never wanted to retire, nor did I ever want to be a nobody. I dreaded losing my family, namely my school and job. That was not for me. I knew that and it would take just a matter of a few days for a newcomer to realize this. I needed to be a somebody no matter what the cost.

When one of my friends retired, I suffered. As we said our goodbyes, we would shake hands or give each other a big man hug. We would smile, laugh, and maybe even shed a tear, and we would always claim to stay in touch. It rarely happened. Each time a former colleague died; I received a call. Now, the calls came more frequently. That was just life.

The memories of these people would also slowly fade. It is important that I should not mislead you. I could be a real pain in the ass. Hell yes, I would fight with you and ultimately seek to punish you. But yet, most times, we would somehow mend the fences and be friends again. People characterized my relationships with others at work, like a marriages. We had our difficulties, but we were in it. And if a divorce was to occur, it would be the other person who packed his or her bags and left.

I thought I had it all. I thought I lived a charmed life.

Chapter Eight
Meet Mr. David James Larue III

That's me. I go by DJ just like my daddy and just like his daddy before him. Somewhere along the way, the spelling changed from Laroux to Larue. The Laroux spelling reflects my Louisiana roots, a nice place to visit, but not such a nice place to live. Being poor and black is bad enough, but being poor and black in Louisiana is just about a death sentence.

My family, besides my parents, comprised me and my two brothers and three sisters. I was the youngest of the three boys and perhaps became more hardened because of the beatings I took from my older brothers. Everyone needed someone to beat on. It was a trickle-down effect. Everyone beat on the person younger. But who did I get to beat on? And if one boy ever raised a hand to one girl in the family, my daddy would whip his butt good. You only had to see that or better still feel that once to fully understand the lay of the land.

My father was a laborer in a mill and my mother worked for the county in a clerical job. They worked hard. We kept our heads barely above water just because of my parent's work ethic. In my family, when you were old enough, you worked. Being the youngest of the group, I escaped regular work until I was about thirteen when I worked trudging groceries home to our neighbors from our grocery store in our small downtown area. My sisters and other brothers held any variety of jobs that children could do. Please do not kid yourself. There were no real child labor laws in Louisiana in my time. In my house, as a child, you did two things. You worked and went to school. Let me correct that. There were three things that you did. You worked, went to school, and, of course, you went to church.

Let me also tell you, you did not miss any of these activities. Breaking one of daddy's rules resulted in you meeting his personal "board of education." That's right, the old board of education, which turned out to be a hand-me-down paddle that was kept hanging by the door in our kitchen. And that same paddle hung in daddy's house and probably his daddy's house. That paddle tanned many Larue butts. It did not matter if you were a girl or a boy, if you broke one of the house rules, your butt tasted that paddle. That paddle now hangs in my oldest brother's house and Larue butts are today, still feeling the pain from this motivational device.

Being the youngest, I could see first-hand how my brothers' and sisters' lives turned out. They were living the Larue life, which comprised working hard and raising a family. Personal happiness was never part of the Larue equation. It was just survival and procreation. For all the Larues, it was really very simple: do the Lord's work and therefore commit another generation to this kind of life. For me, this just did not seem right and perhaps, therefore, that is why I never married or had children. I lost count of my nieces and nephews. It seems like there was always a fresh addition. I could never understand that philosophy because with each new mouth to feed, the family just got poorer and poorer. There was no way out.

Everyone said the Bible raised the Larue children. Daddy's interpretation of the Bible raised us. We changed churches frequently. He always searched for that special fire and brimstone preacher who assisted him in raising us. Our family's discipline structure comprised the old "eye for an eye" mentality. As awful as that manner for raising children sounds, none of the Larue children were in jail or addicted to whatever the "junk" of the day was. But believe me, it was no way to grow up. With the seven of us, someone was always getting his or her butt whipped. Male or female, it did not matter. I always wondered why it was okay for daddy to whip ass on the girls, but if one of us ever raised a hand, there would be hell to pay. In my house, daddy was the boss. daddy was God.

As I grew up, I knew I had to leave. I had to escape. Rural Louisiana was no place for me. I can remember my decision to leave like it was yesterday. The day after my eighteenth birthday, I walked down to the local Army recruiter's office and enlisted. Even though Vietnam was real, I did not care. No matter what the consequences might be, I had to get out. I figured that fighting the Vietnamese would be easier than fighting poverty and being black in the south. I graduated high school in May, and was off to the Army in June. As much as many of my friends were running away from the military in

1966, I ran to the green fatigues and was ready to go. Vietnam did not scare me. I knew that somehow; I was invincible. I survived the Larue household. Vietnam had to be a better place for me than the land I called home.

The next several years were a bit of a whirlwind. I rode a bus up to Fort Polk in northern Louisiana and settled into my eight weeks of basic training. For me, it was quite bearable. I was used to getting up early, working hard and being the obedient child. I ate well and my bed was warm, dry and soft. No drill sergeant could compete with Mr. D.J. Larue II. As boot camp ended, I watched as my friends prayed to get out of the infantry. I prayed to get that assignment. I knew I could get far away from Louisiana and, mostly, use my own skills to survive. And I might just enjoy some of the killing. Both daddy and my sergeants brainwashed me. I was a good at following orders. The drill sergeants merely picked up where daddy left off.

Soon I was in Vietnam, fighting for what I thought was an unknown cause. But that did not matter to me. I was an excellent shot, which I honed shooting squirrels and other small wildlife at home, and I was basically fearless. Perhaps more fearless than any other 18-year-old. I am not proud to say that I did many things that I should not have done in the Army and rationalized them because I was doing it for a cause. I did things because I was told to do them. I never questioned my daddy at home and I questioned no superior in the Army. After a search and destroy mission, I could easily sleep. I earned several medals for my work in Nam including a Purple Heart. I would get patched up and return quickly to the mission. My sergeant knew that when a shitty job had to be done, Larue would do it. My Daddy taught me you did what you were told, and you did what was right. Somehow, I kind of lost that last part of his usual speech: I did what I was told. Right or wrong never mattered to me.

I stayed in Vietnam for about 18 months. Around the beginning of the American withdrawal, I returned to the States. I never told you that to get to Vietnam, they sent us out on a big transport ship with a brief stay in Okinawa. To get home, they threw us onto some refitted cargo planes and we were back in the states the next day. One day, they trained us as killers and the next day; they expected us to go find a job.

I used my separation money from the Army to rent a small apartment in a small community in the northern part of New Jersey, about 20 miles from New York City. The name of the town is Pikesville. It was a small community that not too long ago changed its name to Pikesville. This name change corresponded to the completion of the New Jersey Turnpike in the early 1950s. The Turnpike is the only way to travel by car from New York City to Miami. The town had hoped to capitalize on the commerce moving along this roadway. It did not pan out how they had hoped. It never became that booming metropolis. I did not know how long I would stay there. I was just trying it out. A friend of mine told me that the local school district was looking for a janitor. Yes, a janitor. Black men would be janitors. There was no fancy term for this job. Having no other active leads, I applied and was quickly offered the position. I met the most important qualification, namely I was black, and I had a fairly strong back. So, I gave this job a try. Look at me now. I never left.

Of course, I knew my place in the food chain of the school district. I was at the bottom. I knew how to smile and say, "yes sir." But let me warn you, just because I was this janitor, please do not think that I am stupid because I am not. I also had another remarkable a quality. I could keep my eyes and ears wide open and my mouth shut. When you do that, you can almost survive anything.

And I still had another one of my skill sets, so finely honed in the Army I could and would do any dirty job that I was told to do. Crossing any right or wrong line did not really matter. I did what I was told. I did it fast. I did it right. And I kept my mouth shut.

I have seen some real dummies come in and teach the students. Some who could probably not walk and chew gum at the same time. Some teachers acted like thirteen-year-olds. Others just liked to scream at the kids and boss them around. It was pathetic.

Likewise, I saw my share of incompetent principals and administrators. I would really laugh at this group. They could not manage themselves, let alone manage people. When pay day would come, I would shake my head in amazement when these fools would take home a paycheck. They were the ones truly stealing from the district.

I had another skill set that I perfectly used. I was likeable. I could talk to anyone or any group of folks about anything. I knew who I liked and who I trusted. I never forgot who screwed me or who talked down to me. Another Larue trait was vengeance. "Vengeance is mine, sayeth the Lord." Daddy loved it. Daddy preached it. I learned it.

Chapter Nine
It is always about race

I did not have to learn this lesson. I knew it already. On the day I was born, I probably knew it. I know that race should not make a difference, but it does. And yes, times have changed. It probably makes less of a difference today, but it is always still there. You cannot escape the prejudice. The first thing that you see when you meet me is that I am black. There is no escaping that.

Never kid yourself. When I meet someone, before I open my mouth, the person has already made assumptions about me. Throughout my life, people called me colored, Negro, man of color, black, African American, and many other terms. And, of course, they have referred me to as that "nigger." Now that word has become unspeakable and when talking about it one refers to it merely as the "N-word." This would especially sting when I would hear it, of course, behind my back, from a person who I thought was a friend. Shoot, just like you are white, I am black. One thing I know is that I am a man and a proud American.

Although I dislike it, I can understand that racist bigots exist in the world. They are who they are and will never change. It would really piss me off when a person would put his arm around me like a friend and then, at the local bar, after a few beers, would hear the person refer to me as that nigger. I think I helped some people change their viewpoints. Some left the district because of me. Sorry.

While we are talking about race, understand that when I started in this school district, there were a few black teachers and no black administrators. They would come later to the district. I found this odd because most of our students were black. They sent our black boys a clear message. There is a job for you down the road in our schools and society. You can be a janitor. My presence helped change that as well. I was a change agent without ever realizing it. I would talk to the kids about their future. We would talk about what was needed to escape this hopelessness. I stood up for them. They knew this.

Remember the times when I started. There was a huge racial divide. Blacks stayed on one side of the "tracks" and whites stayed on the other. English was the only language that you heard spoken in the schools. It was interesting to watch this dividing line change and develop. In the 80s, the line moved to a highway that ran through town. In the 90s, the line pushed a bit more north. The racial demarcation line evaporated early in the new century.

Although this not so imaginary line changed in the community, it is important to know that it did not change the tone in the schools. Always remember that I heard everything. I can remember overhearing some old timers talk about their possession of their shotguns in case they needed these guns if the black folk ever crossed one of these imaginary lines. They probably should have drawn a large yellow line down the center of these roads. These feelings ran deep and were hard to change.

Although I was no longer in the deep south, I was tired of being treated like some second-class citizen. I had to do what I could for the next generation. Although change was coming, it was arriving way too slow. Another generation of black and brown children was being set up for failure. I could no longer sit by idly and watch this.

Yes, I was a janitor. Now called a custodian. I guess this title makes the do-gooder liberals feel better. I still cleaned up their kid messes. Of course, I cleaned the puke, the crap and all the other messes one could think. My job had wonderful benefits and decent pay. Most importantly, I enjoyed the companionship my job and school provided. The school became my significant other. My message became clear. DON'T MESS WITH IT.

I was usually the first one to arrive and the last to leave. And I must confess, sometimes I slept there. On most days I ran the school. And believe it or not, most people knew this. It was not the principal, or the teacher's union, it was just me. And yes, I had the power.

I saw many principals come and go and now and then, one would think that they were in charge. I laugh at that thought. They are bright and energetic and think they can change the system. The system changed them. I was the system. I was patient. I had my ways. I was not going anywhere. This was my home.

I once heard someone refer to me as a real school hero. But I am sure that person never fully realized the dark underbelly of the system. They played little individual dramas out daily. Maybe one day someone will write a book of my stories. I had better things to do.

The entire community loved me. You will see. I made the school livable. I made the school great. Yes, I could always keep my school clean, in more ways than the obvious.

Chapter Ten
There's got to be a morning after.

Leroy Peoples existed no more. Now what? What will happen to the school and what will happen to me? And as I sit and think about these questions, the ones that really matter to me concern the school. I did not care about what my fate would be. I did not want to get caught, but if I did, life would go on for everyone and hopefully life would be better for my school.

The next day came like it always does. Things always look differently the day after a significant event. Things are never what they appear to be. Sometimes after a night's sleep, things look better than they are, but most times after that same night's sleep, things look worse. What would this day bring?

The teachers came to school. Mr. Peoples' secretary came to school. The nosy busy-body parents came to drop their kids off and the ass kissers went looking for Peoples to pay their daily homage to him. And just like every other day, the children came to school. I was there early to open the school. When I greeted everyone, I had this unique good feeling about the day. Everyone came to school except Mr. Peoples. He was AWOL. However, I knew exactly where he was.

It is hard to describe, but somehow the school felt different on this day. It was brighter. Sunnier. People seemed to smile more. I heard some laughter from both the kids and the teachers, a sound you rarely heard here. I think it was against his rules that you could actually have fun at school. I hope this was a sound I would hear more frequently in the upcoming days. No one would ever know my secret.

I can remember hearing the garbage truck come to empty the dumpsters. As they pulled away from the school with the ashes from the incinerator, I knew the last remnants of Peoples went to the dump with the rest of the school's garbage. I thought it was a fitting departure. Good riddance. Could the rest of the adults left in the school now rebuild the school the right way? Somewhere along the way, the adults had lost their direction. This school had to be about what was right for the kids, not what was right for the adults. Most times, these two concepts did not intersect.

The funny thing about it, the school ran smoothly without Peoples. The teachers knew what they were doing. Kids never missed him.

Chapter Eleven
Let me introduce to you Mrs. Jane Kelly.

Mrs. Jane Kelly was Mr. Peoples' trusted secretary. She also was a good friend of mine. Earlier in my conversation I said to you I ran the school. That was not really true. Mrs. Kelly and I acted as a team, joined at the hip, for running the school. We could take care of anything and everything. And we did.

One time, I heard our Assistant Superintendent, who you will learn more about later, tell new teachers that the two most powerful people in a school were the head custodian and the principal's secretary. At least he knew this. If any teacher, be they novices, or experienced veterans, ever crossed us, we would get back at them. It did not take them long to learn this way of doing business. It was surely a rule, a rule that was never written, but a rule nonetheless.

Mrs. Kelly was about my age and she had been the secretary in the school for as long as anyone could remember. She kept Peoples afloat. She kept him propped up. She basically did his job. At least the paper end of it. She was married and had a couple of kids that were mostly grown by now. You could tell that her marriage was not a happy one by the way she talked about her husband. I think they stayed married because it was probably too much aggravation to get a divorce. She also doubted her skills. I never thought she was attractive. I never thought she was unattractive. She was just…... Mrs. Kelly.

She and I became friends. We would take our coffee breaks together, chat together (mostly about school) and coexist together in our daily grind. Our other commonality was that we both loved the school. At that point, there was never a doubt about our passion or commitment.

All of this is good background information, but we still had to deal with this one fact. Mr. Peoples was still missing.

Chapter Twelve
After Mr. Peoples Day #1.

Yes, this is day #1. The first day in school after the demise of Mr. Peoples. It was a new day. A new beginning for this school.

This day began like the previous one. Everyone reported for work and school except Peoples. Everyone was wondering about him and I had to laugh. I heard all the phonies express concern, whereas they were internally hoping never to see him again. I also overheard in the teacher's lounge all the jokesters making fun of his unaccounted-for absence. The major theme of these jokes centered on Peoples' forgetfulness that either he forgot how to get to work or forgot what day it was. Everyone enjoyed painting him like some old Mr. Magoo type if character.

And for those of you that do not have a clue about Mr. Magoo, I can share that he was a popular cartoon character most known for his forgetfulness or nearsightedness. I think Peoples could see fine but he acted and even looked a bit like Magoo. I remember the cartoons as I was growing up. Both Peoples and Magoo would talk to themselves. And Magoo would always say when he screwed something up, "Magoo, you have done it again." I could always hear Mrs. Kelly saying to Peoples, "oh Mr. Peoples, you did it again." One day, Peoples asked me where the gym was. For Christ's sake, he had been the principal in this building for years and the gym was the biggest space in the building. On the way to his office, he walked by it every day. Magoo might have been nearsighted but Peoples was working with dementia. I am sure of that.

The parent ass kissers showed concern. However, I am convinced that they showed concern over how his absence might affect each individual's child, not his true well-being. No one really cared.

I always watched in amazement how this group of parents worked. I am convinced that each school had this same set of parents. These parents would do anything, including breaking every rule in the book for their kids. They would trample the next person in line so their own child would be first. I knew that they really did not care about Peoples as a person because they were only worried about how they would now have to cultivate the new principal to give them anything that they wanted. This was a truly selfish lot. Believe me, these parents were a big part of the problem in our school and in our district. These same parents would also be the ones to breed the prejudice in the kids. The kids in this elementary school parroted their parents. Remember, I heard everything.

Mrs. Kelly scrambled. She exhausted an entire laundry list of phone numbers to contact him. She was a nervous wreck. But yet she kept her composure well enough to organize the day for the school. She covered every class and handled every bureaucratic task. I took care of the building. I opened all the necessary doors. All the toilets worked and were clean. I made sure the buses discharged the kids at the right location and every teacher was there to meet his or her class.

It was a smooth day. Maybe it was a smoother day than a day with Peoples present.

Chapter Thirteen
After Peoples Day #2

This is the second day of Peoples' odyssey to the dump. I am sure that he is already there, resting comfortably among all the other garbage. I am sure that his ashes fit right in.

However, today the superintendent sent one minion over to run the school. When I saw who arrived, I had to chuckle because I knew this guy well. When I saw him pull into the parking lot, I whispered to Mrs. Kelly that she should get ready to bring this fool some coffee and watch him kick back with his feet on the desk to read several newspapers. I could even predict what newspapers he would bring to read, and they were not the New York Times or the Wall Street Journal. He started the day reading the New York Daily News and after he finished that; he went right for the New York Post. These two tabloids had the reading level of about a fifth grader. This guy was not a scholar. I predicted he would sit in the office all day, drink coffee, and read several newspapers, which is exactly what he did. He closed the door and pulled the shade down, which revealed a handwritten sign that said "Meeting in Progress, Do Not Disturb." Peoples wrote this in his own handwriting. So, this lock down theory was not a new idea. Peoples had already mastered it. When I emptied the trash, I could take the New York Daily News and the New York Post home with me for my nighttime reading. But Peoples' temporary replacement was not a high-level thinking type of guy. He was merely typical of what the old guard administration looked like: white, old, mentally slow, and lazy.

My other prediction was also right on the money. He was successful in locking out all distractions. The most important thing for me was that he left me alone. Of course, he and I would share our mid-morning coffee break in his office talking sports and telling dirty jokes. I am like a chameleon. I can fit in anywhere. This was all fine with me. I had enormous faith in Mrs. Kelly. I knew that she and I could handle any school related issue.

It was about noontime on this second day of *"the case of the missing Peoples,"* that the police visited. A couple of uniforms came in, talked with a few people, me included, and made out a report. Our police were excellent at filling out reports. Solving crimes or, for that fact, identifying crimes was a different story.

Chapter Fourteen
Life goes on

Like the last two days, the following day began. The kids and staff entered orderly and got about their work. The school was functioning fine. Even though we were just a couple of days into this new routine without Peoples, everyone seemed to know what to do. Kelly and I kept the process of education moving forward. And the funny thing is that between the both of us, there was not one college degree. Now that should tell you something.

At about mid-morning on this third day, a couple of detectives came in for a visit. They rehashed the same items that the uniformed guys covered. They spent some extra time with me hoping that I could re-trace Peoples' last steps. I took them through the boiler room, right past the incinerator. I must brag that this was now the cleanest boiler room in the world. One could eat off of the floor. The incinerator was all scrubbed clean. Our big old furnace glistened in the sunlight that peaked into the room. The place where Peoples took his last breath was where they stood with me. They looked around with me without ever getting dirty. They seemed content with the notion that Peoples just disappeared. I can remember one of them saying to me it seems like "it was just poof, and he was gone." Little did this detective know that his words were quite true. Poof, he evaporated. When these two departed, I was just about sure that they would file the report, spend a few days poking around in the community, and announce that the case was not solvable. I convinced them they did all that they could do. Just like our pinch-hitting principal; they were just lazy. I was counting on that.

The district was not in a rush to fill Peoples' position. Most people believed he would just walk through the door one day like nothing was out of the ordinary and continue just like before, mismanaging the school. They always convinced me that most teachers hoped he would just stay away.

The central office continued to rotate daily substitutes from the central office administrators. You know, a supervisor of this or that, who had no interest in being there. They all had this routine down. Namely, they just hunkered down in the office. The school was running fine.

Mrs. Kelly and me, in combination, made a great principal. You know why? We both cared about the kids and we both knew how to work with people. We had built relationships with everyone. Peoples and most of his fellow administrators never got that concept. Schools are about people. It is as simple as that. All of our well educated high paid administrators don't get this. And I really think that they did not teach this in any graduate school. Most of the administrators were just blockheads and never understood the simplest thing about working with others. Yet a school secretary and a janitor understood this concept well. They could all take a lesson from us.

Chapter Fifteen
The dream team-Kelly and Larue

You now know that the two most important people in the school are the principal's secretary and the head custodian. I already told you that. The real power brokers are us. We can control the flow of information and can control the access to the principal or other administrators. We also control what gets done and when it gets done.

For example, if you were a pain in the ass to Mrs. Kelly, she might lose or delay your supply order. Another example of Kelly's power would be if you needed to see the principal, perhaps about an angry parent, she would not let you near him. You also remember that Peoples loved the privacy and security of his own office. He rarely left it, so to see him, you would have to walk right past Kelly's desk. And getting past Kelly's desk could be a problem all by itself. I bet visitors to a prison had an easier time of access to see the prisoners than what Kelly gave to Peoples. You would hear no complaints from him about that.

Kelly and I ran the school. Everyone knew it.

For me, retribution could be swifter. Piss me off and I would not clean your room. Piss me off and somehow the heat would not function in your room. You get my point. Piss me off...

Mrs. Kelly was a throwback. When I was a student, she reminded me of my school secretary. She could be loud and bossy. She would be a big gossip who loved to hear herself talk. She was very opinionated. Yet her most important quality was that she was extremely loyal. She would give her life for anyone who was in that office. I don't think she had any special liking for Peoples because he would not hesitate to blame her or publicly embarrass her. I think that this is how it probably worked at home. She was subservient to her husband at home and to Peoples at work. There was something in her make-up that allowed her to get into and stay in relationships like that. To me, it was sad. I hurt on the inside for Mrs. Jane Kelly.

All aspects of her life emotionally beat her down. Maybe therefore, we became friends? Could I save her? I mean, save her from both Mr. Peoples and Mr. Kelly. I doubt it because to start with; she had to want to save herself. She had a special affinity for the office of the principal. She probably wanted to be a teacher or a principal, but life did not work out that way for her. So, she settled into this mundane and low paying world of a school secretary. She had no confidence in herself. Hold on, let me take that back. As far as knowing what it took to run this school, she was full of confidence.

We were a great combination. One might laugh at looking at us. She was as white as they come, probably from her Irish descent, and had reddish hair that she would wear woven atop her head. I was a tall, strong, dark complected black man with closely cropped hair, who spoke very little. When people saw us huddled over our coffee, eating her home-baked cookies at break time, they must have laughed. Somehow, in this strange world, we both needed each other.

Kelly was several years younger than me and had two grown children who were her life. I was forever the bachelor with no children and I intended to stay that way. Life held Kelly hostage, yet I was free as a bird.

So, how did we become so close? My best bet is that we were just married to our jobs. We would put our heads together to make sure the school was operating correctly and everyone was in their place.

We could also fight with one another. There were times we did not talk to one another for weeks or maybe months. Somehow, the ice would get broken and we would forget all and we were back to having coffee again. We liked one another. Over the years, we became sort of a team. I never thought our relationship was anything more than work related. I knew she thought the same.

Although the school was running smoothly, Kelly was frantic because of the missing principal. I think somehow, she thought she was going to get yelled at or that some would think it was her fault that Peoples was not there. I ached inside because of her anguish. I wish I could have just told her that Peoples would not be returning to torment her, the teachers, or the kids anymore.

Mrs. Kelly repeatedly called his house and found out that Peoples never came home that night. This was not that odd because he stayed locally with some friends if he did not feel like making his long drive home. She asked me to drive out to his house with her to check on him. We did that, and I faked it really well, gaping into the windows and banging on the doors. I was a talented actor.

The superintendent never missed him and I believed hoped that he would never return. I think that is a telling statement about our schools. Except for the many relationships like Kelly's and mine, mostly, no one cared about anyone else. It also broke down into teams. The teachers did not care about the administrators and the administrators did not care about them. Who cared about the kids? Now, **that** is the question.

Chapter Sixteen
The local police department. Really?

The local police department proved to reflect our society. They did not care about Peoples at all. There was a running feud between the schools and the police. They did not give a hoot about the schools, including all the students. When I would hear people talking about the great relationship between the police and the schools, I would laugh my ass off. It was really sickening watching the two groups of people who supposedly cared about our kids, battle. Was it a battle over power? Over pay? Over work conditions? It was probably some combination of all the above.

Our police department had one black officer. That amazed me. The school district had about 3,600 students, with at least 3,000 of them with black or brown faces.

I also could easily feel the hatred and racism conveyed by most of the PD. The town was changing, and they did not like it. Mr. Peoples was one of the many characters in the school. The police department had its own characters. That, too, would have to change, but that was not my job. The district consumed me.

As far as Mr. Peoples, it was not a matter of race; the police just did not care.

I always viewed the police as just flat out lazy. Like so many others, they as a group worked harder at trying to get out of work than actually solving crimes. Sorry, I meant to say, except solving crimes committed by black kids. They loved solving those crimes. They just loved taking a kid out of school in handcuffs. It did not happen often, but it was always a spectacle. The kids resented the police and the police clearly did not like the kids. You should have seen all the fuss made about walking in the streets. Ok, I get it. The kids should be on the sidewalk. But what if the sidewalk was unusable, or snow covered? The kids fueled the animosity and hate. But who are the adults?

I think I painted the picture of how the police dynamics worked within the community. So now what?

Chapter Seventeen
Meet Beavis and Butthead

I was about ready to take my break for lunch when in sauntered two of our detectives. Believe me, they were your typical stereotypes of poor police officers. Namely, out of shape, both physically and mentally, who were going to just go through the motions. Of course, in this case, they were also white. You might as well have stuck a donut in each one's mouth. I knew these guys from town and they knew me. There was no like or dislike. We were just thrust into this thing together. But for the sake of my story, to myself, I named them Beavis and Butthead after the cartoon characters. And just like the cartoon, these two cops to me were unintelligent wastes of humanity.

Unfortunately, as my story progresses, you will see how these two fools become embedded in my life.

On this visit, they wanted to talk to me about Peoples' habits and specifically to see if I saw anything fishy about that memorable day. I was most cooperative. They opened their little skinny notebooks and took notes. I walked them from Peoples' office, through my boiler room (office) and out into the parking lot. I told them that this was how he left the building every day. From my door you could see his parking space, still with his name and position painted on it with big white letters. He just loved seeing it written, Mr. L. Peoples, Principal. His name and title were all over the building.

We walked the exit route together several times. Do not forget that my boiler room was now squeaky clean. I thought I had done a good job of eliminating every trace of Mr. Peoples. And I did.

Bevis and Butthead left through the same door with notebooks closed. Now I just had to ask myself, was the case closed? Would this just be another of the many unsolved cases of Bevis and Butthead? Believe me, I hoped that would be the case. Once again, solving crimes was not a big priority for these two.

Chapter Eighteen
What about teaching and learning?

We closed out the school year operating with the daily march of the lemons of pinch-hitting administrators. Pinch-hitting fools. If this was a baseball team, it would probably bat about .150. Believe me, this rotating administrator system was fine for everyone. The school looked and felt more like a school. It no longer felt like the prison that we had all gotten used to.

With Peoples gone, we finally got back to the business of teaching and learning. Yes, the teachers were teaching and students were learning. And every day that I could witness this, I felt even better about the job that I had done. Peoples had to go, and we all knew that. I was glad that I could handle that. With Kelly and me in charge, life at the school was good.

Everyone knew the school could not operate without a principal for long. Mrs. Kelly and I would talk about what would be next. We actually never thought that we could ultimately get someone worse than Peoples. Could that be possible? Could someone actually be worse than him? Did I screw up? Should I have just kept mentally torturing the guy? No, he had to die, and he had to die knowing what he did to my school.

The police were inept. The school board was inept. Beavis and Butthead certainly could have done a better job of investigating this crime. They were happy with the thought that Peoples just evaporated into thin air. Hey, I guess they were right in that assessment. He flew off into the night air. I found that thought hilarious. I would hear their conversations at the coffee shop or at the local watering hole. (And it was essential for political survival in this district that you attended both places.) They made a lot of important decisions in these places.

As the days progressed, I knew I was not a suspect. I doubt if anyone was a suspect. Everyone was glad to believe in magic. Someone or something just made Peoples magically disappear. In all conversations, I bought into that theory, as ridiculous as it was. Plus, I was an insider in the school and the community and if the investigation was going somewhere, I would know about it well enough in advance to cover my tracks. And finally, and probably they were plain old lazy dumb sons of bitches and those in the school felt that everyone was better off without Peoples. That I knew.

Chapter Nineteen
Death, taxes and change.

You know as well as I do that the only things that we can be sure of in this life are our ultimate demise and death, paying our taxes, and, of course, constant change. People seem to accept my belief about death and taxes, but somehow cannot get their minds around the concept of change.

One day during the summer, they summoned me to the office where I met a very professional looking young woman. Mrs. Kelly and I were both surprised by her youthfulness. They introduced her to us as our new permanent principal. I immediately thought that manipulating her would be easy and I would still be in control of the school. Her name was Mrs. Lawson, but she quickly told us to call her Angela. I was a bit surprised to see that she was black. Yes, times were a changing, and this was probably the district's attempt at some affirmative action. She was a home run on two accounts: she was black and she was a woman.

She brought a refreshing attitude to the school. She seemed energetic and caring. She was moving slowly to get the lay of the land. I was willing to help. Number one, I had to get in good with her and number two; she was mighty fine to look at and she made it a pleasure to be around her.

She did not let me down. Mrs. Lawson treated the staff warmly and professionally. She listened to them. She recognized each kid for being an individual and actually celebrated their diversity. With this being said, the kids behaved better, and the teachers seemed to work better. I could tell that by the way they came to work every day. Yes, they were smiling and happy. And yes, they came to work regularly. It was not uncommon that under Peoples' leadership, 25-50% of the staff would be absent every Friday and Monday. It was also quite noticeable that the students were behaving better, and the teachers were keeping the kids in their classrooms and handling their problems by themselves. It was not uncommon when Peoples was in charge to have a long line of students sitting outside of the office waiting for Peoples to mete out his form of discipline. It was usually mean spirited. Is suspension from school a fitting punishment for a first-grader? And why did he constantly yell at the kids? I knew in my heart that if we were still in the south, he would have had a paddle adorned in school colors, hanging by his desk for all to see. And I am also sure that he would have loved paddling the behinds of all the black kids. It was just who he was.

After years of being yelled at and abused by Mr. Peoples, Mrs. Lawson's easy and personable style confused the kids. That's right, Mrs. Lawson talked with the students, not at them.

Parents loved Mrs. Lawson. Many of them went to this school when Peoples was their principal. They hated him when they were students and they hated him as an adult. It did not take them long to see the change in the school. Yes, it was getting better every day. Man, I was happy here. I felt as though I went to heaven. I could ride out my entire career here. And who knows, maybe I could make some time with Angela, oops, Mrs. Lawson.

Chapter Twenty
Change hits home

September quickly turned to October, and before long, we were thinking about the Thanksgiving holiday. One day, the boss called me to the office. I thought that they just needed me to clean up someone's mess and as I walked into the office; I saw Mrs. Kelly crying and I could see the superintendent standing in Mrs. Lawson's office. They both smiled nicely at me and quickly asked me to sit down. I was comfortable standing. That being said, they informed me that as of the Monday after Thanksgiving; I was being transferred to the Middle School. I did not want to go, but they sold me a bill of goods or, to be honest, just a load of bullshit. The district needed me. I possessed the "skill set" needed at the middle school. They used this line on others, and I heard it before. I would not fall for that. By the way, what the fuck is a skill set? I was getting shuffled off. I was no longer wanted where I was.

To soothe me, they made me the Head Custodian in my new school, and it paid me a few extra dollars every month. But the building was dirty and a mess. And the group of janitors assembled there never broke a sweat. They spent more time looking to get out of work than they did actually doing any work. Oh well, work was work and what the hell, I needed the job. So, for the next couple of days, I gathered my things and said my goodbyes and prepared to join a new building after the holiday. Could it be all that bad? We will see.

As I left the office after a fake friendly handshake with the superintendent, I returned to work. Why the hell was Mrs. Kelly still crying at her desk? I came to find out that she, too, was going with me. We were a package deal. If we were in major league baseball, I would say they traded us for an old bag of balls and some broken bats. They promised her a promotion to Head Secretary. I think Kelly bought the entire bag of bullshit. Notice how the times were changing. I was no longer called a janitor. I was now a custodian.

Big deal. Call me what you want. I was still cleaning up the messes of other people. Yea, I know it was my job, and I needed to just shut up and take it, but it still troubled me that no matter what you called me, I was still at the bottom of the food chain in the school.

I did not have the heart to tell Mrs. Kelly that their line was a bunch of crap and we were being discarded like an old piece of trash. They viewed us as part of the old regime and for Mrs. Lawson to be successful, Kelly and I had to go. We were like two old shoes that no longer fit. I was a bit saddened because Angela did not stand up for me, or did not even have the guts to tell me about the move unless she was being told what to do. Yet, I knew in my heart that I had to go because I was still a leftover of the Peoples regime. Mrs. Lawson needed to wipe the slate clean. This transfer also affirmed to me she recognized the informal power that both Kelly and I had. Lawson was smart. Although she was young and, yes, inexperienced, she was going to be an excellent principal. She was good for the kids and was exactly what this school needed. The teachers also came alive working with her. I was sad that I could not see this change through to the end (if there is ever an end). I would not be part of this new team and that made me sad.

Oh well, a new adventure awaited.

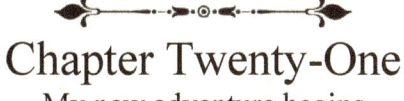

Chapter Twenty-One
My new adventure begins

My Thanksgiving turkey did not taste so good.
I arrived for work in my new school with my additional responsibilities at 6:00 a.m. that Monday. It surprised me to see Mrs. Kelly sitting in her car waiting for me in the parking lot. She was ready for the move, or so she said, but she looked like hell. It scared her to death. I am sure she slept worse than me this weekend and I can almost guarantee that she did not enjoy her Turkey Day meal.

I was proud of her. She acted like a pro. She loved the district. The district did not love her back. For both of us, this was more than a job. It was our lives. But we were small pieces in a bigger machine. And we were both told by many others that we were lucky to have a job. What a crock of shit. We both put so much of our lives into the job, I felt we deserved more. I had to remind myself to grow up and to quit acting like a child. I was a janitor, and she was a clerk. Get over it. Deal with it.

And deal with it, we did. We both, on the surface, settled in nicely. I tried to keep my mouth shut and observe everything. Mrs. Kelly could not help herself. She had a big mouth and struggled to fit in. Eventually she did OK.

I saw quickly that bigger was not always better. Besides a bigger physical plant, there were more staff and more kids. To me, bigger kids always meant bigger problems. They did not let me down. And let me tell you this, the kids were just fucked up. Everyone told me it was their age. I thought to myself, some of them just needed a good kick in the ass or to be taken out to the old woodshed by a parent and have the shit beaten out of them. Thank God I am not a parent. That job was not for me. And you know what, I do not feel cheated, especially where I am at in my life.

I also quickly found out that the internal politics of the school were much more complicated. There were more relationships and many times you really did not know who you were talking to and who they would run back to and tell a twisted version of your conversation. Adults can be quite petty. Some thrive on personal controversy. Some just need to be in some sort of conflict with someone. It was pure drama. Someone could have made a great reality television show about us.

Navigating school would be easy if it were not for the adults there. Nobody tells the truth and nobody wants to hear the truth. That is just the way it is. It is hilarious that people will lie directly to your face and they really think that you believe the bullshit that they are peddling.

There was an interesting power structure in this school. It is really quite complex. One thing I knew was that the principal was not in charge. He may have thought that he was in charge, or that he was the boss, but I realized he was neither the boss nor in charge.

The principal's name was Mr. Warfield. He was a nice guy. I think he liked kids. However, he may have been one of the dumbest individuals on earth. He must have just kissed the right ass at the right time to get this job. We easily manipulated him. The kids snowed him and he was afraid of the parents. The teachers showed him no respect and behind his back he was the butt of many jokes. I was glad to see that Mrs. Kelly was taking charge of the school. Never forget her importance. She controlled both information and access to the pretend boss. And she was a master at using both things.

I think I have time to tell you more about Mrs. Kelly. People seemed to either like her or hate her. There does not seem to be much of an in-between nature of things. People will be nice to her face and ridicule her behind her back. I feel sorry for her in that regard. But please do not spend too much time feeling sorry for Mrs. Kelly, for she is perhaps the most expert manipulator of people I have ever seen. She can remarkably punish people she does not like or punish those that do not kiss her ring.

Kelly holds court regularly at her desk. It has become the official bitching post of the building. Everyone stops by during the day to get caught up on the day's gossip or to fuel the most recent rumor. I know that sometimes, just for the hell of it, I would tell her some crazy rumor that I made up and watch how she and the rest of the fools would spread the word. All the time it was just nonsense that I made up. These antics helped me pass the time. Our personalities and job descriptions linked Kelly and me. I think some called it joined at the hip. I do like her, but I also know how to play with her. As my story goes on, you will see how this all plays out. The more I think of it, the way we play with each other complicates our relationship.

The daily soap opera at the middle school wages on. Day to day, it is the same old shit but told a different way with perhaps different players. Believe me when I tell you this, the district should hire a psychiatrist for the building, but I doubt one person could handle it. There could be a need for several head doctors here because I have found out that each person in this school is nuts. And each nut is different. I think the field of education and the nature of schools attract the mentally ill. Perhaps the schools provide some sort of group therapy, all day, every day. One person is nuttier than the next. I go to bed at night thanking God that I am the sane one.

Months turned to years, and before long, Kelly and I are running this school. I know I am leaving out some parts of the story, but they are probably pretty boring run-of-the-mill stuff. I am trying to give you, my highlights.

Chapter Twenty-Two
The first bump in the road at the middle school-meet Ducky Donaldson

I would always claim that I do not see race. But in reality, everyone sees race. That is just a fact. I will try to call it like it is regardless of the color of one's skin. Or at least I hope I do. It took months, if not a year, for me to realize and know that I must act again. I know that I have to provide old Mr. Peoples with some company wherever that old bastard is. I know one thing for sure that his eternal resting place can't be heaven.

One of my men, one of my custodians, had to go. He was a real pain in the ass. My old friend Mr. Peoples probably would have called him a "lazy, shiftless nigger." And you know what? I would probably agree with him. Look at this, me and Peoples agreeing with one another.

To get an ounce of work out of this man was like pulling teeth. He always had an answer and an excuse for doing something, or in his case, it was probably for not doing something. Old James Donaldson was a disgrace, and he was ruining my school. I also burned inside because this guy was the perfect example of the black stereotype that Peoples held so dear in his heart. Donaldson and his behavior did immense damage to every other black man. I spoke to him about this, but it went in one ear and out the other. He was a dog, no matter the color of his skin.

The guys called him "Ducky" because he walked like a duck. No one wanted to work with or near him. He was that bad. Everyone called him Ducky to his face. It annoyed the hell out of him, and everyone knew this. That made them do it more. Oh, I forgot to tell you I have found that people that work in schools, be they teachers, secretaries, custodians or principals, mostly, have about the maturity level of a third grader. I could most times make more sense out of what the kids said or did as compared to the adults.

Old Ducky had more medical excuses to miss work than one could ever imagine. The art of getting hurt at work was something he had taken to the highest level. He dropped things on his feet, slipped on the floor, tripped on a carpet or lifted something wrong. He would do anything to go to the workers' compensation doctor to get out of work. And mind you that all workers' comp cases did not count against your personal allotment of sick time. Over my time with him, I had watched Ducky work less than half of his required time and get fully paid for it. It was also bad enough that he did this, but he bragged about it. Everyone wanted to kill him. Because when he was out, the other men on the shift had to work harder to cover Ducky's area. He did not care and had no clue about any concept of teamwork.

For as long as I can remember, there was no such thing on the job as limited duty. If you were sick or injured, you either could work or you couldn't. Then one day, some genius board member came up with the idea that it might save the district money if we incorporated a light duty element for our injured custodians. They could work, but maybe not perform all of their given job assignments. Oh, this would work well with my guys. Rules of the game change and you have to change with them. I get that. But it is challenging.

Well, Ducky would come to work and sit around and maybe push a broom a bit while the other men busted their butts. You can only imagine how this played out with the men. I had a minor war on my hands and I had to navigate it daily. It was better when Ducky stayed home. There were a few times some men wanted to physically kick his ass or kill him. It was that bad. Maybe I should have just closed my eyes and let it happen.

It got worse in the winter. Every time it snowed; Ducky would call out sick. If you made up a weather calendar, you could fill in Ducky's absences based upon the weather. He did not care that he was letting his fellow workers down

For the sake of time, I am only giving you a summary of Ducky's work performance. If I went into more depth or length in my stories, I would run out of time.

I spent many sleepless nights thinking about how I could rid myself of Ducky. I knew I also had to make it appropriate for Ducky's behavior. Ducky hated the cold. He had to die an icy death.

It came to me in one of my awake periods about 3:00 o'clock in the morning as I lay thinking about all of his transgressions. Then it hit me. He had to meet his demise in our sub-zero freezer where the district stored all the meats and perishable foods that every school used.

I waited to execute my plan until a long three-day weekend appeared. I chose Presidents' Day. In one way, I wanted to think that George Washington and Abraham Lincoln would somehow be proud of me for ridding the United States of this embarrassment of a man.

Several days before the event, I easily disabled all the emergency procedures for the freezer. It was an old freezer and the maintenance company, when called, never rushed to make a repair. This company was obviously trying to force the district into buying a new freezer. They were here so often that they almost ignored us. I know they would place our call on the bottom of the pile and get to it when they got to it.

That being said, I had to come up with an ingenious way to get Ducky into the freezer alone without being seen. Not that this could be a problem, because, remember, it was hard for me to get him to do any of his own work. He hid from everyone most of his shift. I think I came up with a slick move to make it work.

Ducky worked the night shift, and I dropped in unannounced to make sure the men were working. Because the men worked in different parts of the building, each person could, if they wanted to, work the full shift without being seen. Although the men ate together and took their breaks together, this was not a problem because no one would eat or spend time with Ducky. It was pretty interesting to see how the men would police themselves and quickly ostracize those that did not fit in. And Mr. Donaldson did not fit in with the crew. On break time or mealtime, I knew I could find Ducky alone dozing on the couch in the second-floor faculty lounge.

Prior to work, on this specific night, I made sure Donaldson's area was especially messy. The other men had already left when I put my plan into operation. As we were leaving, I made nice with Ducky as we were exiting the building together. As we passed the freezer, I shared with him that the government sent us a wrong order and there was a lot of extra food in the freezer. The food service manager told me we could help ourselves to the extra. I was letting him in on my little secret, which was a made-up crock of shit. I think he thought I was making friends with him. He was happy that we were bonding on this mission. He was extremely pleased that I chose him, not someone else, for this adventure. When I told him this, his eyes lit up. I am sure that he was already counting the money he could get by selling the stuff in the neighborhoods. Shoot, our people were hungry and, mostly, dirt poor, and I knew a lot of business took place on the streets with merchandise that had "fallen off" delivery trucks. That's the way the economy worked in our community. Everyone knew this, including the police, yet everyone closed their eyes. It was just life. For many, it was just survival.

As we approached the freezer, my pulse quickened. I was getting excited. I opened the freezer door, and he ran in. Donaldson spied the meat in the back of the freezer. He could not wait to get his hands on it. His treasure booty. Shit, he just about ran in, which made my job very easy. He made it to the back, and I could hear him laugh and yell like he just won the lottery. Someone won the lottery that night for sure, but it was not him. The winners were every member in the school, including me. I smiled briefly and shut the door behind him. It closed with a loud thud. I am sure he did not even hear it because he was so tuned in to getting his prize out. After a short time, he made it back to the door and found it locked tightly. Remember that the walls in this freezer are probably six inches thick. And they covered every surface with cold steel. It would be his tomb.

He helplessly looked at me through the small window in the door. He thought I was only playing with him. Remember, we just bonded. We were pals. Or so he thought. I despised him. I hated everything about him. He was just no good. He was an embarrassment to every black man alive. Let's go a step further. He was an embarrassment to every man alive, no matter what they looked like. Everything about him made me sick.

I got great pleasure watching him die. Looking through that small window in the freezer door was like looking into his soul. He begged me to let him out. He begged for forgiveness. He promised me he would work hard in the future. He promised me everything. I just stood and smiled.

I think the temperature in the freezer was somewhere between 0 and -10 degrees. This should not take too long. Soon he shivered. I am convinced that his body temperature was now dropping. That black son of a bitch, I swear, was turning blue. Ice crystals were forming on his hands, eyes, and eyebrows. As he pounded on the door, I could see that his hands were now bleeding and I think that the blood was freezing as quickly as it leaked from his body. I continued to enjoy every minute. In a few minutes, I noticed the most peculiar thing happened. He ran around and stripped off all of his clothes. After the event, I read about freezing to death and stripping off one's clothes is a common thing. I could see him in the back, trying to burrow behind and under some boxes.

After a while, I am convinced that he lost consciousness. I know that there was not much air in there and I also know that there is some dry ice in the back which emits carbon dioxide. Was he suffocating or freezing to death? To me, it did not matter. I was just happy that he was dead. And by the way, I loved watching him suffer.

As I walked out, I took all of Ducky's possessions that he had left on a cafeteria table. I threw them in the dumpster behind the all-night Dunkin' Donuts. I kept his keys. When I got home, I hung his keys next to Peoples' keys on my bulletin board in my kitchen near my phone. I wanted to remember both of them every day for the rest of my life.

I knew that over the long weekend, no one would miss him. His wife divorced him years ago. He was no better at being a husband than he was at being a custodian. I was happy for her and I still believed that she would get his work life insurance. Like everything else that Ducky did, he did it half way. He was too lazy to change his beneficiary. He was just too lazy to do anything but die. In his death, he probably worked the hardest he ever did in his life trying to stay alive.

Chapter Twenty-Three
A busy Tuesday morning

After watching Ducky move on to the great hereafter, I thought a great deal about freezing to death. I have always heard that freezing to death was a good way to go. I was always told that you just fell asleep. After seeing it happen close up, I now know that this is not true. It is a horrible way to go. However horrible it was, it was a perfect ending for one Mr. Ducky Donaldson. I am now convinced of this.

The weekend was enjoyable. I slept well and rarely thought of my dirty deed. I was at peace. I was and still am convinced that I did the school district another favor. I hoped that in the hereafter, both Peoples and Donaldson would talk about their demise. And I hoped even more that they would talk about me. That thought gave me great pleasure and satisfaction.

Tuesday came quickly. Remember that Ducky's mishap in the refrigerator came on Friday night and all schools were closed on Monday. Ducky froze rock solid. I got to work especially early this day. The night before, I rested very well. I hung around the cafeteria looking busy waiting for Mrs. Diaz, our cafeteria manager, to arrive for work and prepare the menu for the week. I felt sorry for her knowing what she would walk in to.

I saw Mrs. Diaz go into the freezer and waited to hear her scream. It would be seconds from now. I counted back in my head, five-four-three-two, and then I heard the scream and the thud. I ran back to the freezer and there was poor Mrs. Diaz passed out on the floor. I slid her out and glanced in the back and saw old Ducky laying there naked and stiff as a board. This was a sight, I assure you. And believe it or not, it froze everything stiff (you get what I mean).

I called the police and then contacted my bosses in the schools. Luckily, it was still early enough to call off school for the students and teachers. We just made up a story about a water line break. It was plausible and it would give the school a day to re-group and open on Wednesday.

Several radio cars responded and sealed off the area. Mrs. Diaz was now laying down in the Nurse's office awaiting medical attention. I greeted the police and helped them seal the area. About an hour later, the two detectives arrived. The police sent the same two detectives that handled the Peoples' disappearance, Beavis and Butthead. I introduced them to the former Ducky Donaldson, now reduced to a black and blue popsicle. I heard them both laugh when they saw him. They made a lot of jokes and wisecracks. I hate to admit it, but it was pretty funny.

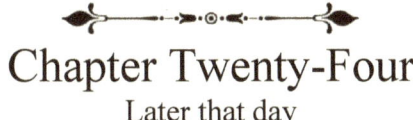

Chapter Twenty-Four
Later that day

The police took my story. It was short and sweet. I explained Ducky worked the night shift that evening and most nights left by himself. At closing time, all the men left. I explained Ducky was a loner, and that I parked my car in my reserved spot near the building's exit. I left through the door leading from the boiler room. I would not have gone through the main lot and hence did not see that his car was still there. I shared with them I did not have a clue as to why Ducky was in the freezer other than he was a bit of a character and it would not have surprised me he went in there to pilfer something. He had the reputation of being an operator and everyone bought this story. So, Beavis and Butthead closed their case, calling it an accidental death. Yes, he died accidentally. Accidentally on purpose, that is.

We all mourned his loss. I was a talented actor. One good thing came of this. The district put a brand-new walk-in freezer in the place of Ducky's death chamber with all the new bells and whistles to help ensure that an accident of this type would never happen again. I also knew that the district kept and used all the frozen food that helped entomb Ducky. After all, the meat never thawed. No harm, no foul.

The local television stations came to cover the story for the evening's news broadcast. I was the one that they interviewed. Boy, I looked good on TV. I made a copy of that news broadcast to watch again and again. This just keeps getting better.

So once again, because of my action, the district improved. We could hire a new guy who had the right work ethic and attitude to do the job correctly. He wanted the job and needed the job. He fit in nicely with the other men, and the school's cleanliness drastically improved. There was once again harmony among the custodial maintenance staff. It is amazing how one person can affect the entire group.

And as I stated before, we got a new state-of-the-art freezer. Mrs. Diaz, our cafeteria manager, recovered physically from her bump on her head and emotionally from finding Ducky. Although I bet, she still sees his frozen naked body in her dreams. I know I do. I found it hilarious and I am sure that for Mrs. Diaz; it proved to be a recurring nightmare. For me, it proved to be a soothing thought that helped put me to sleep. It was better than counting sheep. I had no remorse.

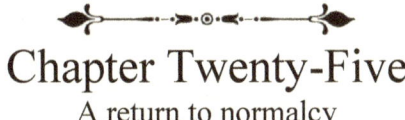

Chapter Twenty-Five
A return to normalcy

Normalcy? What's that?

I found out that the business of schools, in reality, has very little to do with the education of the students. Schools are a playground for the adults. There are so many little dramas that are played out daily. I think that anything a kid learns at school is probably an accident.

Let me back up on that. That statement is not fair. There are many teachers and administrators that come to work every day to positively affect the lives of the students. They come to both teach them and to mentor them. They really want to prepare them for life. Sadly, in my mind, the clowns and fools that come to school every day for the wrong reason overshadow them.

Many are just flat-out nuts. People come to receive mental therapy from their students. Some are on some kind of power trip. Some have other clandestine and, yes, evil reasons for being there. We have already touched on that.

It amazed me to find out how many love affairs played out in the schools. Schools serve as fertile dating sites for those that are single as well as for those that are married.

Believe it or not, people drink or do drugs on the job while the students are there. I do not include those that use the school building as a private hotel or party room for their personal use. I know because I have seen it and I must confess that I have also taken a drink or two on the job, both with others and alone. And yes, I close my eyes to it all. I sit idly by and watch these little dramas play out. I always ask myself, could I or should I stop them? But when these thoughts creep into my mind, they disappear, knowing that if I became the moral police officer on the job, I would soon no longer have a job. For many of the secrets that I hold, in the dark recesses of my brain, involve the higher ups in the district, the board and the city. Yes, knowledge is power, and I know I am powerful.

That all being said, both Mrs. Kelly and I have settled into our new digs. She and I have formed some sort of bond along the way. It is not sexual; it is not some mother / son relationship; it is not like a friendship. I don't know what to call it. It is like we are kindred spirits. Maybe we are both the same person except in different skin. I know one thing for sure is that we both love the district.

I have also now come to serve as her in-school protector of sorts. Believe me, this has nothing to do with being a physical protector because she could probably beat up most people in the school. I have become more of her social protector. If someone messes with Mrs. Kelly, they mess with me, and I will not stand for any nonsense.

I am proud to say that by now everyone knew that Mrs. Kelly and I were the ones really running the school. Mr. Warfield, the principal of the school, was a nice guy but a boob. He could run nothing, let alone a school. He was just good old Mr. Warfield who could and who would screw something up just by touching it. The school's power was right on my doorstep.

At about this time; I became the school's cleaner in more ways than one. I quickly learned how I could punish or reward staff. There are subtle ways to make a point. For example, and I will provide a simple one; if you were on my unpleasant side or needed a lesson taught, your classroom would never get cleaned. If you stayed on this side, your room remained dirty. Perhaps got even dirtier. I made my point.

New people would try to bully Mrs. Kelly. She would turn the tables on them and they became the ones that were bullied. She and I would meet over coffee in the morning and share our tales. I made sure I paid close attention because I wanted to mete out discipline for those that had pissed Mrs. Kelly off. Somehow, they got the message. I found it funny that some of our teachers could not walk and chew gum at the same time, yet they quickly got this power structure. Treating Mrs. Kelly badly would bring swift retribution from me.

I will give you one quick example of how we worked together on this. Mrs. Kelly was in charge of supply acquisition and I was to deliver the supplies to the specific classrooms. Do you think that those that acted like assholes ever got their right supplies? Doubtful. I recall some teachers went a good half of the year never getting a piece of paper. Usually, sometime and somewhere along the way, the thick-headed bastards would get it. Perhaps they would bring Mrs. Kelly a cup of coffee one day or help me subtly as I did my normal duties and wouldn't you know it that soon thereafter, they would receive their long missing supply order. Our justice system worked smoothly. This was a perfect example of one hand washing the other. I liked my hands clean.

Around this time, I noticed I did less and less work around the building and barely got dirty during the day. I now consumed my days making the building work behind the scenes. My hands needed to be clean in more ways than one. And believe me, this was now my full-time job.

Chapter Twenty-Six
Company is coming Mr. Peoples and Ducky

The minute I realized what was happening, I recall throwing up in the garbage can. I did not want to believe it, but I really had no choice. My eyes were not deceiving me. My senses were not playing tricks on me. What I thought was happening was really happening. Although the situation called for drastic measures, I wanted to take my time because I had to make sure I was right.

Mostly, I blended into the walls. I blended into the environment. My work shoes had rubber soles and people never knew when I was coming, unless I wanted them to know.

Let me introduce you to Mr. Singleton, our music teacher. Singleton was the young, cool, happening teacher. He joined us when he was in his early twenties and immediately made an impact. Every kid wanted to have Singleton as a teacher. On the surface, he was a significant find for the school. Not only did the kids love him, the parents loved him. As dumb as Mr. Warfield, the principal was, I knew he was not so fond of Singleton. Warfield and I never discussed this, but somehow, I just knew how Warfield felt. Although Warfield never shared this with me, I knew he had a sixth sense about Singleton. And this sixth sense sent no good vibrations back to Warfield.

Personally, I liked Singleton. I would sneak out into the back with him and smoke a cigarette with him, and I knew he kept a bottle of brandy in that saxophone case of his. I came to find this out late one cold evening after a school play practice when he asked me if I needed a little something to warm me up. When I accepted, we both enjoyed a long pull on the bottle. Singleton was not a pain in the ass at all. I have seen a lot of music teachers come and go and most fit the bill of pain in the ass babies. They would live by the motto, "my way or the highway." Most music teachers were insatiable. The more that you gave them or the more that you did for them, the more they would want. They were just never happy.

Not Singleton. He was fairly easy to work with.

We worked well together until this one day that I walked into his back room in the auditorium where he gave music lessons. When I opened the door, I could not believe my eyes. There was Singleton, half naked, having sex with what I believe was a seventh grader. Remember, I was a silent visitor. I opened the door, and he never saw me. All I could see was his big fat white pass in the air. I slipped back out unnoticed. The first trash can that I saw in the hallway, I recall sticking my head deep down into it and violently throwing up.

I ran back to my office to gather my thoughts. What did I just see? I could not have just seen that. No way. Not Singleton. Everyone loved him. He was a married man, for God's sake. The girl had to be twelve at the oldest. What should I do? What should I have done? What would I do?

First, I know all the second guessers will have a field day with this. They would all profess to being big and bad and tell everyone how they would have physically intervened and probably beat the shit out of Singleton and held his naked ass there until the police arrived. Others would have said they would have told the principal immediately and called the police. I would tell these people to shut up and don't play this game with me. Not until you were there. Not until you saw what I saw. Your mind can't believe your eyes. Second guessing is easy. It is always easy to be the Monday morning quarterback. It is always easy to think about your potential actions. You cannot predict your actions. Please do not think you can. So, stop the bullshitting. Stop the second guessing and stop being so self-righteous. You can never predict how you would react to seeing what I just saw.

That night I did not sleep. I tossed and turned, trying to figure out what I would do. Finally, I decided I would implement a planned surveillance of Mr. Singleton and if what I saw proved to be true, I would set out in my own way to solve this problem. And by now you know my way of solving these types of problems. I solve problems permanently to better the district.

That being said, that Monday, I made sure that I had my quiet shoes on because I would be on a stealth mission. Singleton taught in the auditorium. There was a shortage of space in the school and the auditorium fit just right for the instrumental music program. It also fits just right for Singleton's criminality. There were probably eight small rooms alongside of the stage. The architect designed and constructed these rooms for storage, light panels, staging areas for when an activity was happening on the stage, and for any other reason, one would need these areas for performances. One need was to teach individual students in a classroom. Yet Singleton used these rooms to teach his music lessons. He used these ante rooms to ravage his students.

I now recall how Singleton worked his way back there. It took him several years to beat down Mr. Warfield, the principal, to allow him to work in this location. Singleton was building a little private palace for his molestations. He could not even dream of a better situation. He even began parking his car on the lawn next to his rooms. The man was in heaven. No one would come back there to check on him and he could hear most people coming and, better still, all the rooms worked on a different lock and key system. There was no one with the keys. No one except Singleton and me.

So, within the first few days of my surveillance, when I went on a reconnaissance mission, I heard a noise from an unfamiliar room. These were similar grunts and groans that I had heard the other day. My stomach sank. My worst fear was proving to be true. In my opinion, Singleton was a perverted criminal pedophile. I tiptoed to peer into what he thought was a fully blocked window. Once again, I saw him going at it. I nearly threw up again right there. Once again, I backed out.

I was giving my plan a week. So, later in the week, I went up onto the catwalk to get a bird's-eye view of the auditorium. The catwalk is an area that is above the ceiling. It looks out over the spectators in the auditorium when a performance is on. There are large holes there that allow the spotlights to light the stage. They need a person to adjust the lights for any performance. I worked my way up through the far hatch, one that is seldom used, and cracked it open. To my amazement, I saw Singleton's big ass going at it again. His body twisted and turned. He did not see or hear me. He busied himself ruining another person's life. His huffing, puffing, and moaning drowned out all other noises. He clearly only cared about himself and his momentary pleasure.

On the catwalk, for God's sake! What is with this man? One thing I now knew for sure, Singleton had to go, and he had to go quickly.

Chapter Twenty-Seven
Singleton has to go. But you already knew that!

I had to come up with a plan and I had to come up with this plan right quick. Every day that I delayed, more harm was being done to this child and any others that he was violating. I also wanted to come up with a fitting end for this piece of garbage. It had to look like an accident.

I also had to do this so no student would witness this. However, I had to be there to see his fat face and to tell him why I was doing this.

I had already mentioned that one of the rear rooms off of the stage housed the light board. Our school was old and our lighting equipment was clearly in need of an upgrade. The electric panel looked medieval. It had those large pull handles to control different lights and overall power. I could have filmed an old Frankenstein movie there. It was a little eerie. I knew a bit about electricity from hanging around the maintenance men and did some reading on the topic. It did not take me long to figure out what wire I had to move to make this panel lethal. I figured I could pull this off after school with a few people still around in the building.

I had visited this room on Sunday morning to do my work. I loosened the high voltage connection wire and set it up so I only had a little to do on the day of his planned execution. To this day, I do not think Singleton ever knew that I was aware of what was going on. He was only engaged with himself and his own pleasure. He did not really give a shit about anyone else. He could never get enough, and pleasing himself was the only thing ever on his mind. He smoked, he drank, and he raped. I am convinced he never once thought about the damage he was doing to these kids. And if he did, he did not care. How could he rationalize his own behavior? He never knew that this day would be the last day on this earth.

At the close of school, I asked him to stay and help me with something in the lighting room. I explained to him I needed to have a basic knowledge of the panel because an outside group was renting the space during the upcoming weekend. Basic stage lighting operations were something I had to know. I had completed my lethal re-wiring a little earlier in the day. He fell for it. I also was wet mopping the stage. I called him into the room, and accidentally, on purpose, knocked over my water bucket. It provided a nice little puddle on the floor next to the lighting panel. I had hoped that Singleton would be in a hurry and that he really did not want to be bothered by me for this to work. From here, it was simple. I made sure I stood far enough away in the background. He was smoking his cigarette and not even paying attention to me. He told me that my job would be simple for this upcoming weekend show. To turn the power on, all I had to do was pull this lever down. I asked him to show me exactly what I had to do. That is exactly what he did. As I heard the lever complete the circuit, I instantaneously heard the sizzle and his screams. It was the last thing that he did.

As he stood there screaming, I yelled at him to tell him why this was happening to him and his ultimate punishment was to feel this fire and get used to it because he would feel this fire for eternity. I don't know if he heard me over his screams. I don't know if he processed anything that I said. I really don't care. I got to watch him die, and I enjoyed every minute. Bye, bye Mr. Singleton.

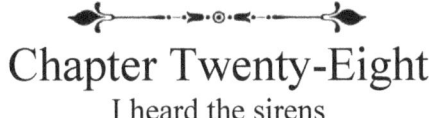

Chapter Twenty-Eight
I heard the sirens

I froze as Singleton sizzled away. It reminded me of a pound of sizzling bacon in a hot skillet. However, the smell was worse as it reminded me of my days in the war. You never forget the smell of burning flesh. I am convinced my demeanor had nothing to do with the horror of watching a man get electrocuted. I can share that both the sight and the smell were horrific. Thinking back, I think that I may have become paralyzed with some sort of joy. Maybe I was getting off on this. I know for a fact that each execution was becoming easier. Easier to plan, easier to carry out and easier to sleep with after the fact. And in each case, I knew in my heart that the district was better off because of my actions.

The aftermath of this execution was a doozy. First, as Singleton lit up, the power in the school tripped out. I guess they did not make the electrical panel for an electrocution. Singleton had taken all the voltage. He was a fat pig, so it didn't surprise me. Smoke and flames also came out of the back room. I heard the smoke alarms and I could hear the sirens coming from a distance. I can only imagine the look of amazement on the firefighters' faces as they arrived. Most times when a smoke alarm went off, it was for some obscure reason like dust in the smoke detector head and the firefighters came with a very pissed off, yet casual demeanor. The school was bothering them again. What else were they doing? Yet I knew the captain would be happy because he got to add a count for a response to his monthly quota. He responded and basically did nothing.

However, this was different. Smoke and flames were now being seen out of the rear door of the stage. And being as this was the auditorium, sprinkler systems sent water now spraying down on all the seats. And there was fatty's body lying there with a surprised look plastered on his face for eternity, his body charred and smoldering.

Because I was there, I picked up a fire extinguisher and starting fighting the flames. I was "Johnny on the spot" and actually received some insignificant burns on my arms to show for my work. When the flames were out, I also coughed a few times to make it look good.

Yes, I became a hero to the school. My swift action prevented a bigger fire. People said that the school was lucky that I was near the scene and could respond with a cool head. The television news feed interviewed me again and I the mayor presented me a medal. How about that?

I never expected that big of a fire, but it proved to be a good omen. The fire destroyed the entire electrical panel, and no one could ever learn that I tampered with it. I cleaned up the mess, yet the smell lingered. The local cops, my old friends Beavis and Butthead, closed the file on this one quickly. They escaped with the minimal amount of effort or work. The old, faulty stage lighting panel caused Singleton's accidental death. Yea, right?

The school and community poured out to mourn his death. He was **the** man. He touched many lives. The community saw him as a savior to our youth. What a crock of shit. If only the townspeople knew how he touched some of them. I was at all the vigils and services and stood in the back at all of them chuckling to myself knowing how he really met his demise. The people canonized him. I had nothing to gain by telling them the truth. Most people probably would not have believed me. However, I hoped that the girls that he was abusing could rest a little easier. I also hoped that someday they would seek the counseling that I knew they would need.

The spirit of Singleton lived on. However, I truly believed that Principal Warfield knew what was happening. He instituted a new policy that no one could use the rooms off of the stage for anything except storage and preparation for performances, not teaching. Thank God. I am convinced that the school made it easy for him to abuse kids. Now, they were trying to pick up the pieces. Everyone was scrambling and everyone seemed complicit. Pedophiles don't change. The school needed to change. I am sure that the student I observed was not the only one. I am not really sure who it was because I never saw her face. I saw a figure and unfortunately Singleton's big white ass.

Chapter Twenty-Nine
Life goes on

One thing is for sure, life goes on. They do not guarantee tomorrow for anyone, yet I can just about guarantee that school will be open tomorrow whether you are there. I saw this concept up close and personal when Peoples passed away and when Ducky left us. The same will be true of Singleton.

It is funny how I think of these deaths. It seems to me like I had nothing to do with them. They exist in my mind kind of like some sort of dream sequence you see in the movies. When I talk about it or even think about Peoples or Ducky, all my actions seem like some slow-motion fog. Shit, I don't know why I feel this way because I provided both of them their ticket to the hereafter. I also happily punched Singleton's ticket to the great beyond. I murdered them. That is a fact. I cleaned the school and that too, is a fact. I won't miss any of them.

Liberation of the school occurred when Peoples passed on. Ducky's passing liberated the custodial staff and Singleton's passing liberated a group of young and innocent 12-year-old girls. And maybe my legacy will be that of the Great Liberator. I like how that sounds. I am noble and my cause is noble.

My murders changed me. Each murder made it easier to do the next one. Each of my murders changed my mindset. I now went to work each day looking for my next target. Man, I have changed!

Chapter Thirty
The passing of time

Singleton's passing occurred in December, and the school soon returned to normal. It sickened me to hear the older teachers talk about Singleton. In their own minds, they made him a teacher and humanitarian of the year. And as each day passed, they made his work more remarkable. It was almost like hearing anglers tell their tales. The fish gets bigger every day. The same was true of Singleton's legacy. It, too, got bigger every day. I listened, but tried my best to ignore it. As I heard all of this background noise, I knew it was real crap. His peers knew about his antics and I knew it. I remain convinced that many of the teachers and yes, old Mr. Warfield knew or sensed it, yet they did nothing to stop it. I don't know how they lived with themselves. Even though I am a murderer, it is easy for me to put my head on the pillow because at least I did something about it. I acted and if that was wrong, so be it.

Schools being what they are, I knew that this issue would soon pass. Today's news in the school, you know that stuff that was on page one in everyone's mind, soon would drift to a deeper section in one's mental newspaper and soon it would be out of print. Schools have a remarkable way of always having "a pot of stew" brewing on the stove. And you always have many cooks cutting up carrots to throw into the mix. Some people can't help themselves. They always have to be throwing something into the pot to cause trouble. They just love it. And soon unbeknownst to me, my next cleaning job would be because of a "soup stirrer" gone awry.

The winter turned to spring, and the spring turned quickly to summer. Although the kids and teachers may bitch about the school year, it really flies by.

Over this year, I really bonded with Mrs. Kelly. No, we were not an item. We never socialized outside of school. I always felt a need to protect her and when some teachers or kids got out of line with her, I could reel them back in. I bought her coffee every day at break time and we would sit and drink this coffee together and talk about the school. It was not uncommon for me to buy her a donut, nor was it uncommon for her to bring in some home-baked goods for us to share at break. We exchanged small gifts at Christmas or on our birthdays and we would help each other out when needed. She kept the books, and I knew if I was running late, she would never mark me tardy or absent. She always kept me in the loop with gossip from the principal's office or the central office. I knew things well before others knew these same things. Never forget that knowledge is power. She knew I would clean her car off on a snowy day or change a flat tire for her. We were workplace friends. I don't want to make more out of this relationship than it was, but we trusted and truly liked one another.

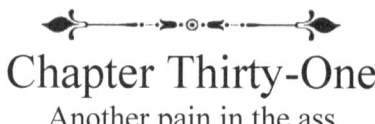

Chapter Thirty-One
Another pain in the ass

One of the other secretaries in the office with Mrs. Kelly was Mrs. Westerman. Now she was a real pain in the ass. She was loud and rude. There were no boundaries for her. She had no real friends, yet she was everyone's friend. Everyone needed her to survive in the school. People tried to stay on her good side because they did not want to get on her nasty side and be the brunt of her mean spirited and hurtful gossip.

Mrs. Westerman was a drama queen. She fought with everyone. Not a person in the building could escape her wrath. Any personal relationship with Mrs. Westerman proved to be cyclical. You fought with her and after a while you made up, but you eventually fought again. These feuds just went on and on. It was just a way of life with Mrs. Westerman. With her, there was always a distasteful encounter just around the corner. She was beyond the normal drama and bullshit one saw in a school. In everything she did, she went over the top. She dressed like a tramp and I always wanted to tell her that no one wanted to see down her shirt. Her cleavage did not turn anyone on. Her face needed a good scrubbing to take all the makeup off and her breath constantly smelled like the cigarettes that fed her addiction. And while we are on the topic of smoking, I know she had many hiding places within the school to sneak a smoke and incompetent Mr. Warfield would never address it. This irritated me to no end because I had to go around cleaning up her cigarettes that she casually discarded in her hiding places. She put out her butts by grinding them into the floor with her foot. Try cleaning that up. I confronted her several times about it and it always became a screaming match between the two of us. There was just no winning with her.

One day at the close of school, I saw Mrs. Kelly sitting at her desk crying. I tried to console her, and she shared with me she just had a bad day with Mrs. Westerman. It was not uncommon for her to have this experience, but for her to cry, it must have been bad. This went on for the next several days and the straw that broke the camel's back was when Westerman purposely broke the picture of Mrs. Kelly's family on her desk. For Mrs. Kelly, the world revolved around her children and their families. She could have cared less about her husband. She shared enough of those tales of woe with me at our coffee breaks. I know people would tire of hearing about her kids, but tough shit to them. Mrs. Kelly was a friendly person who would do anything for anybody, and she did not deserve the bullying treatment from Mrs. Westerman. I felt compelled to act. Mrs. Kelly and the school had to be freed from this shrew. I knew what had to be done. So, on this Friday, I decided. Westerman had to go. The Liberator had to do his thing.

Chapter Thirty-Two
Hatching a plan

Once I decided, there was no turning back. However, I predicted that this liberation would be my hardest yet. How was Westerman gong to meet her end? It had to be appropriate, and she had to know at the end it was because she was such an overall bitch to everyone, especially to Mrs. Kelly.

By now you know I did my best thinking in bed. I would lay there looking at the ceiling trying to figure this one out. I wondered if this was going to be another school accident? On the way home? In her home? I relied on using the school as my place to do my work; the work of the Liberator. I knew the school better than anyone. I knew the hiding places. I knew the exact location of "buried bodies." I knew the ins and outs of the place and how it operated. I studied each person and knew each person's habits. My safety zone and comfort zone of operation were in the school.

I strangled Peoples; I froze Ducky, and I electrocuted Singleton. The school was where I conducted all of my liberations. My repertoire was growing. So how could Westerman join this lucky group?

After several nights of staring at the ceiling, I narrowed it down to two possibilities. She would either have a deadly fall or something would fall on her. Both were risky because I could not be sure that either method would kill her. However, my luck had been very good. I did not want to do something risky or careless and break my streak. My work was good, not because of luck, but because I meticulously planned every detail. I needed a surefire method. Leaving things to chance was not an option.

The old bitch, Westerman, would die doing what she usually did at work; not her job. I figured it out. Something would accidentally fall on her. I knew the exact spot. It would be another fitting end. Now, I just had to do it.

Chapter Thirty-Three
The time was just right

Mrs. Westerman was in charge of procuring teaching supplies, which meant she would spend a certain amount of time in the stockroom. Teachers would place an order with her and she would deliver them at the end of each week. This job allowed her to not work for a full day. She took her time delivering each order to each teacher and used that time to spread her poison throughout the building. She had to be tired. At least her jaws had to be tired because she just never shut her mouth. And mostly, verbal trash was all that ever came out of her big mouth.

I decided that the stockroom would be the place. She would take her last breath under a pile of old, useless trash. I thought this was a fitting way for her to go. This was where she would meet her maker. Yes, she would travel to the great beyond among thousands of #2 yellow pencils and a sea of paper clips. The place was really a mess. They threw shit all over the place. It did not surprise me it looked this way because I had watched Westerman at work. She could lose everything, except, of course, her cigarettes or telephone. I could never figure out how she got anything done. She didn't. Her full-time job was stirring the stew. She always kept the pot bubbling.

Westerman announced to sleepy old Warfield that it was time for her to go to the stockroom. This announcement would always come on a Friday, right before lunch. Then she would spend the entire afternoon there.

I knew it was a big scam, and I am sure others did, too. She may have spent a half an hour readying the supplies for me to help her deliver, and the rest of the time visiting her teacher friends, smoking and talking on the phone. I was always an excellent observer. By this time in my life, I had developed a pretty keen ability to read people. You know it is funny how the malcontents easily find one another. I have heard that misery loves company and, in this school, that dynamic played itself out for all to see. She did not hesitate interrupting classes and the malcontent teachers welcomed her visit. The teacher would stand outside of the door, in the hallway, complaining with Westerman. And of course, the kids, while this was happening, were not learning. I am not sure that the kids cared, and I know that the teacher did not care. But I cared. For Westerman and her cronies, it just did not matter. They certainly did not care. This was a regular game. You could almost set your weekly calendar and watch by these visits. Once again, the kids got cheated. They were the ones losing instructional time. This routine irritated the shit out of me. I am also sure that the kids by the doorway heard all the obscenities that accompanied this visit. They also got a good earful of the gossip of the day, some of which included sordid rumors, including the sex lives of some of their teachers and staff members.

I think that Mr. Warfield welcomed these weekly visits. Because he could spend a quiet afternoon doing some work, if he did any, or take a little nap on the couch in his office. It guaranteed him an afternoon of peace without hearing Mrs. Westerman performing in the outer office. Not only was Westerman a pain in the ass, she was loud and vile. I think I already painted a pretty good picture of her. She was not a woman I would want to bring home to my mother if my mother was still alive, rest her soul.

I had to prepare the stockroom for my plan to work. Tall shelves lined the walls along with the inner aisles. The stockroom missed any annual cleaning. We saved garbage. A six-foot stepladder was in a place that she used to reach items on the top shelf. There were similar free-standing shelves in the center of the room. They were equally high and there were probably three rows of these types of shelves. I certainly do not know if this arrangement would have ever met any national or state safety standards. No one ever checked. When any state, county, or city inspectors visited, we just never took them near this location. The isolated stockroom is in a far corner of the building. Normal school traffic and activity bypassed this place. It was truly out of the flow of traffic. A perfect place for a "liberation."

On some shelves were old ditto and mimeograph machines. You may not recall or perhaps never knew what they used these big contraptions for. We used them to make bulk copies. One thing for sure, I can tell you, is that these bad boys were heavy as hell. Keeping them was ridiculous. Oops, my bad.

I was the one that should have done this job, but right now I was glad that I put it off for another day, hoping that day would never come. Sometimes it pays off to be lazy. They were big and heavy, yet they fit on the center shelves with a bit of an overhang. They also loaded these shelves with heavy paper boxes. If you never have lifted one of these, they are over fifty pounds each. This center row of supplies was to be my murder weapon. This liberation would basically occur in plain sight.

It was Friday afternoon, and I knew Westerman would be there. I had gone into the room the previous night and simply loosened the bolts that held the middle shelves in place. I also disabled the third-floor surveillance cameras. This, too, was not odd. This was easy because half of the cameras in the joint did not operate correctly. It lulled the school into a real false sense of security. I do not know if it was laziness or incompetence of the administration to allow this to happen. But right now, that was not my worry.

Also, in preparation, I moved some of the commonly requested supplies, like pens and pencils, to the highest shelf on the wall near the loosened shelves to ensure that Westerman would partially climb the ladder to reach them.

I was ready to go. It was getting near kickoff time. Westermann's end was near. I did not think about it or worry about it. However, each one of my "liberations" was getting a bit more complicated. And in each case, there was more of a chance of me getting caught. But for the good of the district and for the good of my friend Mrs. Kelly, I had to complete this task. I really felt like I was being driven by a higher power. I questioned my existence on earth. Was it to be the Liberator? It seemed that way.

I hid in the stockroom behind some boxes and waited. Westerman arrived, and instead of filling the orders she took a seat and had a smoke. She also had to make some personal phone calls. I couldn't stand the smoke nor could I stand hearing her screechy voice complaining. I am sure that if anyone saw me, it would have been a comical sight of me hiding behind these boxes while she smoked and chatted. I was saying to myself as I crouched behind the boxes, "God dammit, finish the smoke already," but then I thought she might as well enjoy it because it would be her last cigarette. I sat hiding, looking at my watch, silently imploring her to get going. As each minute passed, I was getting more pissed off. My adrenaline was already pumping through my body and now I had to listen to her whine and complain. One consolation for me was that this would be the last time that I would have to listen to her bullshit.

Finally, she clicked off the phone and began gathering her supplies. As she worked, she sang an oldie tune. She complained out loud about why she had to do this job. She was having a pleasant conversation with herself in two voices. It forced me to listen to her grating voice. Besides holding back my laughter, I was thinking, just get going and shut the fuck up.

When she got to my designated space and climbed the first step of the ladder with her back to me, I gently put my shoulder into the center shelf that I had previously loosened and pushed. Everything came tumbling down upon her. The old ditto machines that probably weighed 150 pounds each crashed into her head. Whack, I heard the steel machine crash into her skull. As my ears processed this, my eyes processed the blood now pouring from the open wound. I was on sensory overload. The other ditto machine clipped her and probably almost 1000 pounds of paper covered her. She did not know what hit her. She did not scream or make any sound. As I ran over to make sure she knew why this was happening, I came to realize that she was already dead. The fall obviously broke her neck. That still did not stop me as I kneeled next to her and whispered in her ears all of her school sins, especially how she treated Mrs. Kelly. I stood there for a minute to make sure that she was dead. She was dead all right. If the head crash of the gigantic machines did not kill her, I think that the boxes and other debris did. Her twisted head was now looking at me at a strange angle. Anguish was her death mask.

I was quite happy that her face was full of this anguish. It was fitting for her to end this way as a payback for all the anguish that she caused. I knew that by her death; the school was better off. Once again, I had to cleanse the school, which was becoming extremely satisfying for me. Now I had to figure out how to slither out without being seen. Because of the isolated location of the stockroom, I know no one heard the crash. It was Friday afternoon. At the close of the day, teachers raced to beat the kids out of the door.

Next to the stockroom was a janitorial closet, which contained a ladder and a hatch leading to the roof. I slithered into the janitor's closet and up to the roof. I then walked across the roof to the hatch at the far end, which I previously had unlocked and made my way down the stairs. Then I made it my business to be seen by as many people as I could. I went to several offices and then down to the gym. I made sure that I chatted with several of the coaches that I considered friends. If they were ever to be questioned by anyone, I am pretty sure that they would not recall the time and would attest to me being where they were.

As I was escaping through the roof hatch, I had to laugh. I laughed because I thought of all the people that used the roof for a variety of reasons. None of which were good. Sometimes people would go to the roof to smoke or drink. Sometimes people would use the roof for some secret meeting and other times people would use the roof just to hide. I had to make my way around all sorts of trash on the roof, including hundreds of cigarette butts and discarded beer and wine bottles. I also believed that the neighborhood kids somehow could get up on the roof to probably do the same things that the adults were doing during the school day. Sometimes the thoughts of both the kids and adults using the roof for the same reason just made me laugh.

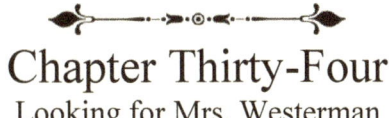

Chapter Thirty-Four
Looking for Mrs. Westerman

The building quickly emptied that day. I did what I normally did. What I became an expert at doing, namely walking around looking busy, but actually doing very little.

It was quitting time, and Mr. Warfield finally came out of the office. He saw that Westermann's desk was more cluttered than usual and her personal items were still there. Mrs. Kelly, who stayed past quitting time daily, was slowly closing up shop. When Mrs. Kelly saw me come into the office, our eyes met. It was kind of eerie. Although nothing more than perhaps my own paranoia, I sensed that when our eyes met; she knew what I had done.

Warfield solicited my help in doing a building-wide hunt for Westerman. I tried to soothe his uneasiness, explaining that she was probably in a teacher's classroom chatting and merely lost track of the time. He bought this for a while and we walked around the building. As we approached the far end of the third floor, my uneasiness grew. We would soon find what I left of Mrs. Westerman.

The walk to the stockroom tired Warfield. I could see it on his face. It was probably the most he walked in a couple of years. He had no clue what waited for him less than twenty feet away. I unlocked the door and held it open for the boss. He probably took about three steps when I heard him scream. It was the first time I ever heard Mr. Warfield swear. I don't know if I ever mentioned it to you that Principal Warfield was a black man. For the first time in my life, I thought I saw a black man turn white. I am not sure if he soiled himself, which would be a shame because he always wore thousand-dollar tailored suits, but I had to use my cat-like quickness to avoid his projectile vomit.

I helped him compose himself and he told me to hurry and call an ambulance. I tried to be delicate, but I told him that an ambulance could not now help poor Mrs. Westerman. That being said, I called the police and reached a friend that I knew on the job, and asked him to respond to the school. I told him what we had on our hands and I would meet him in the back lot. No need for sirens.

Warfield and I accomplished our mission. We found Mrs. Westerman.

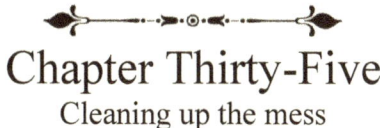

Chapter Thirty-Five
Cleaning up the mess

The radio car arrived using no lights or sirens and parked in a remote location of the lot. I met the uniformed officers there and brought them up to meet Mrs. Westerman. One guy knew her because he went to school here. Before seeing her, he kind of chuckled. Because he, too, had his run-ins with Westy when he was a student here. Mrs. Westerman was a non-discriminatory pain in the ass. She never saw color or status in how she interacted with people. Unless you were in her private little circle, she treated you like crap.

After seeing her, this tough guy cop who was laughing a minute ago, now was in no laughing mood. Just like Mr. Warfield, he started to wretch. I knew then that I had to establish a designated throw up spot, which I did. I put a lined trash barrel out in the hall with a chair and a box of paper towels nearby. There were bottles of water brought up to this spot. This cop would not be the last person to need the designated vomit spot. Others would use it when they arrived on the scene.

The two uniformed cops took the preliminary report and told me to wait for the detectives, my favorite incompetents, Beavis, and Butthead. Upon hearing this, I thought about their arrival and placed a bet with myself about which one would need to throw up first.

It took them a while to arrive, and I held down the fort along with the two uniformed cops. Warfield was in his office, laying down. Some unknown staff member called Westerman's husband. I am convinced her death did not sadden him. When I saw him later that day, I am not sure that the subtle smile on his face was knowing that he would receive her work supplied insurance policy or merely getting rid of her. I think it was probably a little of both.

I felt sorry for the poor son of a bitch. He had to live with her. For us, she eventually went home. For us, we only had her five days of the week, but for this poor bastard, he had her basically 24 /7. I do not know what he did in his prior life to deserve this, but they say there is someone for everyone. I doubt that this is true and let me also say that it is better to be in no relationship rather than a bad one. Unknowingly, in my streak of liberations, I inadvertently liberated Mr. Westerman. He should thank me.

Chapter Thirty-Six
Here comes the calvary

Soon Beavis and Butthead arrived, and I was right. Beavis needed the trash can. Once he saw Westerman's body, he started to wretch. Butthead handled it better. Without beating this to death, no pun intended, Mrs. Westerman was a real sight. It was really hard to describe the look frozen on her face for eternity from her twisted and bleeding head. I am sure that this picture will come to me when I stare at my ceiling at night, but I assure you I did not feel bad about it. I never felt one bit of remorse.

Beavis and Butthead quickly ruled the death was an accident. They surmised Westerman climbed the ladder to cherry pick her supplies and lost her balance and then reached for the center row of shelving to grab to help prevent her from falling. However, her body weight was too heavy for this and instead of breaking her fall, she pulled the shelf over on her and the heavy old copying equipment came crashing down on her head. These two wizards decided accidental blunt force trauma to the head caused that death. However, it looked like perhaps her twisting fall broke her neck. Her head was almost facing backwards. For everyone's purpose, it did not matter. She was dead all the same.

I have to laugh at the stupidity of our local police department. Over several years, this was the third accidental death in the school. Remember how Ducky froze and how Singleton lit up when he fried? And now Westerman fell off the ladder. While we are at it, I am sure that you did not forget that in the other school Mr. Peoples just vanished. The school district probably set the world record for accidental deaths, if there was such a thing. Not one person put two and two together. I was counting on this stupidity and carelessness. However, this was all about to change. I had to cool it for a while.

Things also changed when the board of education's insurance rates skyrocketed and our insurance company was sending into the district a bright young investigator. We will talk about that a little later.

Chapter Thirty-Seven
Kelly and I

After things settled in, we got back to our normal craziness, which was the standard operating procedure for our school on any day. We lived from crisis to crisis, and now we had gotten pretty good at dealing with death. The school community almost became immune to it. This chaos was just normal for us.

Whatever the case may be, I knew things were now different between my good friend Mrs. Kelly and me. Sure, we still took breaks together. I still bought her coffee, and she still brought me my favorite home-baked cookies. There was just something different. You could just feel it. It was like there was that enormous elephant in the room. We knew it was there and yet we never wanted to talk about it. We just couldn't. Both of us knew that. We never talked about it, but I think we both just sensed it. And of all the gruesome things that I did, the only thing that I felt bad about was the change in our relationship. And maybe there was no change. Maybe this was all my problem with my head playing tricks on me. Who knew?

I did not like this change. I miss whatever we had.

One day, as I was working, or should I say walking the halls looking busy, I noticed a job advertised on the bulletin board. The high school needed a Head Custodian. I needed a change.

I ducked Mrs. Kelly. I even hid my request for transfer. I did not want to deal with it. My good bye would be quick and what I hoped would be painless. They granted my request, and I cleaned out my locker and prepared to leave. I was especially good at avoidance and right now I had hoped that this skill would not leave me. A letter in a small envelope fell out of my locker as I was almost out of the door. I opened it and there were only seven words written on school stationery:

I KNOW WHAT YOU DID. THANKS. KELLY.

Shit! God damn it! Son of a bitch!
 Were these to be my last words?

Chapter Thirty-Eight
On the move again

Well, I was on the move again. Probably not a bad idea. I think it was important for me to get out of that school before people speculated on these deaths. It appears everyone was buying the idea that these three deaths were accidental. That tells you a lot about human nature. People believe what they want to believe. And I felt strongly that people in the school community did not think that they had a murderer in their midst. However, no one person could argue that the school, both schools, were not better off because I took care of those people. I have become quite confident that I am the Great Liberator. I wish I could wear some sort of superhero outfit. I lay in bed thinking of what it could be. Superman had his big "S" on his chest and Batman hid behind his cowl. What could I wear? Maybe I will come up with something.

In the past, I dealt with people as they became evident. I never went looking for that pain in the ass. They always became clear. I think somewhere I underwent some sort of change. Now, I am looking for my next liberation. I have justified to myself, in my head, that what I was doing was righteous. I put this information in a locked-up compartment in my brain. It is amazing how the human mind and spirit can adapt.

I must admit, though, I was becoming blood thirsty. I was eagerly awaiting my next mission. However, I forced myself to lie low for a while in my new school. I was going to do a lot of observing and not much talking. I would trust no one.

I found my avoidance difficult because I enjoyed hanging around with some men who were coaches. I was one of the boys. And being one of the boys, opened up some doors for me. I also saw some things I probably should not have seen. Being one of the boys was fun.

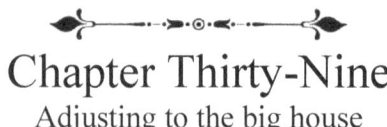
Chapter Thirty-Nine
Adjusting to the big house

Now I was at the biggest building in the district. Some called it the flagship. When I heard that, I had to laugh. I saw it as a sinking ship. I was supervising more men now, and that became difficult. The building was extremely old, and it was dirty. It needed a good scrubbing from top to bottom. The teachers, mostly, were pigs and without question, the students were pigs.

Yes, there was some adjusting I had to do.

The first thing that I observed was that everyone was nuttier in the flagship than in the other schools. It was the big house all right. It was the big nut house. Instead of being the flagship for the district, it was nothing more than a crazy ship of fools. Perhaps more troubling than anything, no one was driving the boat. We were afloat somewhere in "nutsville," with no captain and no rudder on the ship. I will try to explain some antics that I had observed, but I do not think that I will have enough time. But what the heck, I will try. But before I start these tales, I will let you know they are all true. Although most people are liars, I assure you, I am not.

One of my first observations was that most people flat out hated their jobs. They hated kids. And these people really pissed me off because they are the ones that gave the entire teaching profession a bad name. These are the people that became teachers because they thought it was a simple job. They knew the hours were good, and they had their summers off. For this group, there was no overtime. I used to watch the teachers run to the door during dismissal time, almost trampling the kids. I wanted to trip them all.

Others became teachers because they just liked to boss people around. They were on some sort of power trip and for them; they had a captive audience of, say, 25 kids for 45 minutes where they had anointed themselves king. Instead of the king, I should probably say dictator, because that is how they acted. Some teachers really oppressed the kids. They would scream and yell and were overall tyrants. They would work hard at putting the kids down daily. Grades were used to punish the kids that cared. They thoroughly enjoyed failing kids. They would give a kid a grade of 25% say in the first marking period, all the while knowing that for these kids, it sealed their fate by November. Then they would work hard at trying to get the kid removed from their class. I knew this because I would eavesdrop in the faculty dining room and could see for myself as I walked around the building, looking busy. The older kids were easy to bond with. I did this mostly in the students' cafeteria. While trying to keep the place clean, the kids would readily talk to me. Sadly, I was one of the few black adult faces in the building. I became a mentor to many of them. I would attend most of the athletic events and that, too, gave me an opportunity to build trust. They knew I liked them and they knew I respected them. High school kids do not want or need much. They needed to feel respected. I provided that respect, whereas most of the teachers made a business out of disrespect. Believe me, there were some kids that were nothing but a pain in the ass who needed their butts kicked. It was hard for me not to do this.

I settled in and my first year passed by pretty quickly. Before I knew it, I was starting my second year on this journey to nowhere on this ship of fools.

However, I was quietly building my list, only in my head, of future liberations.

Chapter Forty
Facing a genuine dilemma

As time passed, I knew I was about to face a huge moral dilemma. Yes, I have morals. In actuality, perhaps my standards are higher than yours. I think you understand by now how I viewed my actual role. And I knew my actual role was not to sweep floors and clean toilets. I was the savior of this school district. This is my destiny. Being a savior is a full-time job. How could I save each student and the entire district? A place that I loved. Therefore, I had to do my best to keep the district as pure as possible, which I now knew was a true impossibility. So, I just continued to do my best. Many times, I had to save the district from itself. Yes, this institution was alive for me and I could not let it fall into the hands of miscreants that occupied its classrooms, halls, cafeterias, administrative offices and athletic fields.

But now I was seeing some needs that had to be taken care of. And for this one, lying in bed, studying the ceiling did not help. I paced my bedroom and small apartment almost nightly until my body fell victim to exhaustion.

Let me explain my dilemma. There are two parts to this dilemma and as of now, I do not have a simple answer for either part. Would I act on a student? Would I act on one of the "good old boys" that I now befriended? These are two good questions that I still cannot answer.

Let me first share my thinking about the kids. I find out that at the high school there are some genuine problems. In my day, I would have described them as no good bastards that needed a good ass kicking. They ranged in age from 14 to 19 and I can tell you that some of their behaviors were unbelievable. If I ever thought of behaving that way or talking to an adult in the manner that I had become accustomed to hearing, my grandmother or daddy would have taken a stick to me. And I would have deserved every bit. For some of these students, we should call upon the great liberator. But here is the dilemma.

If I am here to make the school better for kids, how can I rationalize doing away with a student? And in this case, I would need to take care of many. Also, I had to believe that kids behave in this way because there are so many other issues affecting their lives. They have no control over these issues, yet these issues help make them who they are and who they will become. So, when I think of it in those terms, kids are off limits. There will be no student liberations. Perhaps I need to move on to parent liberations?

But in another minute of mental clarity, I believe that some of these kids are incapable of change and, therefore, I should eliminate them before they can do any more damage to the school or someone else. This waffling and mental flip flops had to stop. I needed to stay focused on a plan. That focus has kept me successful to this point. I knew that the minute I let my mind scramble, I would screw up.

How would I resolve this?

Next, what do I do about my "good old boys?" Who is more fucked up is not something I can tell you. I have seen them smoke, drink and, yes, screw in the school. I have never in my life seen a group of men that have such strong sexual needs. Some folks will screw anything. And I don't mean to sound sexist, the women are just as bad. You almost needed a scorecard if you wanted to keep track of who was screwing who. There was absolutely no sanctity in wedding vows. They meant nothing. Being married with families did not stop them. I just shook my head in bewilderment at this type of behavior. But they were not hurting anyone but themselves, and if I acted on these folks, I think that there would have been a few adults left in the building.

Also, I have seen them steal just about anything from the building. Some will take anything that is not nailed down. And even then, I am not sure that they would not remove the nails to take something. For example, I watched one of the "good old boys" steal a computer piece by piece. He dismantled it and each day took another component home. I saw him slip the motherboard into his briefcase one afternoon before he left. It amazed me. He looked at me and smiled. For days, no one knew what had happened. He left the shell of the computer behind and I am sure that anyone who walked by assumed that this computer was fully operational. There were absolutely no guts left in it. Eventually, I think that he even took the mouse.

Another time, I watched as a coach stole equipment from the athletic director. He would go into the storage closet with him and trick him into getting up on a ladder to look for something. He would then throw any equipment that he wanted down the stairway and gather it up before the athletic director knew what took place. When I think back on this, I doubt if the AD ever knew anything was missing. He was at the end of his career and most people thought he was senile. Maybe he was, maybe he wasn't. Maybe he knew what was happening all along and just did not care. I am sure that he took that answer to his grave. I had to shut up about this because I too became complicit when I accepted a brand-new pair of sneakers from this coach. It is funny that as I reflect on this; I beat myself up more for accepting the pair of sneakers than I did when I killed someone. The human mind is an amazing thing. I could rationalize and justify to myself a heinous act of killing someone brutally, yet I mentally tortured myself over a pair of sneakers. Go figure.

I think some of the good old boys just felt the need to push the envelope to see what they could get away with before they got caught. They would say or do just about anything. I will let the psychiatrists analyze them. It was just one wacky place.

And these are the guys I called my friends. When I witnessed some sort of violation of the rules, I wonder if I would have acted differently if they weren't my newfound friends. Obviously, that is a good question that I could not answer. What if they crossed some imaginary line in my head? Would the Liberator act?

I needed to establish some rules for my liberations. Establishing these rules and guidelines about my liberations came easily and unknowingly.

My first removal was Mr. Peoples, the racist bigot principal in the elementary school. My second removal was old Ducky Donaldson, who was just a lazy royal pain in the ass, who had become an obstacle for everyone. Next up was Mr. Singleton, the music teacher who was nothing but an evil pedophile who had the entire community bamboozled while he ravaged young kids. His removal was easy. The final removal to date was Mrs. Westerman, who was a nasty, self-centered individual who caused more damage to the school by her constant drama, who finally crossed one of my friends (Good old Mrs. Kelly).

Let's see if any patterns developed. Namely:
- Principal Peoples-racist bigot
- Custodian Donaldson-lazy pain in the ass obstacle
- Teacher Singleton-evil pedophile
- Secretary Westerman-nasty, loud mouth drama queen

It seems as if two categories were emerging. The first being flat out evil people (Peoples and Singleton) and the second category being lazy and nasty people who hurt the school and the people who worked there (Ducky and Westerman).

OK. I could live with those rules. I am sure that they will expand when I see the need.

I was now sure that I would not remove any kids. However, I would have to figure out a way to teach those kids a lesson. Implementing these lessons actually proved to be harder than true liberations. When I gave these lessons, I exposed myself a bit more and made it easier for one to catch me. I also knew that if one of the "good old boys" crossed some sort of line in my head, the Liberator would have acted. No one should have been above the laws that I set down.

I felt as though my role was expanding. I hoped that this expanded role would not cause my demise. I really never worried about getting caught. The school could not survive without me. Because without my work, the evil surely would have taken over. I knew I had carried a very heavy burden on my shoulders. I couldn't fuck it up.

Chapter Forty-One
My first student challenge.

My actual job description contained many tasks that were not very pleasant. To frame it differently, many of my daily tasks just sucked.

One of these was cleaning the toilets. Many of the students acted like animals. I apologize for saying that, but it proved to be true. I know that my pet dog, that I had as a child, had better bathroom manners than some of these kids.

Let me give you an idea of what I saw and then you can make up your own mind on how to describe these kids. For the sake of brevity, I will list some of these things. For example:

- It became impossible to keep the doors on the stalls. Kids would hang on them and swing on them for entertainment. They would also beat the doors up by punching, kicking or attempting to fold the doors in half. Therefore, stalls rarely had privacy doors. What type of quality of life exists when you could not use the toilet to take care of your needs in private?
- It was near impossible to provide soap in the facilities. Whatever we tried ended up a disaster. They ripped soap dispensers from the walls, and if we used bar soap, that disappeared down the toilet.
- It was a rarity that hot water ever existed in the bathrooms. That was not the students' fault. The administration decided it would cost too much to fix and why bother? Because the kids did not take care of the bathrooms, anyway. Nice attitude.
- When smoking was popular, students would put their cigarettes out on the toilet seats. The burnt cigarette butts quickly blackened the toilet seats. Who would want to sit on that?
- It was not uncommon to find soiled feminine products on the floor or stuck to the walls. Now that is a pleasant sight. I challenge any of you to walk into a student restroom and see the walls decorated with used tampons and used sanitary napkins and not get

sick. I challenge each of you not to feel as though you would want to choke someone. Or perhaps maybe kill someone?
- You could not keep a mirror on the walls. It either became graffiti marred or they took it down.
- Overall ventilation was a joke.

I must add that we basically opened the school 24 hours a day. Most every community organization used the facilities. Some of this nonsense occurred after hours. You really needed a matron in the lavatories at all times, and we know that was impossible. I also must add that in the spirit of honesty, the new administration was diligently working to clean it up.

I knew how to solve the problem, but my idea fell like a lead balloon. I should have locked all the adult restrooms and made the adults use the student facilities. The adult presence would have prevented some of these acts of vandalism. I also guarantee that the administration would have treated these facilities differently if it affected them. But in our world, that would never fly.

I would sit and scratch my head in bewilderment at the administrators' attitude regarding the bathrooms. Didn't they know you could judge the quality of life in a school by the restroom facilities? Even I knew that. And who am I? I know I care more deeply about this school district than anyone, even the superintendent and principals. One thing that I could guarantee is that if a Board of Education member's child complained at home about these facilities, they would change. Or perhaps one day, as the enrollment continued to dwindle, the administration might wake up and see the light.

The one issue that forced me to confront my rules was what I will call the case of the "screwing stuffers."

Chapter Forty-Two
The case of the screwy screwing stuffers

I hope that the name that I had given to this situation has piqued your interest. There was a district wide change in the beverage suppliers to the school. The district now sold in the cafeteria and vending machines, 20-ounce bottles of water, iced tea, juice and soda. I knew I heard they cut some deal with the soda manufacturer to provide college scholarship money to the kids for making this switch. Nice, but there was a ripple effect.

Well, we had a group of girls who just loved to take the empty bottles and screw them deep into the toilets. Just visualize that. They had to reach their hands and arms through the toilet water and then they inverted the bottle and screwed it into the opening. They could lodge them so deep into the toilet that no one could get them out. Everyone tried to remove them. Finally, we had to secure an expensive outside contractor to come in and figure it out. He had to take the toilets off of the wall and turn them upside down and use a makeshift tool to unscrew the stuck bottle. Do you realize how costly that was? What a pain in the ass that was? How time-consuming that was?

Yes, I wanted to find the kids and kill them. I was that angry. I had a set of very rigid rules. Breaking my rules was now an option. These kids had to go. But I faced my dilemma about this. How would I catch them? And if I did not kill them, how could I make my point to them? How could I teach them the lesson that they needed? I had to scare the shit out of them. I also had to revisit my rules because I believed these kids deserved the ultimate punishment. Oh, and I forgot to tell you that this behavior went on for years. They obviously started as freshmen and were progressing through their school years all the time torturing me.

I set up cameras near the facilities. I convinced administration to man the female restrooms with teachers at the door to sign in and out students. No luck. About three years into this nightmare, I had a brainstorm. These kids probably averaged one "screw job" a month. There was no rhyme or reason to these acts of vandalism. We could not catch them. I can only visualize these kids having a good laugh. Yes, I took it personally. They were laughing at me, or so I thought.

Chapter Forty-Three
Drastic acts required drastic measures.

I remember being told a tale from many years ago. I am convinced that most people who would have known about it were long gone from the district, retired or dead. It seems as if there was a series of tunnels that transverse the building between the walls. The purpose of these tunnels was to provide access to pipes and conduits. Remember that it was an ancient building. And I recall that people who could gain access used these tunnels just like the people used the roof. Namely, as a place to do what they shouldn't be doing. You name it and people held on to rumors about what went on back there, anything from floating crap games to secret sexual liaisons.

About 25 years ago, I have been told, solving the problem required the district to permanently seal the space. The Director of Building and Grounds opened the catacombs for the plumber or electrician when needed. The only person who had the key to provide access was the Business Administrator. And when access had to be gained, he alone allowed the Director of Building and Grounds into these cave-like structures. Even I did not have a key. One could have probably broken into Fort Knox easier. There is no need for me to get into any of the rumors that surrounded this security. One could see into the restrooms from this vantage point. I will leave it to your imagination.

I had to get in there. That was the only way I could catch the girls who were doing this. As I already stated, I took this personally. It had to stop.

Chapter Forty-Four
Setting the trap

Looking back at it now, it appears I became obsessed with catching these girls. I did. Was it really worth it? Probably not, but I had to take the risk. And I hoped I did not lose control and carry out a student liberation. I knew this would prove to be an excellent test of my self-control. A bigger question came to me on my sleepless nights. What was I to do with these kids when I caught them?

Lucky for me, the vandalism now was only being conducted primarily in one restroom. I think the little bitches were becoming over confident in their exploits. I found an obscure way of gaining access to the tunnels and I set up a rotation where I would slip between the walls at varying times during the day to conduct my undercover surveillance.

Let's back up a little. You remember what I told you about the space between the walls where the pipes ran and what they used it for? When I made my way back into the "belly of this beast," between the walls, I found all sorts of debris, including liquor bottles, old cigars and cigarettes, and a stash of pornography. If I turned a peculiar way, I could see into the restrooms. Besides the other junk that I mentioned to you, there were pillows and a blanket, along with discarded candy bar wrappers and old empty Coke bottles. Obviously, the administration was so quick to wall this tunnel off that they never sent someone in to clean it out. The nest / perch was waiting for its owner to return. Time just froze this space.

Since I had no desire to watch anyone use the bathroom, I would just sit quietly waiting to hear the sounds of vandalism and then I would look. Yes, the sounds of vandalism. When you have done my job as long as I did, you could actually tell by the laughs, shouts and giggles what the students were doing without ever seeing the action.

And so, my vigil begun. Please don't underestimate the difficulty of this surveillance because I still had to do my job and, of course, I had to conduct the surveillance with no one ever seeing me. By the way, I cleaned up the space and got rid of all the trash. I did not want anyone thinking that this trash, including the pornography, was mine. That was not my thing, and I would want no one to think that I would look at it.

Alone, I would look at my ceiling, thinking if I could set some sort of trap for these kids. I could never think of one, so I would just lie awake thinking about what I would do to them when I caught them. I was confident that I would be successful in my quest. Failure was never a thought for me. I just had to be patient.

Sometimes I would be in bed and have no reservation in my mind that I would just somehow kill these kids, but then I would think of the rules that I had set up. I kept reminding myself of the work to be done. I had to make life better for the kids and teachers. It became almost a mantra for me. "Doing it for the kids"

I would also lie awake thinking about my selective set of morals. I had no difficulty killing someone who I thought needed to be killed, but I would never think of looking at the pornography that I found in the walls or, dare I say, watch the girls use the bathroom. Yes, I am righteous!

Chapter Forty-Five
Got you!

Then one day it happened. As I sat among the rat feces and dusty, stale air, I heard that laugh that I told you about. I got them. I heard them talking, and I heard them juggling their 20—ounce empty soda bottles.

Their giddy voices told me why they were doing it. They were really just teasing their principal. I know he thought he could solve any problem, and the kids knew this too. When he was investigating some unpleasant student behavior, he would brag about his success rate solving these petty crimes. And I must admit that he was pretty good at this task. But these students really had the tiger by the tail and they were pulling this tail now for months, if not years.

I watched them perform their task. They reached in the toilet and I was right, they would screw the bottles into the openings. They had to put all of their weight down on the bottle while they screwed it in. Each toilet took two bottles, and they were basically impossible to extract without major toilet surgery.

Chapter Forty-Six
Public enemy #1 and #2

It did not surprise me to see who the culprits were. It would have been an easy guess. These two young ladies were sisters who were probably the worst two students in the building. Every student in the building was afraid of them. And I meant every student, boy and girl. If anyone tangled with them, they would end up hurting. You get my picture. They equally intimidated most of the faculty and they were equally afraid of these kids. These kids were in school to do everything but learn. They were a menace and needed to be dealt with. I felt sorry for the administration. They did their best. They would suspend the kids for an offense and then they came back meaner than before. These kids needed to be expelled. They really needed to be extinguished. I don't want to revisit that again. I had to just follow my rules.

Chapter Forty-Seven
Trouble on the horizon.

While I was thinking about how to rid the school of this vermin, I received some notes from my good friend, Mrs. Kelly. You remember her? My friend, the secretary. These notes were troubling. Reading between the lines, I sensed that Mrs. Kelly wanted something more out of our relationship. Something that I was not prepared to give.

I had no time or desire for romance. And if I did, in all candor, it would not be with Mrs. Kelly. I basically just ignored the notes and did not say a word to her or to anyone else. However, the last note was especially troubling because she profusely thanked me for "liberating" her from Mrs. Westerman. Those are my words, not hers, but the note showed that she clearly knew that I was behind her death.

Shit! Now I was going to have to somehow deal with this. I certainly did not want to kill her, but I did not want to get romantically involved with her. Shit, shit and more shit.

I was now going to juggle this bullshit. But first, I had to think of what to do with my "toilet screwers." That was the most pressing thing on my mind now.

Chapter Forty-Eight
I hatched the plan

I had to get rid of these kids, and I needed to do it quickly. Killing them would have been easy, and really, that is what they deserved. Sorry, I am beating a dead horse.

I thought I had a foolproof plan. I filled two of the 20-ounce Coke bottles with individual packages of cocaine. If you knew where to look in our community, getting drugs or guns was easy. I had cut the soda bottles around the top and painted the inside of the bottles a light brown to resemble Coke. I then reassembled the bottles. It looked pretty good. I had two bottles filled with cocaine and any passerby would just assume it was Coke if they looked. I placed these bottles in the girls' lockers, which were right next to each other, along with a stack of ten- and twenty-dollar bills. This plot cost me almost one thousand dollars to execute. But cost was never an issue for me. I had to do what I had to do!

I made sure that the girls were in school and in class, and then I placed these bottles securely in their lockers. I then ran to the principal's office and told him what I had seen. I told him I just saw the girls put the bottles there and overheard conversations with other students about when their "store" was to open.

The principal was excited. This was like Christmas to him. I was handing him the two worst kids in the school on a silver platter. Now I just had to have confidence that he would not blow it. I could sit back and quietly chuckle.

The plan went off without a hitch. He sent for the girls with our security guards and then took them to their lockers for a search. I was nearby, leaning on my broom pretending to work again (I had that routine down pat!), but I was there to see the look on these little bitches' faces as they prepared to take the fall as drug dealers. It was not ironic that I would place the cocaine in these bottles. They were just like the ones the girls used to torture me. Now, the principal could really have the last laugh.

The girls went nuts when the principal removed the bottles from the lockers. They used every curse word available. They put together some interesting sentences using the word "fuck" and "motherfucker." I chuckled to myself. They physically went after the principal and had to be restrained. What a scene. What a show for all to see. Eventually, the police arrived and took the perpetrators out in handcuffs for all to see.

As I pushed my broom around in circles cleaning nothing, I quietly chuckled as they left kicking and screaming. I accomplished my task differently. I liberated the school but certainly not the greater society because I am sure that they will go somewhere and resume their menacing ways. These kids would not change. In some ways, I regret not taking them out to join the others that I had to deal with. I remain ever fearful that these young ladies will procreate. When this happens, the world will be in for more trouble. I pity the principal that will get those kids one day.

I do not believe kids like that are capable of change and they will doom society to deal with the results of their antics. For that specific time period, I could only worry about the school district. That was a big enough challenge for the Liberator. Yes, I was now comfortable calling myself by that name.

The girls never returned to school. You know, it seemed as if everyone was happy. The kids, the staff, the principal and, yes, me. Here, the Liberator chose not to end their lives. When they left the school, the liberation succeeded.

And by the way, I never had to remove a soda bottle from a toilet again.

Chalk another one up for the Liberator.

Chapter Forty-Nine
Change-A rather strange phenomenon

I think I had already told you I had the uncanny ability to melt into the walls. I saw and heard things that others did not see or hear. Over time, I had become almost an expert on reading the body language of people. For me, it has always been a fact that people say so much more with their bodies than their mouths. People can communicate mountains of information without ever opening their mouths.

For example, I am reading you right now as I tell my story. You are skeptical of my tales and me. You certainly do not trust me and you are not sure if my stories are true, or if some of these stories are just bullshit? Or perhaps you feel I am just flat out crazy and have no contact with reality. I assure you what I speak is the truth.

Am I right? Did I read you correctly?

Do not answer that, it does not matter. Should I go on? I still have a great deal to share with you and I know that I have so little time left.

Well, change is hard. I am sure you heard that and you have probably have experienced a radical change in your life. People get nervous with change. Not me. I could easily roll with the punches. For me, it did not matter who was in charge. I just did my job. New people to me only became a problem when I saw they were hurting this school district. My personal antennae were always fine-tuned to this.

Let me share with you a story about change. This is a story that contained a very likable character. From the start, he never had a chance in the district. Listen, this district that I speak so highly of has its warts. A big wart is the notion that "outsiders are not welcome." Believe me, it is not a notion. They might as well put a big sign on the lawn of all the schools shouting this out for all to hear. It should be the banner on the website. Yes, we need you to work here, but you will probably not succeed because you are not from here. This entire concept is incestuous, but real. I have also noticed that the level of acceptance is less when the importance of the job is more. What I mean by this is that you have a greater chance of acceptance as a custodian or secretary than you do as a principal or superintendent. And saying this brings me to tell you the story of this likable naïve soul who became our high school principal.

I knew this poor fellow was in for trouble when I heard of his appointment and I cemented my knowledge when I saw him. This black guy had zero chance of success. He had two strikes against him right out of the gate. Before he pissed someone off or make an unpopular decision, he was behind the eight ball. He was an outsider, and he was black. Good luck my friend. (And he needed every bit of my well wishes.)

I think this man was a good guy and probably a decent educator. A nice guy with good intentions. However, I do not think that he was the brightest bulb. Instead of keeping his eyes and ears wide open and his mouth shut, learning the people in the school and the people in the town, he came in thinking that he was going to be a change agent. He thought he could save the world. Although he may have been smart enough, he was not savvy enough to be that agent of change. He quickly imploded in the position. He was in over his head and it showed.

He probably made two huge mistakes that ultimately cost him. First, he attempted to transform the school into being more Afro-centric overnight. This was probably not a bad idea because the school was overwhelming black now and the kids perhaps needed this dose of Afro-centricity. But, and this is a big but, he forgot that the town and the power brokers in the town and in the school were still predominantly white. They did not want to hear street talk being spoken in the hallways by the administration, nor did they want to hear a graduation speech filled with grammatical errors that sounded like talk directly from the streets. Is this racist? Of course, it is. But it was what the climate was. It would take time and a special nuance to change this, and this new principal did not have it.

Second, for whatever reason, he lived in the school. Yes, you heard me correctly. He bedded down in the school. He slept on a couch in his office and showered in the locker rooms. It appeared he would rather play basketball with kids and staff than run the school.

Yes, another racist stereotype. Just like Ducky Donaldson, he was a living stereotype of the black man. People thought of him as nothing more than an uneducated black man who only wanted to play basketball. I wanted to shake him. I wanted so badly for him to succeed, but I saw he was incapable of grasping the negative situation he had gotten himself into. He just could never earn the respect of the community. Yes, the community was partially to blame, but so was he.

Before long, the big bosses unceremoniously fired him and ran him out of town. Of course, the black community did not like this and it took some time to settle the situation. Eventually, the only way they calmed it was returning to one of the good old boys to run the school. The entire escapade was embarrassing for the district and embarrassing for all black constituents. I think most people agreed that the school would be better off without him, yet the change set back race relations within the district.

To close out my thoughts on change now would be perhaps be premature. I saw people viewed change as hard and perhaps needless. I held many teachers' hands as they cried at the end of the year because they were told that they were now teaching third grade instead of fourth. More tears came when they were told that they would change their classroom. And if you wanted to see a death-defying scene, tell a teacher that they were being transferred to another school within the district. I have seen people given bad news, like the death of a spouse or a sudden trip to the hospital for a spouse or child, and take this type of news better than one of my earlier mentioned moves. My examples that I shared are elementary school based and my secondary school brethren act just as bad if they are told that they will teach grade ten English next year instead of a level that they have been used to. And very few if anyone wants to teach ninth graders. It is ridiculous.

Likewise, when a new superintendent or principal takes over, people will live in fear for months before the new boss takes over. The gossip mills spin at full speed and I have seen people actually get sick and vomit all over the place (that I had to clean, thank you very much) because of the dread of a new boss.

Forget about changing teaching styles. When I overheard a principal talk to a teacher about his overuse of the lecture method, his reaction was like I just absconded with his wife. Yes, a black man with his white wife would cause him less stress. One might expect an LOL here, but sadly, that will not happen.

Let me send one message to the staff—GROW UP!

Chapter Fifty
Here comes trouble—again

Yes, I need to be cautious. I see two different fronts that I now had to deal with.

The first one being Mrs. Kelly. She had become a bit of a pain in the ass. I have tried to steer clear, but it has turned out to be impossible. I feel as though I am caught between a rock and a hard place. On one hand, we had a special type of relationship. I liked her. However, we both had different definitions of the term special. For me, it was nothing more than we were friends. We were loyal to one another. I felt as though we were navigating the same journey together. We both cared about the school and we both, in our own ways, worked to keep the school the way we liked it.

Even though we were now in different schools, I still tried to maintain our friendship. I still would visit at break time and we would do an occasional lunch. Maintaining our friendship was fine and dandy, but I really needed to keep her close to me. In this way, I could closely monitor her and let's face reality, she was a fountain of information. She knew the news while the ink was still wet on the paper. Ok, I admit it. I had to use her for this and no; I did not feel too bad about it.

For her, I saw the relationship change. After I had liberated her from Mrs. Westerman, everything changed. If you recall, she sent me that note upon my departure stating that she knew what I did. I could also tell by the way she looked at me that something was different. I had to sort this out. But how? Did she really know? I am losing some sleep about this. Either I had to confront it or I had to forget about it. I think that you have figured out by now; I am kind of a confrontational guy. Perhaps, confrontational is not a good word to describe me because I rarely show people my emotions and even in a dispute with someone, I am not apt to raise my voice. Perhaps the better word to describe my demeanor is controlling. Right now, I have to be in charge of my situation. I was not sure I was in charge of Mrs. Kelly. I had to think more about this.

The second thing that troubled me was that several days ago, I saw an army of suits walking around the building. I had heard that they also visited the middle school and the elementary school where I took care of Peoples. Who were they and what were they doing? I had to get my sources on this and unfortunately, the person who would know this was Mrs. Kelly, which just added to my grief. Screw it, I had to know. Kelly would know what was in the newspaper before the any paper hit the streets.

I figured out that the next time I would bring the coffee in for our coffee break, I would sort this out.

As we sipped our coffee and made some small talk, I got right to my point and asked about this entourage of suits. Of course, she knew all about them. The district's insurance company was thinking about doing an investigation of what they believed was the many serious accidents in the district.

Yes, this bothered me, but yet I did not feel as though it was a fundamental change. What could they know and who knows if I would ever see them again? I knew how these things worked in our district. Let me put it this way, here today and gone tomorrow. No need for me to worry. There was no way that they could find me.

Chapter Fifty-One
A fool's paradise

Do you think that you really know what crap I was dealing with daily? I doubt it. To paint you a better picture, I will give you some examples.

The first thing that you should know is that very few people had any common sense. And if someone possessed common sense, they rarely used it. This goes across the board from administrators to teachers, right down to the lowest rung of the food chain, custodians.

As you learn of my story, I trust you can see that I am far from stupid. My brain is good and I use it. I could have and should have gone to college, but those options were not available for me. I also have common sense and I use it. You can tell by my liberations that I am a good problem solver. You have also seen that I know how to keep my eyes and ears open and my mouth shut. And perhaps my biggest skill is that I understand human dynamics. I can work any room with the best of them. And never kid yourself, this political skill is the winner. If you have this, you can survive anywhere.

I am sure that you will enjoy this story. I wish it was one that I had made up, but I assure you it was true and it happened exactly like I said it did. It was the start of the summer cleaning regimen. I had about six of my guys up on the third-floor scrubbing and cleaning. The only students present were the summer school kids and a small limited number of staff. In one room, an old couch had to be removed. My group of custodians decided that the easiest way to get this couch out of the building was to merely throw it out of the window. They figured that once the couch was down on the ground, probably broken into many pieces, it would be easier to move. So, "operation couch" was now in effect. The six fools hoisted the couch up and pitched it out of the window. They did not realize their own strength and instead of the couch simply dropping to the ground, it actually flew to land on a teacher's car that was parked in the lot. I would have loved to have been a passerby and to have seen this couch fly. I can only visualize the bored kids half asleep in summer school seeing this couch fly by the windows. They now had a story to tell.

Just think, if it hit someone walking below the couch. It would have killed him or her. I also have to chuckle a bit when I think of it. What if you were walking to your car and saw this flying couch spinning downward towards your head? Were you headed to Oz? You now knew how the wicked witch felt as she saw Dorothy's house spinning in her direction.

Of course, they called me on the carpet for this. These fools were mine. They were my pride and joy. The look on their faces was priceless. Once we sorted it all out, I found it funny. The men did not get fired, although they could have. They suspended them all for some time and lost some wages. They all returned to work a little wiser. And no, this type of incident has not happened again.

My crew of gentle lovable morons!

The next thing that you will find funny is a story of a teacher who did not have one ounce of the brains that God had given him. He was a good-natured fool. Most kids liked him. He was one of the best bullshit artists ever created. He could mesmerize a seventh grader with a story with the kid never knowing that it was all made up. Most knew him well enough to call him on it when he tried to bullshit the adults.

One winter, his car got stuck before work at a local café. He was fueling up for the day. There was probably ten inches of snow on the ground. Once he saw he could not get his car out of the snow, he caught a ride back to the school and "borrowed" the school district's twenty passenger school bus to push his car out of the snow. He had access to the keys and drove this bus as part of some extra duty position. He never had permission to use his bus as a plow or tow truck.

Guessing the outcome of this story is easy. In this adventure, not only did he crack up the bus, he damaged his own car and got the bus stuck along with his car. Once again, my man became the laughingstock of the district. This was not his last embarrassing act. Once again, the district showed its inability to get rid of the fools and kept him on with some disciplinary notes in his file. This was a very forgiving district and gave fools second chances all the time. Do you think The Liberator would get a second chance? After all, I was just doing the job that they should have been doing by getting rid of dead wood, no pun intended. Shit, maybe I could get promoted.

Chapter Fifty-Two
Back to Mrs. Kelly

Well, after much thought, I decided that holding this type of conversation was best held off campus. We need to take lunch off site for a change. I had to pry more to find out exactly what Mrs. Kelly knew and how she knew it. I did not want it to seem like it was a date of some sort. On a monthly basis, Mrs. Kelly had to take petty cash to the bank, and I usually accompanied her to provide a bit of safety for the process. It was easy to suggest a lunch tied to this task.

She dove directly into the topic that I did not want to talk about, thanking me for Mrs. Westermann's removal. I claimed I had nothing to do with this, but I still probed deeper, asking her how she thought this was possible. Her answer surprised me. First, she told me I was full of shit and she just knew. She could read my body language. This stunned me. Did I give it away somehow? Was someone actually as good as me reading people? It seemed as this was so. Of course, denial was the only way to go. If you deny long enough, people will only hear that and end up believing you. I went down this road without overdoing it. I tried to change the subject, and it worked. However, a little twinkle remained in Mrs. Kelly's eyes. A twinkle that I did not like. As I was clearing the table, her hand laid atop mine and I felt a little squeeze. This little squeeze and that woman's twinkle in her told me I was in trouble. Deep trouble.

This was not good. This would require some action. I sensed I was not in control here. I knew what I was going to think about. I hoped my ceiling would provide me with an answer.

I needed a direction. I needed a plan.

Chapter Fifty-Three
An old nemesis returns

It wasn't bad enough that I had Mrs. Kelly thinking crazy. I had just learned that one of my "favorite" teachers was being transferred back to this school. Mr. Solomon was coming home to roost. I am sure that you have heard the saying, "when it rains, it pours." I was now amid a brief shower in my life. Mr. Solomon was a meek, effeminate math teacher who was black. And yes, this man disgusted me. Just like Ducky he gave all black men a bad name.

I think that I already told you about the teachers that used the roof for a variety of reasons. Mr. Henry, one of the most seasoned math teachers, used to sneak a smoke between classes. He was just addicted to nicotine. I had actually seen him smoke two cigarettes in his mouth at one time. Now, that is a sight. He had a hard time lasting one 45-minute class period without having a smoke. Everyone liked him and wanted to help him out. The principal assigned his classroom to the third floor, right across from the closet that contained the roof hatch to get a person on top of the school. Between periods, this fellow would climb the ladder, open the hatch and stick his head out for a smoke between periods. Like the delivery of the mail, neither rain nor snow would prevent him from taking care of his nicotine addiction. I think everyone knew about that and did not give a damn about it. Unfortunately, the principal assigned the room directly next to the closet to Mr. Solomon. What was he thinking?

No one cared about Mr. Henry's antics, except Mr. Solomon. He was just a royal pain in the ass. However, Mr. Solomon was a pain in the ass to everyone. It did not matter to him who you might be. Whether you were a student, teacher, administrator, parent or custodian, he was just a royal pain in the ass. You could have been white, black, brown or yellow. It did not matter; he was just a pain in the ass. One thing that I will give him credit for is that he was a nondiscriminatory fool. I am being nice when I call him a fool. Most people, when they described good old Mr. Solomon, they referred to him as a nasty little wimp.

I cannot believe that some fool married him. I felt sorry for his wife.

He was now my problem. The principal at his former school must have really paid to get rid of him. Perhaps the superintendent was just pissed off at the high school principal. Or maybe this was just the march of the lemons and it was now this building's turn to have Mr. Solomon.

During my career, I saw principals and superintendents use power in a remarkable number of ways. Some of these folks were so trivial and vengeful, I could not believe that they ran the schools. Although, I did not see it, or perhaps did not want to see it, these folks did not take this vengefulness out on the students. However, most would not think twice about being vengeful, jealous, and spiteful to their colleagues. That spoke volumes about the morale of the district. The overall culture of each building needed a kick-start. Terminating everyone was probably the best answer. The hiring process could start all over again from square one.

Sorry, I got off of the topic a bit. Let me get back to that wimp, Mr. Solomon. He was like a little witch that flew in on a broomstick on one sunny Monday morning and his appearance immediately affected the culture of the school. Those who knew him knew to stay away. I found it funny when I heard the older teachers telling the new teachers to avoid him. I did not find it funny when I saw a group of his old cronies welcome him. Yes, misery loves company and if you were to take one message away from my story is that each one of us, every morning, before our feet hit the floor, can choose our attitude for the day. Some folks love to choose to be miserable. Yes, Mr. Solomon had some friends. What is a group of witches called? A coven, right? Well, we sadly had a coven in our school and it was basically dormant until Mr. Solomon arrived. I needed to set aside a portion of the parking lot specifically for broom parking. He was the chief warlock among the witches.

It didn't take long for him to start with me. His room was never clean enough. Let me assure you that to keep him off of my back, I made sure his room was extra clean. I am glad that the rest of the faculty did not get angry with me for giving him special treatment. But I think they knew I was just trying to survive. And I had always lived with the notion that if you put a little extra thought and effort into a problem on the front side, you would spend less time picking up the pieces when everything fell apart. And I knew for sure that in the world of Mr. Solomon everything could and would quickly fall apart.

It was not long before the room cleanliness became a secondary complaint and his concern about the air quality in his room replaced it. For God's sake, it was an old school and although he was a math teacher; they housed him in the science wing of the building. That is just the way it was. Sometimes the science wing of the school would have certain unpleasant smells. I could tell what time of the year it was by these smells. In the fall, the ninth graders dissected frogs, and the offensive smell of the preservative stunk up the building. Likewise, in the spring, the chemistry students were doing some sort of basic chemical analysis and that too would have a distinct odor. It was just the way it was in our school and I am sure it was like that in probably all schools. Mr. Solomon needed to get a life. Perhaps his sense of smell was so keen he could have somehow claimed a medical disability and retired? Although nothing surprised me, I never heard of your sense of smell causing you to stop working.

His behavior and needs caused a lot of grief. I felt sorry for the principal. I could do nothing to satisfy Solomon.

For me, it came to a head when he sent kids out of the class and to the office because of the perfume or cologne that they wore. He would stand at the door and, instead of welcoming the kids as they entered his class, he would sniff them. If they did not pass the sniff test, he would not allow them in the room.

There were several periods in the day that he may have had five students in his class because the others did not pass the sniff test. I found this funny because at this age many of the kids smelled of body odor, or their clothes may have stunk because they did not have the means to do regular laundry. This nut of a teacher was sending kids out because they were trying to smell good. I can tell you that this routine did not last long because it now was ruffling the feathers of the principal and vice principals. The parents were also getting pissed. And if there is anything that will get an administrator's attention is an angry parent.

Kids were switching classes or flat out dropping this math class because of him. It was also a family thing. If an older sibling had this teacher, no way parents would let this teacher torture another one of their children. Basically, his classes comprised kids who were new to the district of who did not have an adult at home that would have advocated for them. The situation was sad.

    The man was evil. He was hurting the school, and he was hurting kids. He had to go. To be frank, I could not stand the wimp. The Liberator gladly accepted this new challenge. I feel as though there should be some sort of signal to call out the Liberator. You know, like the "bat signal" that Commissioner Gordon used to call Batman. Okay, now you know, I loved Batman as a kid, and could not get enough of this show on television. I regularly think about my liberations. Perhaps I unconsciously modeled my work after my childhood hero.

Chapter Fifty-Four
Too much to think about

Maybe I am biting off more than I can chew. Multitasking or doing too many things at once could be my downfall. I had to take a deep breath, and I made sure that I would only do one thing at a time and make sure it was right. I constantly reminded myself to pay attention to the details.

I now lay in bed thinking about what I could do with Mrs. Kelly, who somehow now was making me her love interest, and that wimp Solomon, who every day came to work to torture not only the kids but the adults.

I forgot to tell you Solomon had now reported the school to a variety of state and federal regulators regarding a healthy work environment. So now we had more layers of inspectors and air sample readings being taken. By the way, all air sample results came back satisfactory. I think he really enjoyed busting our balls.

I had to somehow tap dance with Mrs. Kelly. Although this was an unwanted pain in the ass, I thought I could manage it. Saying that, I turned my attention to the elimination of Solomon. I had to come up with something creative. I was now being greedy, but for my pleasure, I wanted it to be painful. A little suffering on his behalf might just make my day.

Above it all, Solomon had to go!

Chapter Fifty-Five
The final sniff tests

I had to come up with a method of elimination that was fitting for Mr. Solomon.

I think you know by now through my story that although I am nothing more than a janitor, oops, sorry, custodian; I am not stupid. With a little simple research, I found my method for this liberation. In theory, it was a most appropriate way for Solomon to go. However, translating this theory into action was going to be hard. I had to build upon some of my past liberations, and hope for the best. I needed to do some meticulous planning and then cross my fingers for a little luck. I had to get Mr. Solomon into the chemical stockroom behind his classroom alone. That was going to be difficult.

My plan theoretically was simple. I was going to mix bleach with vinegar to form some chlorine gas. For good measure, I was going to slip some drain cleaner into the mix to hopefully speed the reaction and to make it more powerful. Yes, I was going to re-enact a good battlefield scene from World War I. If successful, his death would be because of him doing his "sniff" test one last time.

It was a known fact that Mr. Solomon kept bleach in his stock room against the directives of the administration. I had to get rid of all the bleach in the building years ago. We used bleach regularly as a cleaning agent. Several years ago, some government agency, without thinking, banned it. Let's not kid each other. I had plenty of it still in the building that I used in tough cases. I know that when I had to disinfect an area, I would pull my bleach out of its hiding place and use it when no one was around. The principal gave me his wink of approval. He just wanted the mess cleaned and really did not care how I did it.

To make it look legit, I needed to have other people exposed to cause some minor damage to make it look like some sort of accident. I waited for a professional development day. On these days, the students and staff are not in that part of the building. The day had finally arrived.

I asked Mr. Solomon if he could come up to his room and show me where he felt any extraneous smells were coming from. He had previously told me he smelled cigarette smoke coming from the vents, along with cooking odors from the microwave in the faculty room. Remember, he was obsessed with smells.

I had my trusty mop and bucket with me filled with bleach. When he arrived in the stockroom to show me the vents that he believed were bringing in smells to the room, he smiled when he smelled my bleach. He loved bleach. It was his personal "go to" cleaning solution. I had previously placed a half gallon of vinegar in the cabinet below the sink in the stockroom, along with a can of our most powerful drain cleaner. I got him up on the stepladder for him to show me the exact spot of concern. When he was up on the ladder and with his back to me, I quickly emptied the vinegar in to my bucket. For good measure, I could sneak in a quantity of drain cleaner. I almost immediately smelled the gas. I slithered out of the room and held the door shut.

Solomon yelled and screamed. No one was ever going to hear him. I held my body weight against the door. Although he pushed and struggled for a bit of time, the fumes overcame him. The wimp was no match for me. He passed out while I was watching. I watched him take his last breath. I was a bit surprised as he turned a bright shade of red as he took this final breath. You know, I felt pretty good about that.

I left the area for a while and then returned to the scene of my crime so I could report it. The fumes overcame me as soon as I opened the stockroom door. I stumbled into the hallway and called 911. They evacuated the rest of the building. The ambulance took me to the hospital, which treated me for some minor inhalation burning of my lungs. A little dose of oxygen was all I needed. They quickly released me to go home.

Mr. Solomon was, in fact, dead. Several firefighters and police officers had to be treated for inhalation issues. Because Mr. Solomon was such a nut and cleanliness kook, they later assumed that he was in one of his paranoid phases and concocted the vinegar and bleach mixture to get things extra clean. Upon chemical analysis of the death concoction, they assumed I left the drain cleaner in my bucket and Solomon was in such a rush to clean things, he never saw it. I have already explained the ineptness of the police and they were happy to close the case.

The manner in which he died surprised no one. His death, and the manner of his death, did not surprise his wife. She was happy that he went out doing something that he really loved doing, scrubbing and cleaning. She told us he just loved the smell of bleach. All I could think of with hearing that statement was seeing the two of them in an intimate embrace with an open bottle of Clorox in the room. Some couples will light some aromatic candles for romance. He opened a bottle of bleach. To each their own. Live and let live. Right?

Another successful liberation

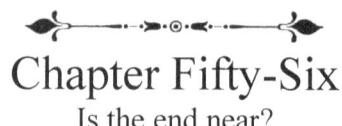

Chapter Fifty-Six
Is the end near?

That now makes five liberations (Peoples, Ducky, Singleton, Westerman, Solomon). I had this strange feeling that my luck could run out. This school district needed my dirty little deeds. I really believed that my liberations allowed this district to survive. It now convinced me I had this higher calling.

I was sure that without me, these evil people would go on hurting kids.

As I lay awake at night, I thought of the terrible impact that these folks had not only on the kids, but on their peers, who came to work every day looking to do the right thing. Other people knew the impact of my now deceased "fab five." People like this sullied the reputation of all the others in the district who possessed wholesome hearts.

Working in a school was a special calling. The good Lord summoned you to this type of work. I saw this calling almost like a calling to be a priest, minister or nun. When you worked in a school, you did not care about money, promotion or recognition. You were in it to make the lives of kids better. If this was not your reason, you had to go. And if you were not ready to go voluntarily, I was always there to help you exit. However, I am sure you would not like my help. Go ask Ducky? Go ask Solomon? You get my point.

Two things were now happening.
- Kelly was not going away
- The district's insurance company sent a full-time investigator to the district.

Yes, I was invincible. (OR WAS I?)

Chapter Fifty-Seven
The magnificent Mary

If you recall, I told you about the posse of insurance people that visited the school. Obviously, our insurance claims were staggering with all the deaths besides the other bullshit type of claims. Although I could not quote for you any exact statistics, I could just about guarantee that of any ten claims submitted to our Worker's Compensation Board or our liability insurance carrier, eight were total bullshit. Go pull old Ducky Donaldson's file if you don't believe me. Just like Ducky, many of our staff spent more time on trying to figure out how to get out of work than they did on actually doing their assigned work. I also could probably point to some numbers to show you that by eliminating Mr. Ducky, our Worker's Comp. cases that we filed went down.

I saw the stir of activity one day and some unfamiliar faces. I had to find out what was cooking and although our relationship was now somewhat strained, I had to turn to Mrs. Kelly to find out what "pot of soup" was brewing on the stove. She knew it all. Because of all of our accidents, the insurance company was assigning a claims investigator to the district full time. Once again, Kelly's dirt proved to be true. Office space in our building and the middle school was being cleared for this person or persons. I had to put my news antennae out to find out exactly what was up.

Sure enough, at the end of the week, this thirty something woman arrived to set up shop. She was tall and attractive. I immediately drew my eyes to her long, flowing red hair and her green eyes that could drill a hole right through you. She carried herself well. Just by watching her walk, I could see that she was confident and sure of herself. I could also tell that she was a no-nonsense type of person. Somehow, I sensed a certain type of power emanated from her. Her body language told it all. This was not a person to be messed with. She was a young woman on the way up and nothing was going to stand in her way and if you did somehow get in her way, she would trample you. She took no prisoners. Her name was Mary Magdalena.

What are you kidding me? Was I now going to do battle with Mary Magdalene, Jesus' girl? I had told you earlier that my church was very important to me. I had done my homework there and studied my Bible. After I paced around at night, I read my Bible. Sleep regularly eluded me. When my mind raced, my Bible soothed me. You know I do my best thinking at night. I sleep very little. The Bible fills my time. That being said, my understanding of Mary Magdalene is pretty comprehensive. I believe Mary was a trusted advisor and confidante of Jesus. She may have been Jesus' wife. Some have believed that she was a repentant prostitute. Some believed that Jesus and Mary Magdalene had some sort of sexual involvement. People have said that they saw Jesus and Mary kiss. Although no one is sure who Mary was, some things seem fairly certain. Namely, that she was a devoted follower of Jesus. She very well could have been his closest advisor. Was she the "apostle of apostles?" Mary stayed with Jesus at his crucifixion and witnessed his burial. Was she the first to see him upon his resurrection?

Who the hell knows who exactly she was? One thing I know is that she was one powerful woman who knew how to handle herself in a world of men. Am I in trouble? Will this woman bring me down? I don't believe in coincidences. I believe there is a reason for everything. Our insurance investigator's name is Mary Magdalena. Is there some coincidence or reason for this? I believe in my heart that there is surely a reason she is here. I know I am not done with my liberations and I am driven, because that is a reason that I am here.

Let's get ready to rumble!

Chapter Fifty-Eight
Two women to juggle

So, now I had two women in my life. And to be candid with you, I wanted neither one. I knew from my friends that one woman was just about impossible to handle. I also knew from many of my friends that I would never handle two women. For many women, it was merely a matter of sex. But for me, at this time, it was a matter of survival. Let's look at my dilemma.

First, I had Kelly, who I had known for years. She had become, for me, one of my only loyal friends. We were friends. Good friends, nothing more. However, as you now know, she wanted to take this relationship to a new level. I did not want to date Kelly. I did not want to marry her, and I did not want to sleep with her. So, on this end, I had a potential to deal with a woman scorned and rejected. She was dangerous.

She was also proving to be diabolical. She teased me. Not in a sexual sense, but with what she believed was her secret to my work. I saw a side of her I did not think existed. Would she really bring me down? Who knows?

Should I have just banged her and kept a little side action going and led her on? In the end, would I be able to eliminate her?

Should I just ignore her? She had no proof. If she brought up the topic or threatened to go state's evidence, I could encourage her to do it and let's get it over with already? But if I did that, would somehow something leak out and then my entire career as the Liberator would be over? Would the dumb ass police finally put two and two together and not get five? I felt as though my head was already on some silver platter.

I saw no straightforward answer. So, I guess my inaction would be my action. As a man of action, I was not happy with this plan and I knew I had to think about it a great deal more. Well, at least I laid out several options, none too appealing.

I knew I had to somehow compartmentalize all of this in my brain and turn my attention to the magnificent one, Mary Magdalena, our now in-house, permanently placed insurance investigator.

Now, unlike Kelly, I would have loved to have thrown a hump into her. But I had to face it. I was too old and probably too black.

Miss Mary was going to be dangerous. She was young, driven, and ambitious. She was looking to make a name for herself. Looking to make that big splash. And I sensed she did not care who she crushed along the way. Mary would not take any prisoners. Somehow, I think she would have viewed crushed bodies along the way like some sort of merit badge. I could see my scalp being clipped somehow to her belt next to all the other fools that she had brought down.

Besides being attractive, she was smart. What could be more dangerous than a smart, attractive woman? I saw early on that she could flirt with the best of them. She easily played men like a piano. A look, a touch or a twirl of the hair could seduce even a cold-hearted soul like me. She also knew how to dress. She knew how to use her appearance and her style to her advantage. While I am on the topic, her shoes could kill. When I looked at her shoes, I somehow wanted to ravage her. Shoes make the woman. For you ladies out there, looking to trap your man, never forget that, nor where you heard that from. I don't want to paint the wrong impression of her. She maintained her professionalism but knew how to use her feminine qualities to her advantage. OK. Enough talk about Mary. Just know that for me, she represented a killer shark.

It was easy to see how things were developing with her. She seemed to have connected with our Assistant Superintendent who I will call Big Lou. A nice guy. A member of the old boy's network. A young man on his way up. Just like Mary, he was smart and dangerous. They were becoming a team. What else do assistant superintendents have to do all day? From the outside looking in, I always thought they had the best job in the district. He or she could hide all day and stay in the background. In our district, they highly paid him, with little accountability. However, I could see that when he became interested in a project, he would dive in headfirst. Just like Miss Magdalena, he was smart and ambitious. He could be dangerous.

Shit, I now had a team working against me. Were they going to be the new Murtaugh and Riggs? The new Turner and Hooch?

Hopefully, this team of Mary and Lou would be more like Maxwell Smart and Agent 86 from *Get Smart*, that old comical spy spoof television series of the 60s. We would see.

Chapter Fifty-Nine
Is the handwriting on the wall?

So, now it looked as though it was going to be a battle of the wits. Each side drew that imaginary line in the sand. Each side stood firm. It would be me vs. the team of Lou and Mary. Maybe a battle of the wills. I knew I could win that battle.

I saw the two of them bonding. They were inseparable. Attached at the hip. Mary and Lou. A crime-fighting force to be reckoned with. I am being sarcastic. I hope. They were smart and, yes, ambitious. But I had experience and guile on my side. I could be a slick son of a bitch. Although I hope they underestimated their foe, I knew they could not bring me down. I've got right on my side. I am virtuous.

The first thing that they were doing was touring the buildings. They were trying to get a lay of the land. But do not forget that I knew these buildings better than anyone. I am confident that I have left no evidence. I was also confident that I could mislead them off of any trail.

I had to determine what my mindset was going to be. Was I going to be a cooperative soul, or was I going to be an obstacle? There were distinct advantages of choosing either side. If I was cooperative, I could somehow make myself part of their team. I might learn from the inside what their strategy was going to be. Where were they headed mentally?

Of if I was their adversary, I could mislead and perhaps get them so caught up with me they would lose their focus on their mission. This required some thought. This required some rumination from me as I stared at my bedroom ceiling at night.

All I knew was that the world still turned and our district still needed me. I already had my eye on my next target. Perhaps my biggest score yet. We will see.

Chapter Sixty
Setting the scene- the undercurrents that remain strong

I think it is important that for you to fully understand the story; you need to understand the community a bit more and understand some dynamics that exist within in the confines of this two-mile square soap opera.

As I told you earlier, the schools were in a constant state of transition. We had rapidly turned into a school where the black and brown faces clearly outnumbered the white faces.

That should have been no big deal, but for this town, it was. You see that the political power brokers in the community remained white, hopelessly locked in the 1960s. For this black man, the 60s were not that good. That, too, should tell you a great deal. Someone once told me, and I think it was Big Lou, our assistant superintendent, that a sociologist once told him, it amazed them how quick this transition happened. The community change was not unexpected, but the rapidity of it was. That only compounded the issue. Change is hard, and it hurts.

Remember that I told you that Big Lou, our Assistant Superintendent, was one of the good old boys and as an equal member of this club we could talk. Within the "good old boys," there was no rank or pecking order. Once in the club, we were all equal. School position, age, or skin color did not matter. Our relationship helped determine as to the direction that I take as the investigation begins. I felt I could easily pump him for information. He was too trusting and open, but I always respected his intelligence. I think that he never saw the nasty side of people. I don't take that necessarily for a weakness, but I think it is a trait that I could use to my advantage. Could I easily manipulate him? Maybe.

Let me try to explain the "good old boys" and how it applied to this community. Foremost, this informal club was all male and for years was all white. I was one of the first "colored boys" allowed in. (I hope you see my sarcasm here.) There is no application form or by-laws. You just kind of know when you have made it. The "good old boys" let me into this fraternity. Once in, everyone was equal.

No, I didn't have to dance or shine shoes or get everyone coffee. I was now an insider. I was now privileged to hear inside gossip and allowed to go places with this group. Within the town, no one questioned this group. People scoffed at them behind their backs. And yet everyone envied them. That same guy that would be the biggest critic of the group yearned for inclusion in this group. They ate at the same local cafes and only drank at certain bars. I knew the mayor would hold weekly court every Saturday morning for breakfast. It was kind of funny, but everyone knew that at 10:00 in the morning every Saturday, where this group ate and conducted business. This group welcomed no one here unless someone invited you or you were part of the mayor's inner circle. I used to laugh when I would drive by each Saturday morning and see whose car was in the lot. It was equally comical to see those that were expelled from this club doing their community and family chores when in the past they would have been eating eggs and bacon. It became embarrassing for the expelled to be seen at the bank or cleaners because then everyone knew you were now on the outs with the mayor. Small towns and small-town politics—you have to love them.

These guys could easily communicate with one another without ever saying a word. They were masterful at using winks and nods. A tilt of the head could have a meaning for them. They also had a nickname for everyone. They called me "The Preacher" because of my involvement with my church, and I would also quote scripture when I found it applicable. I have to laugh because I had already given myself a nickname, an alter-ego if you will, "The Liberator." Not bad. I was the liberating preacher. And you could see from my discussion here the difficulty I would have if the time came when I would have to act on one of the good old boys. I still stand by what I said earlier to you. It all depends upon what the issue was. I knew in my heart if I ever found one of my club members messing with a kid like old Mr. Singleton, I knew I could act and act quickly and decisively. No questions asked.

So, this was my slice of middle America. One man, the mayor, who was, in my opinion, a master politician and a master manipulator, controlled politically the town. By the same token, he was power hungry. He wanted you to kiss his ring. You had to genuflect at his altar. I used to laugh that at any event he would find a seat in a prominent location and, as people entered, they would have to make their way to this guy for the ceremonial ring kissing. Please don't take my tone to infer that I was above it all. I wasn't. I did my share of ring kissing and genuflecting.

Believe me, it was comedic in the way some people would kiss his butt. Others had their head so far up his ass I am sure that the boss could not even pass some gas. It was that bad. And if you were around long enough, you would see the make-up of this group constantly change. You always knew who was in or out of the loop. It was that obvious.

It was also very sad to see those that wanted to be part of the group grovel and demean themselves, hoping to gain entry and access. You also must know that you did not get a promotion in the school district if someone did not somehow connect you to this group. Watching the same group of guys get passed over for every opportunity was sad. Oh, they may have been qualified, but they did not possess the most important quality, namely membership in the "good old boys." Some of these guys went to their graves wondering why this group excluded them. They just did not have it. And one of the most important qualities needed to get in was one's knowledge of sports. You either had to play, coach, gamble or somehow be able to understand and talk this lingo. In part, this prevented many women from ever gaining access. It really wasn't what was or wasn't between their legs. It was one's ability to dissect the sports page and comment on what was being talked about on the afternoon sports talk shows. Some of these guys tried to fake it. It was sad and comical. I would get chills up and down my spine watching this. Their behavior was an embarrassment.

Let's get back to the mayor. He could smile at you to your face and stick a shiv in your back at the same time. People regularly stabbed each other in the back. Many times, the victim never realized it. You could then walk away and never realize a knife was in your back. He was mayor for at least 25 years and called all the shots. His puppets comprised his town council. The few black guys on the town council made me sick. They would speak to the community, especially the black community and feign that they were on their side and, in reality, they were perfect Uncle Tom caricatures. I was sure that at council meetings, the mayor would ask them to do a little tap dance as entertainment, and they would willingly oblige him. Believe me, it was really sickening. They shined his shoes and kissed his ass. I knew I would rather deal with some white racist son of a bitch than them. At least with the white bigot, you knew what you were getting. It always remained in the back corner of my mind that these "Toms" were getting paid off. It had to be. I always wondered why they would sell their souls to this bastard. Was this sell-out for power or money? I guess probably both. Although I thought it, yes, felt it, I could never prove it.

You know what? I was really not angry with them. I pitied them. I felt sorry for them. These guys sold out. They sold their souls to the devil. For what? A few dollars? For some perceived power when in reality they had none? For some sort of false validation, who they were as black men? These guys just sickened me.

The mayor was attempting to rebuild the town. A noble cause. When you looked at a picture from, say, 1968, the downtown area was thriving. Vibrant stores on every corner and every block. When you turned the clock ahead, say thirty years, you saw a ghost town. Vacant stores, graffiti and garbage everywhere. Broken windows and broken-down buildings were everywhere. Crime was not a huge issue. The town was a ghost town. This small town was like thousands of others across America.

You also have to realize that this group conducted no business of any worth in public venues. When I say that, I mean all school or town official business. They made important decisions at the café, bar, or in someone's car. That is just the way it was. You had to basically like it or lump it. Some faces may have changed, but the rules and practices remained the same. I also wonder about this group's sobriety. Was sobriety a requirement for decision making? Not for this. I knew I had a limited frame of reference. But I wondered exactly how much liquor residents consumed in this tiny two square mile community. If all towns operated in this manner, the distilleries and beer manufacturers should never have to worry about going out of business. Our town alone could push stocks to new highs. We liked our beer. We liked our wine, and we liked our whiskey. This was just a fact.

But despite all of this bull, the mayor's initiative yielded results. Old buildings were being razed and new ones rose in their place. I really did not care who was getting rich off of these projects. And I had a strong hunch that some people I have already mentioned to you were making a fortune. New things breed other new things and the first thing that reared its ugly head was person-to-person street crime. I used to hear some kids brag in the lunchroom about their recent thefts and conquests. They would lie in wait in the dark as someone got off the train or ventured out of their new apartments. They talked about knocking a guy down and then "running his pockets." That meant stripping him of everything that he had in his pockets, from a cell phone to cash, to his watch and briefcase. I also heard of cases when other out-of-town youth appeared. They, too, would be subject to the tax that these hooligans would put on every newcomer. As part of this robbery and assault, thieves regularly took the outsider's coat or sneakers. For every stride the town was trying to take, it seemed to take two steps back in public opinion. And believe me, sadly, people wanted to believe that the schools were a mess and out of control, which was the furthest thing from the truth.

I give the teachers and administrators credit. They worked hard at keeping the schools fairly safe and orderly. Despite all the crap happening on the outside, our kids were still graduating, and some were going to some of the best colleges and universities in the country. Others would succumb to the streets.

However, if you ever drove by the high school at dismissal time, you would see a very scary group of young men ages 18-22, no longer enrolled in the schools, hanging around the building. And, of course, we were battling the emerging gang crisis that was spreading throughout the country. You could see the kids leave the building, walk down the street a block, and take their bandanas out of their pocket to display their colors. In the ongoing struggle of gangs that ravaged our country, the Bloods claimed Pikesville as their turf. All was fine until a new student might arrive from a town which was considered "Crip." All hell could break out. It was fun going to a basketball game or a football game against a rival gang. Sadly, a sign of the changing community was seeing patrons enter sporting events through metal detectors. Some games had to be played at crazy hours and at secret locations. Sometimes with no spectators, including the exclusion of the parents. I was fortunate that I was in "the club" and could work security for the events. I was good at it. No one messed with me. Times change and change is painful.

It amazed me the first time I saw a student with tattooed dog paws walking up her leg. I went over and complimented her on how nice they looked. It was really interesting. Little did I realize these tattoos were gang symbols. Times were a changing.

Thank God that the school district had me. I was the only one that seemed to hold it together. I would guarantee that if you took a representative survey of the community about my actions, they would have approved. The people that I took out needed taking out.

Was I just kidding myself?

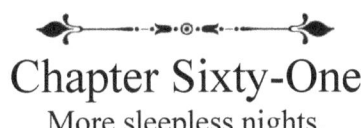

Chapter Sixty-One
More sleepless nights.

I had some new thoughts rush through my mind as I tried to fall asleep. I thought often about my legacy. Was greatness part of this legacy? I hoped so. Certain things were sure to happen. I will get caught or I will die of old age and then people can piece together anything that they may think of to pin the crimes on me. I thought about the need to chronicle my actions. Did I need to explain it to the community? Were they entitled to know the whys behind my actions? Was there a bit of a personal need to take credit for my gifts to this community? Did I want some credit for my sacrifices? You bet I did!

That being said, I kept a journal of my actions. Looking back, I made two big mistakes. I kept this journal, and I kept a souvenir of each liberation. I kept each person's key ring. Looking back, I had some fascination with keys. For me, keys represented power. The bigger the key ring you had, the more power you possessed. And never forget that I had the biggest key ring in the entire district. Keys equal power. When I took your keys, and by the way, your life, I was taking your power. Your power left you as your last breath left you. Now, I had it.

I would think that I was nothing more than some sort of predator. Was I some sort of desperate serial killer? Was I the black Ted Bundy? John Wayne Gacy? Charles Manson? I don't think so because I got no pleasure out of doing my deeds. Each one of my eliminations was for the school district. I wanted a school or an athletic field named in my honor. Because, let's face it, I did more for this district than any old president or war hero did. I saved it.

When I thought like this, sleep came to me. Tomorrow will be another great day.

Chapter Sixty-Two
Investigation update

I was right. Miss Mary and Big Lou were becoming an item. I hope for Lou's sake he was getting a little slice of that. She was fine. No matter how fine she was, and no matter that Big Lou was a member of the good old boys, they were now my adversaries. Although they did not know it, they were trying to bring me down and yes, stick that needle in my arm. After what seemed like a brief hiatus, the state could not wait to stick a needle in another person's arm, especially when he was black. For that, I am sure.

Mrs. Kelly had already told me that one of the first things that the pair did was to generate a listing of all the staff at each building when each liberation occurred. This could be the first sign of trouble for me. I was at each school. No doubt about that. I had to think and think hard. Who was going to be more of a problem for me, Miss Mary and Big Lou or Mrs. Kelly? I caution you, please do not be quick to answer that one. Because I believe that Mrs. Kelly was going to be my downfall. What did she know? I mean, really know? What was she guessing about? Did she just have a feeling about how I handled her nemesis, Mrs. Westerman, or did she really know something? I had to find this out.

Chapter Sixty-Three
The destructive bitches

In the meantime, I had my eye on a next potential evil person who needed to go. One of our board of education members was becoming a real pain in the ass. And, of course, this person was connected with the local politicos. City politics were incestuous. Several years ago, the political machine helped elect the town council president's wife to the board of education. Her name was Mrs. Black. And yes, I found this humorous, or perhaps ironic, that Mrs. Black was black. For the first term, she pretty much fell in line and behaved. She slowly felt her oats in her second term. I really believed the problem was all generated out of intense love for her husband. She saw from a distance how the mayor had treated him. She was smarter than her husband. His behavior consistently embarrassed her. He was the perfect ass-kisser. I think the modern term for that would be a sycophant. He was black, but wanted so much to be white. They would talk about the demeaning behaviors of the mayor until late in the night. His wife was always encouraging him to be a man. A proud black man and to stop this ass kissing. It never seemed to bother him. I knew some folks had a thick skin but underneath it all they would suffer. Mr. Black's behavior never humiliated him. He was clueless about this perception. It humiliated his better half. She wanted him to stand up for what he believed. She was the strong one in their relationship. I could see her somehow someday on the Jerry Springer Show carrying on and airing all of their dirty laundry. She was tough and she could be mean. I kept my distance from her and when I saw her, I did my best "yes mam" show that I could put on. I was courteous and helpful. And yes, I would do a quick little tap dance for her when needed. There is nothing worse than a smart, angry black woman. Take my word for that.

Although I had no proof, I could not help but wonder what the council president's pay-off was. He had to be getting a kickback somewhere along the way. The city was now booming with redevelopment. He was getting his palm greased somewhere. If I only knew, I could use that information against him and ultimately his wife. As time passed, I felt like shaking him. Shaking him and yelling that he needed to grow his balls back and get control of his wife. But you know, he was probably smarter than me because the more she became involved with the school board; she had less time to be a pain in the ass to him. He let her have her toy; the board of education. So, who is the real fool now? Me, of course.

She seems to have made the board her personal playground or a tool to torment the mayor. Perhaps to just further torment and embarrass her husband. Maybe she behaved this way just to make a point to him. Who knew her motivation and no matter what it was, did it really matter to me? She was a power-hungry bitch. That is all that I knew. That is all that I saw.

Ultimately, the board elected her president and from that point forward, everything in the district worsened. She now had more power. Not that I really care about our new superintendent, but she was now torturing her. It was almost comical watching this superintendent quake in her shoes as this woman sent her on many wild goose chases. They have always said what goes around comes around and this superintendent should have a brief memory because she came in like a terror and demon and now, she was getting a wonderful taste of her own medicine.

This became a side drama for me. I had to cover my tracks, and I had more work to do. Although we were never the greatest school district, it is sad to see how these two power hungry women decided, probably covertly, to bring the district down. Because of all of this side drama going on, I am convinced that no education was going on. I will tell you more about that in a few minutes.

Chapter Sixty-Four
Drama, drama everywhere

Let's get one thing straight. I could not care less about the mayor. I could not care less about the council president. I could not care less about his wife, and I could not care less about the superintendent. Each one had his or her own personal agenda. And none of these agendas have anything to do with education or teaching and learning. I hear from my administrator friends that test scores keep going down and no one seems to care. What really upsets me is that both the board president and superintendent are fiddling with the status quo. Mostly, this status quo works well for me. And you know by now that when I see a persistent problem, I address it. And this goes well beyond me. I think that this status quo has worked fine for the district to date. We were doing Ok. Of course, we weren't the best school district, but we certainly were not the worst. The new board president and the new superintendent led the district directly into the toilet. Everyone saw this coming.

Something also bothered the hell out of me. These two power hungry bitches picked away at the old boy's network. They knew it existed and both of them hated it. Although these two shrews hated each other, somehow, they bonded over this. I think that they just wanted to eliminate all men from the district. At one time, the administrative team was mostly all men. Now it was going to be all women. A few of the old-timers were getting squeezed. These were my friends. I really can't remember the last man that was hired. These two bitches viewed themselves as the modern woman. They made it their mission to right 100 years of discrimination against women. And perhaps worse, a black modern woman with some power. If things did not settle down, I could have accurately predicted that I would soon call The Liberator into action.

It was interesting, and yes, for me, somewhat sad watching the trickle-down politics play out. The board president would beat up the superintendent, who would beat up the closest administrator, and they would then beat up the first teacher that needed a beat down. And as I am sure you would predict, these beaten down teachers would turn to the kids to provide the beating that they deserved, whether or not they needed it. Everyone just wanted to piss on someone. They did not care who it may be. This was now the culture of the district. I blamed both of the women on top. For me, it was as simple as that.

The kids got screwed. Isn't that how it always is? The weakest link in the chain gets stretched and twisted until it breaks. These two fools forgot what schools were about. Schools must be about the kids, not the adults, and yet I watched this war play out daily.

I actually went to board meetings to watch the dynamics on a public stage. Going to a board of education meeting was better than watching television. You could always count on some drama. You just never knew how it would start and who would be most affected. I regretted they did not sell popcorn and soda at the meetings. Going to a meeting would have been a cheap date.

Teachers and administrators knew the game. The city fathers worked on a system of reprisals. School administrators knew this. This system rendered them helpless. If you stirred the soup, you could expect a beat down.

Some of my administrator friends, yes, good old boys, would tell me that when the superintendent was angry at them, she would just ignore them. She would exclude them from important meetings. For example, I can recall one principal telling me she would not let him into a meeting that all other principals attended about the school budget. He was totally disempowered. This superintendent could write the book on how to marginalize someone. She just loved cutting guys' balls off. And for these guys that still cared, this management style ate away at them. Were they the best principals? Probably not. But they still cared. How do you think that individual principal's school made out at budget time? The system totally screwed them. But the boss certainly did not care. She tried to push these guys out of the door. Some left on their own for other jobs. Some retired early, and some just stayed to get pissed on. I wish The Liberator could take care of two birds with one stone. Wouldn't that be great? I wanted so desperately to wake up one morning with the satisfaction of a completed liberation. Both of them were never to be heard of again. This thought gave me some chills. Could I make this happen? I will have to really think about that one.

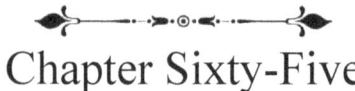

Chapter Sixty-Five
Trouble ahead-three rivers flowing into one?

As I lay in bed, staring once again at the ceiling, I now saw that I had three distinct problems bubbling up at once. It was almost like watching three rivers winding down a mountainside ultimately joining to form a big river emptying into the ocean. I felt myself floating down one of these rivers. And yes, they were getting closer together. And yes, my river was about to spit me into a black hole.

How was I going to slow these rivers down when they were all gaining steam? All gaining momentum. The waters I could see were becoming quite rough. I was about to head into the rapids. Into the whirlpools. I always marveled at watching the Olympic kayakers compete and navigate their choppy course. They strapped these athletes into these, what appears to be flimsy kayaks and race down a dangerous course. I would see these kayakers roll over and continue down the course upside down with their head and shoulders submerged under water, only to see them reappear bobbing upright later in the course to finish their run. I think I was now like this upended kayaker; my head was under water. Would I be able to pop up like them and finish my run down the rapids? Would I be able to keep my head above water and not drown?

Okay. I had to gather myself. Keep my wits about me and figure out my next steps. My three rivers await me. I had the River Kelly, The River Miss Mary and Big Lou and the River Bitches (superintendent and board president). Each river presenting me with some interesting and unique navigational challenges.

Chapter Sixty-Six
The River Mary Lou

I have said little about the investigative team because they were really trying to fly under the radar. When they spoke to me, I tried to baffle them with bullshit. I am pretty good at that.

I already knew that they knew I was the only one in every building when the "liberations" occurred. Okay, that is a bit incriminating, but not insurmountable. The lack of interest by the police made my cover much easier. The police are still happy writing each of the deaths off as an accident. Good, that is exactly what I wanted them to think. As I have already told you, their laziness and incompetence played right into my hands. I do not see that changing.

Miss Mary and Big Lou had commandeered a spare classroom in my building to use as their home. Someone well equipped it. It had all the technology available along with many of the comforts of home, including a couch. They also had the locks changed by a locksmith that the insurance company sent to do the job. That was an interesting move. It told me they clearly did not trust me or anyone in the building. It also told me they did not trust any of our local locksmiths. I told you they were smart. Changing locks in the district was a joke. Local locksmiths or our maintenance crew regularly siphoned off keys to distribute to political friends or family members. Normally, possessing a key was easy. Not in this case. Nothing in this district is private. I learned that long ago.

For example, if you wanted to see someone's private personnel file, I could get a copy of that for you by the end of the day. If you wanted to know about a student or staff disciplinary matter, that too was easy. No sweat. Your school e-mails were also at my fingertips. I could get them, although that was a bit more difficult for me, but still not impossible. This is another important reason you should never use your work e-mails for personal business. My tentacles reached deep into the underbelly of the district. I could also get my hands on the health benefits folder, which provided access to the prescription drugs that people were taking and the district was paying for. I laughed when I saw all the tough guys that were taking Viagra. Likewise, I never realized how many people were taking anti-depressants. You get my point. I could get any piece of information that I wanted. This was all good information to have in case I needed to help "persuade" or convince someone of my point of view.

Key security was a real joke. We should never even have bothered to lock any doors. Most of the people in the community had a spare secret key stashed away for whatever reason. We were careless with keys. No one attempted to reclaim keys from terminated or retired employees. Those that retired or died, I guess, took their keys to the great beyond. The wonderful Miss Mary changed all of that. Now, both internal and external doors were computer card driven. And your card only gave you access to certain areas. It limited you to areas that you had a reason to be in. A computer read out every night would follow your actions.

I saw where they were going with this. Big brother would be always watching now. I had to assume that they now knew that I had access to every place where one of my staged accidents occurred. But so did a hundred other people. They would not get me on that one. Okay, in the future I had to be more careful, but I still could get whatever I wanted, whenever I wanted it. Procuring information and access were still my greatest powers. No one else had this skill. I was proud of that. But don't forget, it took me years to master.

Miss Mary also had her tech crew come in and install a comprehensive series of cameras in living color, monitoring every square inch of the building. Finding a dark spot was going to be difficult. Not impossible, but difficult.

For some, as I have already said, keys are power. However, information is more powerful. I already had the keys, and mostly, I could always get the information. I had developed a comprehensive series of spies. My spies were the school secretaries. They liked to feel important. I could squeeze most anything out of them. For some of these folks, it took me years to cultivate. For others, my task was ridiculously easy. I had found over the course of my career that secretaries, mostly, were blabber mouths. And they collectively just loved to reveal secrets. Anger directed at their boss heightened this apathetic attitude. They would sell him or her out for the approval of others in a second. When they felt beaten-up, they needed their self-esteem boosted by someone like me. They just loved to hear themselves talk. And I had become a master at striking while the iron was hot. I had developed a sixth sense of sorts that I just knew when one of my spies needed to talk.

However, nurturing all of my people could be a full-time job. Sometimes I came to work and did nothing all day but "work" my people. I felt like a farmer cultivating my crops. I would water and feed them as needed, and they would ultimately provide me a bountiful harvest of information and access.

Chapter Sixty-Seven
The River Kelly

I knew I could manage the River Mary Lou. I knew its direction. On the other hand, I saw problems navigating the River Kelly.

I am not sure if Kelly was panicking over the situation as it was developing with Miss Mary and Big Lou. They were constantly pressuring and pestering her. And she was just becoming so miserable in her marriage that she now saw this as an opportunity to do something about it. I think she hoped I would ultimately liberate her from her marriage.

Over the last few months, I saw Kelly transform herself. First, she started with a new haircut with a new color shade. It looked pretty good. Next, she dropped some weight and firmed up some of the extra weight she carried. I noticed our lunches were being skipped and when we ate; she brought a much healthier selection from home. Sadly, my cookie treats from her became a thing of the past. That was unfortunate because her cookies were a real treat. And finally, she was buying herself a new wardrobe. This new wardrobe had also included a new selection of shoes. I must admit that I love seeing a woman in a sexy pair of shoes. And believe me when I tell you I am no foot pervert. I just like shoes. Most women do not put enough time into shoe selection. In this way, Kelly was much like Miss Mary Lou. Maybe Kelly was just trying to copy the younger woman. Maybe they, too, were having secret meetings and conversations. Kelly was investing her time and money in her appearance. Perhaps I am flattering myself, but I really felt as though she was doing this for me. I knew she wasn't doing it for her husband.

So, now I had Kelly dolling herself up. Here comes the trouble.

And trouble sure found me on our next trip to the bank. She dropped off the money and jumped back into the car, but before I could even start the car; she was all over me. I hate to admit it, but she felt good, looked good and smelled very good. Then she opened her mouth. She was trying to undress me. She took time to whisper in my ear and remind me about her gratitude for the elimination of her nemesis, that pain in the ass, Westerman. All I thought was I needed to use a stall tactic. I needed some time to think. Her disappearance allowed everyone to rejoice. I bet even her husband had a big favor handed to him and he was outwardly enjoying every minute of his freedom as I watched him piss away her insurance money at the local watering holes. He was also spending a great deal of time in Atlantic City at the casinos. Good for him. He put up with that whiny, cigarette smoking bitch for a long time. Let's just say he was enjoying his newfound freedom.

But let us get back to Mrs. Kelly. I calmed her down and cooled her off. I would not bang her in broad daylight in the parking lot of the bank. With a promise, I could put her off. I was using the old four corner stall that basketball teams used to use when they wanted to freeze out the opponent. They just played keep away. I was now trying to play keep away from Kelly. It worked. She cooled off. We set up a date. A date? Is that what you call what I was walking into? For me, it could very well be a date with the executioner.

Next weekend would be the time and place for some action. What action, however, I was not too sure about. This needed some more thought.

We drove back to the school in silence. She fluffed her clothes up, and I did the same to mine. I dropped her off at the doorway. She entered the school with a newfound hope.

After parking my car, I entered via a remote doorway. I would be lying to you if I told you I used these extra minutes to think of my plan. I used these extra minutes to just take in the scent of Kelly's new perfume mixed with the scent of heated passion. I have to tell you; it felt pretty damn good and pretty exciting.

I entered my school with dread and concern. I also entered with a new sense of exhilaration.

Chapter Sixty-Eight
The River Bitches

Okay. Now I must turn my thoughts to the third river monster that I had to deal with, The River Bitches. Namely, the Board President, Cruella De Ville and the Superintendent who I will refer to as Ursula. It strikes me funny that I name both people after Disney villainesses. Mrs. Black, the board president, had all the features of Cruella. She dressed like her and carried herself like her. When she opened her mouth, I could hear Cruella. The poor Dalmatians. Our poor school.

Likewise, the Superintendent looked like Ursula the sea witch, or sea hag from the Little Mermaid. For Christ's sake, that woman was making over $200,000 a year and dressed like a pauper. I have seen restroom attendants dress better. When she and her friend Mrs. Black walked around, you could see the difference from miles away. You can also see that I am watching too much of the Disney Channel on cable. Believe it or not, I find I can slip out of the real world when I put the Disney Channel on. It became an escape for me.

It was hard for me to comprehend when I saw them together that they could have formed such a bond. They looked so different. They sounded so different, yet they were both evil. Here is another lesson to be learned from my story. Namely, evil comes in all shapes and sizes and all colors. Evil does not discriminate. I guess they shared power rather than fighting with each other. Over time, I knew this could not last and they both would ultimately destroy each other. But I could not wait this long. The district could not wait that long.

And the first question that came to my mind was very simple. By trying to address both of them, was I biting off more than I could chew? Did I have to liberate the school from both of them? Or could I just liberate the school from the most dangerous one? The one that seemed to be the most destructive.

Anyone easily saw that the superintendent was just a court jester for Mrs. Black. She pulled her strings like a puppeteer makes his or her marionettes dance. When they walked together, the superintendent stayed two steps behind the board president. Although this was probably never formally orchestrated, it just was the way it was. And believe me, it was obvious. When they were in a room together, the superintendent always played second fiddle. Speculation was just speculation. It was as simple as that. I always waited around to hear the board president boss the superintendent around. It was embarrassing and demeaning. I almost felt bad for the superintendent. I said almost, because she was evil in her own way.

Other than their bitchy attitude, what was really bothering me about these two? How were each one of them negatively affecting the school? When I actually thought about it rationally, changing the status quo pissed me off. Change is hard. Change is hard for everyone. Everyone reacts to it differently. Implementing change in a nasty and disrespectful way makes change much harder. Neither one of them ever thought that it was important for them to bring the masses along with them. They never gave two shits about the average person, the common worker in the district. They never would listen to the commoner's voice. One thing I knew for sure about leadership, you cannot leave the average person out of it and you cannot be a prick to everyone. I knew some of the fragged lieutenants in Viet Nam that I am sure in the great beyond wished they knew this lesson before it was too late for them.

Maybe I was just pissed because they were women. Probably more pissed that in both subtle and not-so-subtle ways, they were trying to eliminate the "good old boy" network. And in reality, times had changed and maybe the "good old boy" network had to go. But it didn't have to go the way they had planned. It worked well for many years. Yes, I know that for me, the system worked very well. I can't comment for all of those brothers that were qualified and passed over for leadership opportunities because of this new female centric environment. For them, it sucked. The pink ceiling was crumbling. I knew I could never let that happen. Sorry about that.

Chapter Sixty-Nine
An epiphany at midnight

One night it just happened. The thought came to me like a lightning bolt. Why didn't I see it earlier? I was pacing and thinking about the scripture that I had just read and then, BAM, it just hit me.

I had to get someone else to do my dirty work. And I had a few thoughts on this topic. I knew there were more than several people primed to do the job. My role would be to push them in the right direction. And with my bullshitting skills, I knew I could do it. I just mentioned what I had to do. I had to get someone to frag them.

Fragging was the ultimate show of disrespect. When one threw a fragmentation grenade in to an area to kill a superior officer, people referred to it as fragging. And usually, your intended target was your asshole lieutenant. The explosion of shrapnel would usually kill anyone around the explosion. And what was important about this method, no one could ever identify the thrower because they would lose all evidence and prints in the dust. The problem for the perpetrator was if someone had seen him throw the grenade.

Another way to carry out a "fragging" event would be to have a stray bullet hit the intended target in a firefight. No one could ever determine where the bullet came from. A bit more personal. And it worked. For some that used the shooting method, they just had to feel it. They wanted it to be personal.

I had my plan. Now I had to pick the person who would unwittingly carry it out. And I would unnecessarily sacrifice this person for my cause. Oh well, you remember I told you that every battle has some collateral damage. You just hope that it isn't you.

Chapter Seventy
Paranoia everywhere

I think that I have already told you about some crazies that walked the halls in the schools. I am talking about the adults here, not the kids. Mental illness was rampant. Although I had no real frame of reference, because I had spent just about my entire adult working in life in the schools in this district, I always found it hard to understand why so many crazy people existed in the schools. The schools attracted them.

I mention paranoia here because it is relevant, and it is something that will eventually help me. Every year, administrators get more paranoid. I have seen some of my boys get so squirrelly at the end of their careers that they went to extremes to ease some of their fears, worries, or concerns.

For example, we had one boss long ago who would keep a listing of your associates. His list confirmed the notion of guilt by association. You could just be standing in the parking lot, chatting with a colleague about the weather, who the boss did not like, and if the boss would ride by and see you, you would make his enemy list. You made the shit list. He was taking names. And once you made this guy's list, it was hard to get off of it. Some guys finished their career, never being spoken to or acknowledged by this guy. There were times I actually saw him write names in his little black book. He also starting wearing a pen on a string around his neck so he always had it handy to mark down a name in his book. It was hilarious. Everyone laughed at him behind his back.

I can't really remember the sequence of leaders but after pen man left, we had a guy who became so crazy that he made everyone in his inner circle sign a loyalty oath. Eventually, there was an internal outcry, and this practice ceased. However, his paranoia never did. You had to openly and publicly declare your loyalties. Failure to do so forced your exile or termination. He trusted very few people. Also, he thoroughly enjoyed berating people. He liked to embarrass you. And after the ass-chewing, he would huddle with his few friends and laugh about it. I stayed clear of him. He knew how to torture you.

I don't want to leave out this next guy who worked by marginalization. He excluded you when you annoyed or angered him. If you cared about your job, this hurt. I used to watch one of his administrators sit and cry in her office when he excluded her from a meeting. She sat crying in isolation at her desk while others of her same rank met. The boss told her to stay away. That hurt. And please don't infer by this tale that it was only women that he brought to tears. I saw many men sit and cry after dealing with him, too. I felt bad for these folks. They were basically good people but were in over their heads in their job. Treating people in this way is just mean and useless.

I really felt sorry for the people that just wanted to come in to work and do their jobs. These folks did not care who the boss was. They knew they had a job to do and were just going to do it. These were the actual warriors who could put all of this other bullshit behind them and focus on what was right for the kids. I could visually see how this bullshit affected them. Yet they trudged on. I dedicate my liberating work to these folks and I still believe that if these people knew what I was doing, they would probably give me some sort of medal.

If I had a nickel for each crying jag I had seen by the adults in the building, I would be a rich man by now. I remember Big Lou telling me one time he spent most of his days dealing with some sort of staff nuttiness. He was right. It was always something. And most times it just reminded me of some middle school kids' problem. Stuff such as this one was talking about me, or this one took my material or this one gave me a dirty look over something. It was just the same old bullshit that wasted everyone's time. And don't forget that it was the kids that paid the price for this nonsense.

Now it was my turn to use this nuttiness to my advantage. I had three pigeons lined up who I thought I could push over the edge to frag the generals.

Chapter Seventy-One

Wanted: Mentally unbalanced teacher willing to sacrifice for the district.
Applicants, please fall in line.

Okay, I had my candidates to carry out this job in my head. I knew I had to be slick, very slick to make this work. I could not rush it.

My first candidate was Mr. Gonzalez. I heard him tell his story before. Everyone has heard him tell his story before, probably more than once.

Mr. Gonzalez and his family fled the government's oppression in Cuba. He still spoke with a heavy accent and I could never understand him. God only knows how the kids could understand him in class. Mostly, he would just close his door and try to teach. He was also mean to the kids. And saying that, you can only imagine how the kids responded to him. They tortured him. His usual "M.O." would be to pick out one of the mentally weaker students and unleash all of his wrath on him or her. Most times, these kids that he targeted were genuine pains in the ass. He could not deal with them. He was high strung. He would walk the halls, staying close to the wall as his eyes would rapidly scan back and forth, looking for trouble. For every two steps he took forward, he would glance behind him for anyone who was following him. His demeanor defined paranoia.

Several times, he asked me to move his car around the parking lot during the day because he knew he was being followed by someone from Cuba. I assumed it was one of Castro's loyalists (yea, right). He came to work several times late as he tried to elude them. He made police reports all the time. They ignored him. One time he ran his car aground in a local park, trying to make an elusive maneuver. He missed the lake by about 20 yards. That would have been an actual sight. I overheard his police reports. They were comical. It was hard not to laugh out loud.

Big Lou told me one time that Mr. Gonzalez accused him of being an agent for Castro. They went around and around about this and ultimately the board suspended Mr. Gonzalez and required him to undergo a medical evaluation, including a psychological exam. I believe in my heart these exams were big scams. It cleared him to return to work. He would be good for a while and then it would all start over again.

I knew I could rev him up. I could fire up his paranoia pretty easily. I knew I could make him believe that the board president was an agent for Fidel. That could work for my plan, but I had other nuts to review. The district was just full of squirrels. I just had to pick the right one.

Squirrel number two was Ms. Walsh. Her paranoid mental illness was that every male in the district wanted to have sex with her. When it was my turn to be accused, I just went right back at her. She knew not to pull that shit with me. She preyed on men who exhibited some kind of weakness. She was a career wrecker. She was a life wrecker. I saw more than my share of men, yes good men, chased from the district because of her. I would tell them to tell her to go fuck herself and give her a good barking and she would run away. However, the men she chose for this harassment were just not strong enough to do this.

Times being what they were in society, the boss had to take her seriously. So, when she complained, an internal investigation had to take place and each man would deny these allegations. It was so hard because it always ended up as a "he said, she said" event. Who knew where the truth was? From the onset of this bullshit, I knew where the truth was. Not with her. She fabricated all of it. Did she enjoy it? I am sure that she did. She played the victim while they left these men swinging in the wind. The cherry on top of this shit sundae came when she wore a coach's whistle around her neck, and if a man was in the same hallway with her, she would loudly blow this whistle. To tell you it was disruptive would be an understatement. The first time I heard this, I almost shit my pants. It scared everyone. This lasted until Big Lou, after he jumped through many hoops with her, had to really sit on her. Not literally, figuratively. She might have liked a run with Big Lou. Who knows? Like so many others, she was not discriminatory about who she picked to hassle. She was an equal rights assassin. She picked on black men and white men equally. If they were young or old, she didn't care. It made no difference. She just enjoyed ruining lives.

I knew I could press her buttons to tip her over the edge. However, I thought that my plan would have been more easily executed by a man. I think Walsh proudly hated all men. I wonder what happened to her along the way? Obviously, it had to be something bad. Terrible.

Squirrel number three was another real whacko. His name was Mr. Kowalski. Fallout from the nuclear accident years ago in Russia worried him. If you recall years and years ago, the Russian Chernobyl accident set him off into outer space, never to return. Yet he stood in front of six classes a day, twenty-five students in each class lecturing them. There was not a time that I passed his classroom when he was not ranting about Russia. I think that the administration really fumbled this one. He was certifiable. He would wear camo into school and also look around, searching for these make-believe gremlins. I could probably use this time for him to payback the district because he was about to retire. Payback for those that haunted him for years.

I had a great deal of thinking to do. Which squirrel would be my pigeon? You want to take a guess?

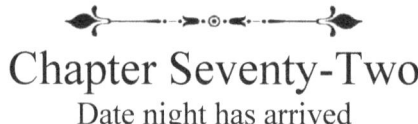

Chapter Seventy-Two
Date night has arrived

Well, the River Kelly keeps meandering through my thoughts at night. Now I am staying awake thinking of her. I can't stop smelling her perfume. I can't stop feeling the heat of her passion. And I must confess that while I lay there in bed thinking of this, I get aroused thinking about her. Thinking about some secret and dirty liaison. Although I told you before that sex was never very important to me, but after all, I am still a man. A man with certain needs and desires. And right now, Mrs. Kelly was both a need and a desire. This shit keeps getting crazier. But on this one, my body wants what my body wants and right now, my body wants her.

We set it up for the upcoming weekend. She told her husband that she was working at the school play. He never cared. He was a blob. We went for a cozy dinner where her hands were all over me under the table and ended up at a motel on the interstate close to the school. No one would see us there. If someone did, the rumors would fly.

We both had a couple of drinks with dinner and we could barely wait to get into the room. I had a hard time registering. I don't mean to be cute on this one, but I really had a hard time. You get what I mean. Right?

I think by the time that we had entered the room, our clothes were already half off. Without going into all the details, Mrs. Kelly did not disappoint. In the first few minutes of our sexual encounter, she released all of her pent-up sexual anxieties. We rested a bit and I can share that the second go around was as good as the first.

But this trip is not necessarily about sex. I needed to know what she knew about my liberations. Did she have any facts besides her intuitions? Well, some information came out in some of our pillow talk. I skillfully manipulated the conversation in that direction. I think I told you earlier that I liked to keep a small souvenir from each liberation. The keys I chose were mine. For everyone that I took care of, I took that person's key ring. It turns out Kelly saw me with Westermann's keys. She also saw me with Mr. Peoples' key ring. As some sort of thrill, I would carry one with me, hooked onto my key ring every day. Kelly recognized the keys.

I admitted nothing. I just stayed evasive.

Believe or not, before we left, inasmuch we were not staying the night, we went at it for a third time. It surprised me I still had it. I think that deserves a LOL.

We both left satisfied. This satisfaction for me included my new knowledge of what she exactly knew. I certainly won't kid you, but I enjoyed the sex, too.

We both agreed this would happen again, and we both agreed that we had to be discreet. No one could know about us.

For me, I was going to enjoy the ride, once again, no pun intended.

Chapter Seventy-Three
A time for reflection

This machine needed to be slowed down. I felt as if I was running on a treadmill. There was too much going on at the same time. I knew myself well enough to know that when this mental overcrowding takes place; it is time to step back. Okay, what is exactly on my plate right now? Let me see if I can briefly list them:

- I will start with Mrs. Kelly. Like it or not, I was now in some sort of romantic affair with her. Not only did she sense my guilt, she saw my key collection and if she looked closer, she would see the key rings of my other liberations. This was not good, but I think as long as I was playing her and giving her little pieces of me, I would be safe. And I said before, she was good in bed. I could feel and sense all of her pent-up desires and fantasies, either being played out now or soon to be played in the future. In a lot of ways, I was also liberating Kelly. But instead of killing her, I was freeing her. The Liberator strikes again.
- Miss Mary and Big Lou were now sniffing around everything. It appeared Big Lou put his regular job on hold and was now working overtime on each one of my liberations. Was he really working hard on my liberations, or was he really working hard with Miss Mary? Now that is a good question. It appeared they were not even trying to keep their "extra-curricular" activity a secret. I was happy for the big guy, but still troubled by his carelessness. It just proves another point that I have learned that the "man with no mind" between a guy's legs was overpowering. If you need another example, just look at me.
- I was trying to figure out how to liberate the district from the board president and, if I was lucky, the superintendent. I could not be greedy, and I knew that the board president just had to go.
- Beavis and Butthead, our friendly incompetent detectives, were nowhere to be seen. That was a good thing. The police

really did not care and were out of the loop. It just proves that the people that were eliminated were really pains in the ass and I truly believe the elimination of these two thrilled everyone. This also clearly proved the competency, or should I more accurately say, the incompetency of the local police department.

- I was revisiting my internal policy of not eliminating the kids. Some of them were so bad and disrespectful that I truly do not know how the teachers came to work every day. Some of these kids just needed a good punch in the mouth, a kick in the ass, or the flight out of a third-floor window, straight down to the pavement, hopefully landing on their heads. I would not miss these individuals at all. I believed their parents would not even miss them. And the schools would be a lot better. It is sad that I am seeing this behavior in children at a much earlier age. I especially feel bad for the teachers that are intimidated, are old and tired, or for the ones that are not skillful enough to manage this lot. These folks loved teaching and still could be outstanding teachers if it wasn't for this group of nasty assholes. This certainly needs more consideration.

- And while all of this shit was going down, I had to manage the politics of the district and community. This was a full-time job on a quiet day. Now, with all the other crap I was dealing with, managing life became more and more difficult. It was even difficult for me: that suave politician. However, I had no thought of ever giving up my reign as the master politician and kingmaker in the district.

Life is good. But life is hard.

Chapter Seventy-Four
And the winner is....

After some long and hard consideration, I concluded that the easiest squirrel for me to manipulate was Mr. Gonzalez. Not only was he nuts, he was angry nuts. Believe me, many people are crazy, but few people hold on to his anger like Gonzalez. I knew I could push his buttons the right way for him to somehow do my dirty work for me.

Although I would not be doing the deed, getting him to do it was still going to be difficult. In my manipulations, I did not want him to turn and take me out along the way. I still liked life, and I knew I had more work to do in this district. So, I basically had to subcontract this liberation.

As I told you, Gonzalez had this weird fear of Fidel Castro and his Cuban regime. Even though Fidel was dead, this powerful fear still dominated Gonzalez' thinking. I think his parents and possibly he as a child experienced some of the worst things one would hear about Castro and the methodologies of his rule. I knew he escaped with his mother, leaving his father and other family members behind. His father was an intellectual and I believe he did not meet a pleasant end. I never heard Gonzalez speak of his older brothers. I believe that they just went missing after an involuntary conscription into the Cuban Army. Gonzalez and his mother ended up in America and somehow, he ended up teaching in our district. His employment in our district was obvious. He spoke and taught Spanish, and we needed Spanish teachers. I think I told you that our district was changing. In the future, I could see that teachers were basically going to be bilingual to survive. Just think about how the good old white boys felt about this. The resentment was obvious. I knew I could use this resentment to fuel Gonzalez' hate. I did not need to throw a lot of gasoline onto his fire of anger, because his hatred was always simmering near the surface. When the kids pissed him off, I saw it bubble over. It was not a pretty sight. This is where I will start.

I knew I had to befriend Gonzalez. We were really not on speaking terms, so my brainwashing process would not be easy. We would smile at each other and maybe say hello and yet other times he would distance himself from me mumbling under his breath. At these times, I doubt if he ever saw me in the hallway. Although, I saw very early in this process that his personality and his paranoia were going to help me.

So, I began at what I saw as the beginning. I said hello to him. We talked about cars. He loved his car. Although it was a piece of shit, it was his treasure. It was a big Oldsmobile from the early seventies, basically held together by pieces of rust and duct tape. It reminded me of the cars that I would see in pictures of Havana streets. When he was outside of the building, he always wore his Cuban fedora. There was always a chewed cigar stump hanging from his lips. I always wondered if these cigars were from some secret stash.

I also started cleaning his room. Although, as the custodial supervisor, I barely lifted a finger, I would go to his room before the start of the school day to straighten up. It gave me an opening to bond with him. It started out pretty simply with some idle banter. I would praise his car, commiserate about the unruly students, or rip the administration with him. This phony bullshit was always difficult because I could barely understand him through his thick accent. God only knows how the kids could understand him. Perhaps that is why they seemed to pick on him. Probably the only good thing this man got out of teaching in this school was his paycheck. And I think I could fuck with that too, as this process moved down the road. I believed I could drive him over the edge. No, now I was sure of that. I found him very easy to manipulate.

I brought him coffee in the morning and I found a café in town that now specialized in Cuban fare and I would periodically bring him a strong Cuban coffee that I knew reminded him of home. He would tell me about the good things at home. One day, he handed me a small package and when I opened it; I saw a bundle of six Cuban cigars tied together with a bow. I thanked him and one day after work drove around enjoying the pleasures of a good cigar. Yes, we were bonding.

For the sake of time, I am leaving out all the crazy rants that he would share with me. He believed Big Lou was an arm of the Castro regime and was here to inflict some sort of deadly harm on him. I shifted his thinking and told him it was not Big Lou, but the crazy bitch superintendent that had it in for him. I told him I heard her say that. His eyes twirled as I could see. Yes, he was processing my fake information. She arrived in our district and I got him to believe that she was going to destroy him. I claimed that she also jeopardized his remaining family. I knew she came from the educational system in Florida where her mission was to put out any stray Cuban dissenters and bring them to some sort of justice. W   What the hell did I know? Justice for what? The bullshit just kept rolling out of my mouth. He was buying every bit, whether it was right or wrong. You know I found people will believe all the lies that you tell them if you tell them repeatedly and tell them with conviction. The liar soon believes he or she is not even lying anymore. This is where I had Mr. Gonzalez.

One day before school, I had made it a point to come in very early that day. I had my ladder up in Gonzalez' room with the face off of the public address speaker in his classroom. Because we had changed the public address system several times over the last thirty years, there was what seemed to be an endless supply of dead wires still behind the scenes. I found some old abandoned wires and connected them to an old fluorescent bulb light starter. I connected some dead red and green wire to this D-battery sized object and made it look real. And when Gonzalez walked into his classroom that morning, I was up on the ladder slowly disconnecting this phony mechanism that I just connected. I showed both excitement and surprise when I exclaimed to him the "I found it." I told him I found a listening device embedded in his classroom so the superintendent could hear every message. He fell for it hook, line and sinker. I do not know if it was shock or anger, but his face immediately changed color to a crimson red and just as quickly to a gray pallor. He spoke uncontrollably in both Spanish and English and I could make out only a few words he kept repeating, "… just like Castro, just like Castro, just like Castro." Mental fatigue overcame him.

To sum it all up, I was playing with his fears of the real or imagined boogeyman in Cuba and how this boogeyman had tentacles that reached into our tiny district to flesh him out. He assured me he already knew this, and he also assured me he would not be going away easily. If they were going to get him, they were going to have to carry him out on a gurney. I just about had him hooked. For this, I was sure.

He was getting close. My pump was being primed. I suggested that he and I do some late-night surveillance on the school board president, chief of police, and the superintendent. He eagerly agreed. So, we spent many a late-night watching shadows pass before us while I filled his head with imaginary stories. This cloak and dagger bullshit was tedious but, hilarious. I would see something or hear something and make up some quick story about what was happening. I never realized that I was such an excellent storyteller.

I also quickly found out how sleep deprivation could screw you up. Shit, I would have made an excellent spy. Maybe I would have been a great interrogator. Why didn't the army see this skill in me? I never had to touch the guy. There were no beatings with a hose or bamboo shoots under the fingernails. I did not have to go get my car battery and attach it to his balls to give him a good jolt. All I did was fuck with his mind. I guess the experts would say that I had a straightforward job because his mind was so messed up to begin with. Who knows? I don't care. It was working for me and my hands were never getting dirty.

We both would come to work after these late-night excursions, asleep on our feet. It was easy for me to go hide for a while and take a nap. I could basically sleep the day away. I already have done this in my career many times and it was easy. He had to stand before six classes daily and I would come in around noon. And I must add that these were not honors classes. Most students were just in his class because of a state language requirement and these same youngsters could give two shits about Spanish. Instead, they just loved making Mr. Gonzalez' life miserable.

It came to a head one day after one of our nighttime operations. One of our wise guy kids pushed the right button and Gonzalez hauled off and belted him. I wish I would have seen it. The kid was an asshole who deserved it, but now it played right into my hands.

I could now see the light at the end of this tunnel. My work with Gonzalez was coming to a head. It would not be long now.

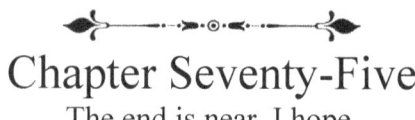

Chapter Seventy-Five
The end is near. I hope.

I got to the scene fairly quickly to see the action. They escorted the kid to the nurse and, ultimately; the kid had to go to the hospital to have his broken nose repaired. Gonzalez may have done the kid a favor. Maybe the kid would use this punch in the nose to straighten out. Who knows? If he did not, this would not be his last trip to the hospital to get stitched up or repaired. For some assholes, it only takes one broken nose. For other assholes, they never get it and many of these end up dead. Time would only tell about our young friend. Would he be a one and done client? Or a frequent flier? Like I said, time would tell.

Security managed the scene and escorted Mr. Gonzalez from the building. The school district suspended him pending police charges and an official hearing. There was never any doubt about his guilt. There were probably about 25 witnesses who saw the whole thing go down. Gonzalez never disputed it. It was one quick hard punch landing squarely on the nose. His claim was a weak one, namely that he just could not take this kid anymore. The kid was a constant irritant to not only Gonzalez, but to other teachers as well. Shit, half the building wanted to thank Gonzalez. I could help escort him to his car. I used this time to stoke the fire in Gonzalez' belly while it was still burning. I told him that this kid was a neighbor of the board president and I knew she had asked him to set up Gonzalez with the superintendent's blessing. I told him that the kid he punched was nothing more than a stooge doing the boss' dirty deeds for them. And because Gonzalez now knew that the board president was part of a Cuban scheme, it did not take Gonzalez too long to put two and two together and come up with five.

I told Gonzalez that we were just like they were in Nazi Germany, where the kids readily turned on the adults. They regularly escorted parents and teachers to the public courtyard for a hanging spectacle. I told him that the board president was using the same tactics. She saw herself as the new Fuhrer and the superintendent was her next in command, a combination of Hermann Goring and Heinrich Himmler, the loyal number two. Yes, of course I was digging deep for this bullshit. It just popped into my head and let's face it; I really didn't know all that much about Cuban history, so I had no real frame of reference. I just pulled some shit out of the air. Something that I remembered from my eleventh-grade history class. Wow!

I knew that I just had to play on Gonzalez' fears and paranoia. I thought I was going to have to put on my boots to wade through all of this bullshit.

This approach worked. I hoped it did not work too well. I had to keep him calm until his full board hearing took place. That is when the climax would occur.

I only hoped that after that meeting, we would sing "ding dong the witches are gone."

Chapter Seventy-Six
D-Day

After his 45-day suspension from work, the board of education scheduled his hearing. It was all but assured that the board wanted to unceremoniously fire Gonzalez and take his teaching certificate. I had used this time wisely, putting every lie I could into his head, and I had instilled more hatred for the system and for those in charge of his psyche. I dug deep. I almost felt bad.

Everyone believed that this would be the case. And because Gonzalez did not have many friends, no one really cared. If this happened to a more popular teacher, or perhaps one of the good old boys, the community's reaction would have been entirely different. They would have vilified the kid and looked for every reason to forgive Gonzalez and save him.

Believe me, I have seen this act before. One thing you should always remember is that in school districts, justice is not always fair or appropriate. The system treated people differently. Punishments vary depending on who you know and who you blow. Whether punishments are right or just does not matter. (That, of course, is figurative. On second thought, maybe it isn't. I can now recall cases where it was all about someone getting blown.) That is the system like it or not. Sometimes it may be racial persecution, gender persecution, life style choice persecution or age persecution. It just did not matter. But the reality of things is this; all the various persecutions that I just mentioned are secondary to my first postulate about justice and maybe life in the school system. It is all about who you know and who you blow. Never forget it.

I saw one last obstacle I had to figure out before the hearing. By law, in these cases, it was a requirement that the defendant, Gonzalez, would have to sit through a psychiatric examination. Gonzalez' sanity became the issue. In this kangaroo court, his sanity became the determining factor for his punishment. I could not let this happen.

One good thing that I had in my favor was that the doctor was a puppet. He was a puppet for the board of education. They appointed him and he gave them any answer that they wanted. He was told what to do. The board wanted to get rid of Gonzalez at any cost and they would put the screws to this doctor to make it benefit them. That was a given. I can recall that the football coach one time needed a star player classified as a student with special needs. This would enable this player to be eligible, regardless of the student's grades or age. The coach told us at the bar after the examination that the doctor came to the meeting with two determinations written up, with each one stashed in a different breast jacket pocket. As the coach was entering the hearing, the doctor was hanging outside of the door, catching another cigarette before the meeting started. He asked the coach to read each write-up and pick the one that would help him the most. Done deal. The player was eligible and had a stellar season padding the win column of the coach. Also padding his massive ego. (I never said that. LOL)

And so, the same thing happened with Gonzalez. This crackpot doctor found him totally sane and competent to take part in his hearing. What a joke. Gonzalez was probably crazier than many of the people stashed away involuntarily committed to the state's psychiatric hospital. I am sure that we will see who is right on this matter.

They set the stage for the hearing. Gonzalez put on a suit and tie, circa 1965, and sat with the union delegate who put absolutely no energy in to defending him. If it was me, I would have had Gonzalez in some psychiatric hospital recovering from a breakdown. We would have dealt with his punishment, if there was ever to be any, down the road. But that wasn't the case. I set this night up to bid good riddance to Mr. Gonzalez.

He came in with his suit on, carrying his battered briefcase. After the board got done beating him up, he spoke. But before that, his lame delegate gave a half-hearted speech and asked the board to give Gonzalez a second chance.

I thought I had created a lean, mean fighting machine, but I sat there feeling sorry for him and guilty of my manipulations. He was really a pathetic character. Insane and now clearly in some psychotic break. Who knows what he and his family really went through? We never walked in his shoes. It was sad. I was sad. But I had to do what was right for the schools. To me, the end justified all means. Some had to sacrifice. I never felt remorse.

Gonzalez got up, went to the podium and gave a ranting speech about the Cuban regime that had persecuted and tortured his family, and now the agents of Castro had followed him here to America and continued his political persecution. He wanted to be treated as a political prisoner. He dammed the United States for allowing this to happen and dammed the board president and the superintendent. I knew what was coming. Shit, I helped him plan it. He stood tall, opened his tattered briefcase and took out an old revolver, probably from the family, directly from Cuba, aimed and fired at the board president. I saw two bullets hit her, one bullet missed and splintered the blackboard behind her, two bullets then hit the superintendent and with the last bullet, Gonzalez slowly put the pistol to his temple and fired. His brains ended up splattering the audience and messing up the bulletin board in the room. He had a wry smile on his face. For once in a very long, long time, I think he was happy and finally at peace.

No one would persecute Mr. Gonzalez anymore. His gunshot wound to his head chased all demons, both real and imagined.

Even though this outcome was what I expected, I still sat stunned. I had seen a lot of death in my day and took part in and handled a lot of killings and yet this was, in fact, the most stunning. It might have been the noise. Maybe it was the smell of death and gunfire. Perhaps it was the screams of the victims and the audience. Perhaps it was the look on the board president's face at the split second she knew what was coming. It was pure terror and fright. When I killed people, they were all caught by surprise and, mostly, did not know what hit them. This one was different for me. I don't know why, but it was moving. In that instant, I thought I would cease being the Liberator. On second thought, the district still needed me.

It seemed like it took hours for the police to arrive, but I am sure it was only minutes. Some in the crowd ran to the two women that were shot. On the spot, the board president died. The shots critically wounded the superintendent. The ambulance rushed her barely alive body to the hospital. Blood and guts were everywhere and on most people. Gonzalez was dead as a doornail. As Gonzalez laid dead on the floor from his self-inflicted gunshot wound, he looked peaceful.

Unfortunately for the superintendent, and fortunately for the district, the ambulance did not make it in time. An emergency room doctor pronounced her dead. I am told that the emergency room staff valiantly worked to save her, but she, too, was now gone. Her guilt and ultimate sentence turned out to be that she blindly aligned herself to an evil person. I don't really know if she would have been a better person without the board president, but one will never know the answer to that one. Being included in the local political groups made her feel good. She sauntered around the city with the board president like some big wheel. When she was just some flunky or lackey for the evil queen. Who knows? But it is an excellent lesson for all number twos. You know, the loyal sycophants that can't get far enough up the boss' ass. Sometimes the results can be fatal.

Some in the crowd threw up. Some wet and crapped in their pants. Most were crying. That bastard association delegate sat stunned and I think in shock while he wiped brains from his brow. For how he defended Gonzalez, he deserved every bit. I stood in the room's rear and watched the theater. It was some show.

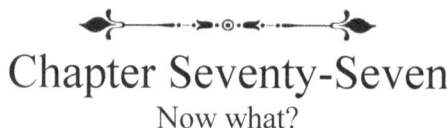

Chapter Seventy-Seven
Now what?

After a swarm of uniformed police officers arrived and sequestered all of us in a nearby classroom, the EMTs arrived to provide any comfort and treatment to any of the spectators who needed it. Someone made a pot of coffee and we all sat there in some state of mindlessness. Because I knew what was coming, I had to somehow fake it. Although Gonzalez killing himself was not part of the initial plan, I planted enough seeds in his head to know that once he got himself worked up, he could never turn back. It turned out that his suicide actually helped me. He could now never reveal my role in all of this. I am just lucky that I did not get a bullet up my ass. I think old Mr. Gonzalez left this earth happy that in his mind he was fighting against Castro and his regime. Don't laugh or shake your head "no" because you do not know how crazy and psychotic Gonzalez was.

I find it amazing that Gonzalez lasted in the classroom for as long as he did. He could have easily come in and killed a bunch of kids or staff for some bizarre reason only known to himself. As I sat there, waiting to be questioned once again by the police, I thought of how many other Gonzalez' were walking around in our district and because our district does not differ from other school districts; I sat in amazement, thinking of the number of teachers and administrators who could do this. It is astonishing. How do these crazy folks keep slipping through the cracks? Another question came to my head to think about. Did the schools attract the crazies or did the school make vulnerable people go flat out nuts? I need to think long and hard on that one.

And yet, as I thought of all the nuts that walked our halls, I actually assigned faces to my list of crazies. My list was startling, especially because some of the good old boys were on that list, along with some of my other friends. I reflected on my life. I believed district employees thought I was incapable of this type of violence. They trusted me.

Am I crazy? Should I be on the top of everyone's list? Well, of course I would be if everyone knew what I did to people over the course of my career. However, as I sat there in my solitude, I thought perhaps I was the only sane one in the district. I say that because everyone knew about the harm that the crazy people were doing to kids and no one did anything about it. And no one could ever argue that perhaps after each of my liberations, the district became better. I was better than the rest because I had the balls to act and do something about it. The system never could act or never wanted to act. Who knows? Ineffective principals and superintendents kept coming and going and no one could solve the problems like the Liberator. I was a doer. End of discussion.

No, I never thought that I was crazy, but I was clearly angry. And as I sat there, I drifted in and out of sleep. As I told you in the past, I did my best thinking as I lay in bed, drifting in and out of sleep. As I sat there, I felt myself drifting and thinking.

Maybe I am in some sort of dream sequence right now, like some kind of movie. Maybe I was just going to wake up and find that my life story that I have been telling you was just a dream. I also know that my police friends told me that the guilty suspects would fall asleep on breaks in the interrogation process. Maybe my guilt is showing through my actions.

I lived my life as an angry man. What a waste. In this deep reflection, each day I woke up angry at something. And it was the same way I went to bed, angry. I seemed to have it all, and I still was not happy. Overall, people could never really please me and I could never please myself. I would get easily pissed off at my friends and colleagues over nothing. It was an adventure driving with me in traffic, especially when an asshole driver would appear. I personified road rage. I am surprised that no one shot me in traffic. However, I had many altercations of some sort with other angry drivers.

Perhaps that is why I do not have a significant other as we speak. (Is Mrs. Kelly becoming somehow this significant other in my life?) I would not be telling the truth if I told you I had no feelings for her. I do. But I just don't know what to do with those feelings.

As I drifted in and out of sleep contemplating these heavy thoughts, I felt a tap on my shoulder. I looked up and saw my old friends, Beavis and Butthead. Our local detectives.

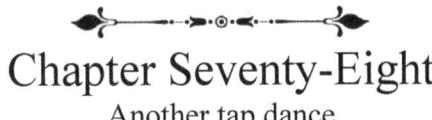

Chapter Seventy-Eight
Another tap dance

Over the years, Beavis, Butthead and I did a good job of tap dancing with each other. I would lead the discussion and at other times I would let them lead the dance. They were too stupid to know any different.

We went through the details of the night's events fairly quickly, and then they sprung their final key question to me. They asked me why I seemed to be in every tragedy. Was it a coincidence or was there some reason?

I paused a beat. I hoped they did not infer that my pause was some sort of statement of guilt. Just like a poker player, I hoped that my brief pause did not tip my hand. It is these little subtle things that will screw you up. Did I just make my first mistake? Who knows?

However, if I were sitting in their shoes, I would have interpreted my behavior in the same way. I verbally stumbled a bit and told them I was at most district events, good ones and bad ones. I joked with them and told them I was omnipresent. I don't know if they knew what that word meant. I told them I had no life and if they wanted to make some sort of inference into that, they would be wrong. Very wrong.

They chuckled and folded up their long skinny notebooks and placed them back in the breast pockets and prepared to leave.

As they dismissed me, I saw a small, sinister bit of eye contact between the two of them.

Was my goose cooked?

Chapter Seventy-Nine
Another country heard from

I almost forgot about little Miss Mary, the insurance investigator. Big Lou was keeping her very busy giving her the high hard one. I am sure that you know what I mean. They had become the item that I expected back when she first appeared. It is hard to spend that much time with someone and not get romantically involved. You know, that small touch or insignificant bump, they mean something. Likewise, you could see that secret brief look that they shared or that laugh that only someone who was knowledgeable would laugh about. I would almost bet that at meetings, they would play footsie underneath the table. Lou and Mary were basically inseparable. Their late meetings and late dinners together were becoming the talk of the district. I saw it and so did everyone else. I do not think that they cared. They were behaving like two teenagers in love. And that was fine with me. Let them worry about each other and forget about their task at hand. I think that the only thing that they have been investigating was each other. I know they did not want to solve any of my liberations because if they did, it would be the end of their little daily dalliance.

They made a cute couple. Big Lou just had gotten a divorce and Miss Mary was single. She started out as the young upwardly mobile female who started out really not caring about the opposite sex. Breaking the glass ceiling for every woman drove her. She believed she was on the fast track to success. Personal derailment was never an option. That was all true until she met Big Lou.

Over time, I saw it develop. It all started innocently and professionally. That lasted a few weeks and then I saw that old man / woman chemistry working. They both wanted each other. They should have just worn a big sign announcing it. But just like in my work as the Liberator, the pursuit and the chase energize you.

Enough love stories. Shit was a happening. Shit was changing. And I could sense it was moving fast. Well, the first thing that happened, Big Lou slid into the top chair. Initially, I felt some relief. A good old boy in the top chair. They set us up for a good run. But behind every good man is a good woman. Right? If you ask most men if that was true, I am sure they would word that statement something like this. Behind every successful man, there is a pain in the ass woman. Big Lou was ready to let these "accidents" drop. He was ready to start his tenure as superintendent with a clean slate. Little Miss Mary would not let that happen. She actually set up shop now in an office directly next to the new boss with a separate and private door that provided an easy in and out for both of them. Did I just make a joke? An easy in and out? I am cracking myself up. Sorry.

It wasn't long before they summoned me to this new office for a meeting. I swaggered in with my confident manner and what I saw shocked me. They had all of my recent murders posted on a large white board with pictures and tons of facts. I saw my name listed under each murder. It looked just like one of my favorite crime dramas on television. Was I now part of some *Law and Order* marathon? I was shocked and, I must admit to you, frightened.

Okay, I was smarter and slicker than either of them; or so I thought. Instead of them interviewing me, I tried to interview them. The only thing they really had was that I was at each accident, or incident, or, for that fact, murder. You can decide what to call my liberations. I know for sure that my liberations were cleansing. I wish I could have done more of them. Even though I was working diligently to purge these people from the district, my list grew. However, I am only human.

I also learned what they found out. They never found the keys of the dead folks. I saw on the white board written "missing keys" highlighted and underlined in purple. I was pretty impressed. They picked that up. In all the craziness around each crime, these two figured out that the keys were missing. And never forget, most people working in a school had a ton of keys. There were just so many locks in a building and everyone had keys on top of keys. I think I told you earlier those keys somehow represented power. Don't forget that. And now, with all the technology, I would have needed a wagon to carry all of my keys around. Shit, they should have asked me. I had all the keys neatly arranged on a display in my house. Each dead person's key ring, which I sometimes carried with me, fascinated me. These key rings gave me a sense of some of that dead individual's power. I thought that maybe some sort of mystical energy was transferring to me from the rings.

I wish I could show them to you, but since I can't, I will try to describe them.

Mr. Peoples had a small bronze Confederate Flag key chain holding his buildings keys. When I got a close-up look, I nearly peed my pants with laughter. It was really fitting that the racist son of a bitch had that medallion on his keys. He could never, ever change with the times. He is better off dead.

Ducky Donaldson had a big silver money sign holding his keys. The money sign had fake diamonds embedded in it. I think Donaldson thought he was some super fly pimp. He was just a super fly fool.

Still, to this day, I have absolutely no regret killing both of them. I felt no remorse at all. So, I am two for two.

Mr. Singleton, that music teacher child molester, had a gold saxophone attached to his keys. That was his instrument, and I heard him play often. He was a damn talented musician. Too bad he was so fucked up. I just wonder how many kids he abused. How many lives did he ruin? Probably too many to comprehend. He was like the wolf in the chicken coop. He had his pick of the pack. He could find the most vulnerable. He preyed on that. The man could not keep his dick in his pants. I wish I could have cut it off with him being alive while I did it. Death was too good of a punishment for him.

I did Secretary Westerman for Mrs. Kelly. It was my gift to her. I did not really have that big of a beef with her. Yes, she was a pain in the ass. I could ignore her. Others could not. And sometimes you just had to do a favor for a friend. When I first saw Westermann's key ring, I did not know what it was. I had to really study it. Maybe I am too old and out of the loop, but after some long studying, I could come up with my answer. She had a small roach clip with a green marijuana leaf on it where it clipped to the keys. Not only was she a pain in the ass, she was a pothead. I have no tolerance for drugs. The clip was very nice. Some artisan did a good job on that one. She probably bought it at some rock concert or folk festival.

Fittingly, Mr. Solomon, the screw ball math teacher, had nothing more than a small bottle of Purell clipped to his keys. His hands were probably like prunes and alligator skin, knowing how much of that crap he used. He could not get enough. The little plastic bottle was refillable. There were several huge pump bottles in his room. He never ran out of Purell. He just ran out of air. He was a mean bastard. I am glad he is dead. He won't hurt any of my kids anymore.

I had more work to do. I had to get the keys from the board president and the superintendent. Before they summoned me for my discussion with the police on that frightful night, I just had to get the keys off of the new victims. I now felt myself obsessed with getting these keys. Way back in my mind, I figured that the liberation was not complete until I possessed something of the victim. Look at me now. I am psychoanalyzing myself. Yup, I am as nutty as the rest of them.

Amid the confusion and chaos surrounding Mr. Gonzalez' artwork, and yes, his killing of the two bitches was a piece of art, I could sneak up around the bodies of the two beauties that laid on the floor. The board president was obviously dead, but people were scurrying around the superintendent. I scurried also and during all the confusion; I could swipe her keys off of the table. The board president's keys were a bit more difficult to procure. I found them deeply embedded in the dark confines of her pocketbook. I had to be slick because I did not want it to seem that I was "running the pockets" of a dead body. So, I thought on my feet and thought quickly. I knocked her pocketbook to the floor, and the contents ended up scrambled on the floor. I acted like the good Samaritan that I am, and bent over to pick up all of her garbage and, in the process, I pocketed her key ring. It was successful.

Collecting my souvenir keys now drove me. This strong desire amazed me. I had a huge adrenaline rush. And as I stood there, I got an enormous rush, thinking how great it would be if I could score Gonzalez' keys. I knew that I only had a minute to act, so I hurried. I tiptoed through the blood and brains and lo-and-behold, his key ring sat on the podium that he used to hold his notes and briefcase. I used the old backhand cup technique to swoop the keys off of the top shelf and into my pocket. I felt like I was a twelve-year-old seventh grader stealing candy from the corner candy store. But just like when I was twelve years old and needed that sugar fix, I needed those keys.

I had three more sets of keys to add to my collection. Gonzalez held his keys together with a piece of leather with an arm and fist raised in a power salute burned into it. I think that probably had something to do with his hatred for the revolution and the Castro regime in Cuba. He could never let it go. I think it defined his life and his death proved to be some sort of symbol of martyrdom for him.

The superintendent had a funny little peace sign stamped on some sort of cheap metal. That was not a surprise. She was cheapskate frozen in a different decade. I found it ironic because she carried a peace sign on her keyring. She was never about peace. Her own power and survival drove her and worked day and night to secure her status with the local politicians. It was almost funny that in life she had crawled up the board president's ass and in death they were side by side, almost on top of one another. I found a bit of comic irony in this. You dance with the girl you brought to the dance and in this case; they danced together in life and ended up dancing together in death.

I found the board president's key chain and perhaps these keys proved to be the most interesting. She had a small rectangular Lucite key chain. I found the quote printed on it interesting. "Politics has no relation to morals." The superintendent lived and died following those words. Of course, I did not know who said that and had to think a bit about what it meant. The next day, I looked that quote up and it came from Niccolò Machiavelli. Man, for this woman, it was fitting and appropriate. She lived her political life with absolutely no morals. And she and the superintendent would fuck you every chance they got. They had already proven that to the school community. With both of their deaths, the district benefitted.

The more I thought about my set of keys, I thought about what our keys say about us. You hear that stuff all the time about judging a book by its cover. But in reality, maybe we are who are keys say we are. I had to pause and inspect my keys. Holding my keys together, I had the Geek letters of Alpha and Omega joined. They made the symbol of gold that had lost most of its shine through time and use. I picked up this key ring years and years ago and basically forgot all about it. In the Book of Revelation, Jesus says of himself, "I am the Alpha and the Omega, the First and Last, the Beginning and the End." For those that do not read the Bible and I believe it is most of you, the Alpha is the first letter of the Geek alphabet and the Omega is the last. Putting the two letters together symbolizes the eternity of Christ as the Son of God. Yes, this is who I am. This is the Liberator doing God's work.

Chapter Eighty
A return to normalcy

Yes, we slowly returned to normal again. We are good at returning to normal. I have to say it was a breath of fresh air having Big Lou in charge. At least he would say hello to you and civilly speak to you. These two very simple things, saying hello and civilly speaking, were not in the previous now deceased superintendent's skill set.

I say we returned to normal. But I really don't know if that was such a good thing. What was good about normal on this ship of fools? I always had a theory about students. When the good old boys would talk together, we would speculate about what the district would be like without some of the bad kids. You know, some of the really belligerent and nasty assholes. We almost had created an informal most wanted list of students. And let me assure you that if a student got on this list, one of our security officers would be sure to get you. This one guy could target a kid and would be relentless. Everywhere the kid went, this guy would show up. It was almost magical. He had a sixth sense. Well, he would ride this kid long enough that either this pressure on the kid, or the kid just being who he was, would just slip up. The security guy would wait there with this shit-eating grin on his face. Then the principal could and would suspend him or her. I think I shared with you before that an asshole did not see gender or race. There were white assholes and black assholes. There were both male and female assholes. It just proved one of points, an asshole will always be an asshole. Let me get back to the point I was trying to make. If three of the top ten trouble makers just stopped showing up, because or expulsion or just quitting school, three yet unidentified assholes would quickly take their place on that list. I use my same student asshole logic theory to teachers and other adults in the building. When one asshole departed, another would somehow rise to the top and fill that departed person's place on the asshole list. It just always worked that way. So, yes, as we returned to normal, we still had our share of assholes. We just added some fresh faces.

Miss Mary was clearly now the unappointed number two in the district. How the hell did an insurance investigator, who was not even on the district's payroll, get there? If you needed to ask that question, you would have surely lost my respect. Always remember that it is not what you know, but who you blow that matters. Yet, now, because of this cozy little situation, I did not think that Big Lou and Mary Magdala ever wanted to solve any of these cases. Although they had to show that they were making some headway, they never wanted this to end. They were loving every minute. I never saw Big Lou so happy and Miss Mary loosened up. Many a night, I would lay awake thinking about Lou and Mary going at it. I had visions of her being a real firecracker, one who always wanted to be in charge, and Big Lou just lying there enjoying every minute. Yes, I must admit it, that I would not have minded trading places with him for one of these adventures.

With all that being said, they were making some progress on the case and reading between the lines. The fingers were pointing at me.

I needed to get an assessment of things. I needed to get out in front of things again. Since the Tuesday night massacre at the board meeting, I kind of let myself slip behind in my intelligence gathering. I needed a date with Mrs. Kelly.

Chapter Eighty-One
Friday date night

I walked out of work on Friday, knowing that I was probably going to have a crazy night ahead of me. If my past rendezvous with Mrs. Kelly was any sign of it. With that said, I needed a nap. I fell asleep easily, with pleasurable thoughts ahead.

I picked Kelly up, and we dined at a small restaurant sharing almost two bottles of my BYOB inexpensive red wine. Dinner talk was trivial. We both had our minds on the dessert. And I was not talking about ice cream here. You know exactly what was on my mind.

Kelly was a bit more talkative at dinner and she posed some questions about some liberations. Of course, she focused on the demise of Westerman, and I made a quick decision to share some details of this. I figured she knew anyway, so why not give her a little something to chew on? It also did not hurt that she knew I had the wherewithal to act on these thoughts. I hope she thought about the possibility of me acting upon her one day. She seemed to eat up every minute. She wanted to know every detail.

After dinner, we headed directly to the Comfort Inn on the interstate that we used the last time. Because I knew where we were going to end up that evening, I took the extra ten minutes after work to register. We got the same room as last time with an easy exit out right into the parking lot. There was never a need to navigate any hallway. That was good. No extra person needed to see us. The room looked the same and had the same antiseptic smell. I wondered how many other people used the room and the bed for a secret meeting. On one hand, the thought disgusted me and yet it seemed to exhilarate me.

My nap waited for these ten minutes, but it was worth the wait. The anticipation of the evening just gave me some pleasurable thoughts for a change to think about before I headed off for my afternoon siesta. Rest came easily for me. I guess people would refer to my nap as a power nap. I would have to agree because I was powering up for an electric evening.

The ride to the motel was steamy. We were not in the room for ten minutes and we both were fully undressed and ready to go. And go, we did. It amazed me at the drive of that woman. Wow, she wanted it and wanted it now and often. Shit, I am making up for her deprivation for many years. It was okay with me. I hate to say that I was having trouble keeping up.

I noticed she talked a bit more about each session. As I was trying to rest and get ready for another session, she seemed to want to babble away. I needed the break to gather up some more steam. I think you know what I mean. For whatever reason, Kelly focused on Donaldson. You remember that fool custodian who froze to death in the freezer? She craved information. And being caught in the high of the red wine and the crazy sex I stupidly shared with her Ducky's last few minutes. She casually laughed and soon fell asleep. We both slept for about an hour before we showered and prepared to drive her home.

My wine buzz and the initial exhilaration of the sex evaporated. My brain crushing headache arrived. We drove in silence. I would not be telling you the truth if I told you that the sex was not good. It was great. Kelly did not let me down, and she continued to surprise with her minx-like antics. However, I replayed the night over in my head and kicked myself squarely in the ass. I talked too much. I revealed too much. Was I now a dead man walking?

We said goodbye, and she tiptoed into the house. I did not know now what the dynamics were with her husband. Nor did I care. That was their business. I had enough trouble now worrying about myself.

Chapter Eighty-Two
No sleep for the weary

After hearing much of my story by now, I am sure that you guessed I did not sleep well that night. If I could have beaten myself up, I would have. I needed a good ass kicking. How could I be that stupid? Was the sex that good? Why did I run my mouth so much? I knew I had just broken one of my most important rules that I have lived my life by. Namely, I kept my mouth shut and listened more than I spoke. I really fucked up. The man with no mind between my legs was controlling my big mouth. I deserved to get caught.

Now to answer my two questions that I posed to myself. Yes, I was that stupid and yes; the sex was that good. As I lay there in bed staring at the ceiling in my all too familiar way, the thoughts of me opening my big mouth were being pushed aside by the thoughts of the fantastic sex that we just had. If you would have asked me several years ago about the capabilities of Mrs. Kelly in the bedroom, I would have laughed. But she had proven me wrong. Now, I just can't get enough. And as she remade herself physically, she unleashed a tiger sexually. She could not get enough. Both of us should be ashamed of ourselves. There we were, two grown-ups acting like some teenagers that walk the halls in the buildings in which we work. We were acting like two young kids that just had sex for the first time; like this was our first sexual experience. Yet in some ways in was.

The intense physicality of the sex was liberating for Mrs. Kelly. I guess there were more ways than one in which the Liberator worked. Yet for me, I could not distinguish between the pleasure I got from the sex with Kelly from the rush and pleasure I received from killing someone. As I lay there thinking of this thought, I realized how fucked up I must be. Maybe someday some big shot psychiatrist will analyze me. He or she can write a book about the Liberator and make a boatload of money off of my life. However, I still dream of perhaps dying on the job with no one ever finding out about my acts of liberation.

Chapter Eighty-Three
Time for a status report

Beavis and Butthead—Nowhere to be found.
Miss Mary and Big Lou-Fucking too much to be found.
Kelly-Hornier than ever. It appears our little act is becoming an every Friday night event.

So, I guess for me life is good. Big Lou is running the district nicely since taking over from the old bitch. He is keeping Mary satisfied and employed in the district. Shit, he does not want to see this end. He enjoys having Miss Mary next door to meet his every need. And the more I think about it, I think Big Lou and I are in a similar boat. We are both hooked up with two horny things that are just sapping our energy. As long as we are both consumed with satisfying these women, we can't really put all of our focus into the workplace. Luckily, I can nap on the job. I do not think Big Lou has this same opportunity.

The new board president is fine. It seems as if everyone is internally retreating to the good old days when the good old boys ran the district. There is some sense to that. People clamor for change. Change comes and they dislike it, so they clamor for a return to the past. At least in the past, they knew the players and everyone kind of knew not to rock the boat. Everyone knew the politics of the district. They knew whose ass to kiss. The district, time and time again, exemplified dysfunction. But it was ours, and everyone in the city knew it.

Everyone was back to being just happy in our little community. This dysfunction wrapped us up in some sort of bubble. Almost like some snow globe you break out of storage at Christmastime. You shake it up and it snows. But the snow eventually settles again and you are back at peace within this little world. The group is fine until someone rocks the boat. Some may rock the boat because they actually see the dysfunction and want to change the district to improve it. They want to help the kids. However, I have found that over time, few change agents grasp on to this altruistic notion. Wouldn't it be nice to make a change for the right reason? However, that is rarely the case. People want a change because they got pissed off at someone. Or perhaps promotions passed them by. Others merely wanted an easier assignment. Another common complaint that I have heard is that someone disrespected them. And finally, some may clamor for change because they have actually become too crazy to function normally in a specific culture. Somewhere along the way, they lost their sense of reality. We already saw how that worked with Mr. Gonzalez. Although he has left this world, there are others that will quickly and unintentionally fill his spot on the list of crazies in the district. We are never short of these crazies. I wonder if other districts work this way? Do they have their own crazies unique to their own school and town? I think they do.

It is funny, but I must digress a bit here. It is interesting to see how the rank and file will defend and protect our crazies. They will protect them until they just can't anymore. They probably left you scratching your head with that statement. I believe there comes a time when it boils down to you or that crazy person. If you defend them or protect them too vigorously, others will see you as crazy too, and you surely don't want that to happen. Because you are never the crazy one. (Oh yeah, according to who? By then you are probably as loony as the person who you were protecting.) When looking at it this way, people will quickly throw the nutcase under the bus. I hope that makes sense to you because it is the best that I can do to explain it. The kids do the same thing. They will torture and pick on everyone, except that student or teacher who is really nuts. Then they, too, will hunker down and protect that individual. I have watched this go on for years. Maybe it is as simple as they do not want the nutcase picking on them. So, they just stay away, or actually defend the nut from others. It is an interesting phenomenon.

I think I told you this before, but it is worth repeating. For most of the adults working in a school, they couldn't care less about the kids. The adults will spend 24 hours a day thinking about ways to make the school better for the adults. This is a real selfish and shitty way of doing business in the schools. Maybe some school districts have found a way to beat it, but ours has not. We cannot seem to break this cycle.

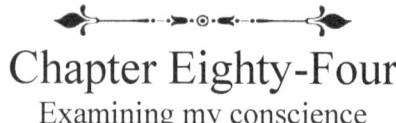

Chapter Eighty-Four
Examining my conscience

Although I am not Catholic, I am a Christian and I believe strongly in a God and my faith. My Catholic friends, especially when I was in elementary school, would tell me about a process they would go through before confessing his or her sins to the priest, called examining your conscience. Before talking to the priest, one conducted a little mental inventory of all of your sins. I certainly don't want to criticize other religions, but to me it sounded a bit of a ridiculous contrived process. It has become a time for me to examine my conscience relative to all the liberations. I thought I was just about perfect in my execution of my tasks, but I felt like a noose was tightening around my neck.

I purposely made all of my liberations look like accidents. I book ended those with the disappearance of Principal Peoples and the last execution of the superintendent and the board president.

Where were my mistakes?

First, I wish I would have made up a better story about Peoples' disappearance. However, his disappearance shows how easy it is to become anonymous, especially when you do not have a significant other.

Second, I kept everyone's keys as a bit of a prize for each successful liberation. These insignificant keys reminded me of winning a prize at a fair or carnival for knocking down some weighted bottles. Maybe we can talk about the symbolism of this a little later if there is time. It does not matter to anyone the reason I kept these keys. Just know that I have a key from every victim.

Next, I have told Mrs. Kelly too much. I did not use my brain here at all. On second thought, that little man below my belt was doing all the thinking for me on this topic. I could see this as my major failure. I saw how information turned Kelly on and that translated to better sex. When I fed her bits and pieces, it turned her into a more ravenous being. She became a being that a man could only dream about. Oh, that man with no mind. You can't live with him and you certainly don't want to live without him.

Next, in each case, I have been consistently telling my stories, whether they be to Big Lou and Miss Mary or Beavis and Butthead. Consistency is key and I give myself an A grade in this category. But I know that one minor slip of my lips will sink my ship. I can feel these outside parties trying to trip me up. I better be careful.

My planning has been meticulous and flawless. Although I was around the scene of each death, although it may have seemed coincidental, I had business to conduct in each area. One could view me as being lucky or unlucky to see each liberation. By me being "Johnny on The Spot" for each killing was circumstantial. But was it good evidence of wrongdoing? Juries convicted people on much less evidence all the time. At these accidents, I could always explain my presence.

If the officials found any type of trace evidence, such as fingerprints or hairs, each building was my building. My fingerprints, hair and DNA would be all over the place. No worry here.

Chapter Eighty-Five
Another Friday Night

You know the routine by now. It has changed little. Please do not make an inference there that I am bored by it. I am not. Likewise, do not think that I don't really enjoy it and look forward to it. I do.

That being said, we completed our same ritual in the same way. Dinner, wine and some very sexy conversation. I still cannot believe how Kelly hid this secret side of her for these years. Each week is a fresh surprise and each week I am left panting and wanting more. I do not need to go into all the details, although I am sure that you would enjoy them. It is unnecessary.

However, one thing I did notice, which seemed to be different this time around, was Kelly's need for more information. The details of my liberations heightened her sexuality and desires. I enjoyed every minute. Now I realized she was "getting off" on these details. And as the "man with no mind" between my legs could not think clearly, I know in the heat of passion that I talked too much. Hey, listen to me. Details drove her to unknown places of discovery. Places that I surely wanted to go. And so, there we went. I was not sorry. I was only thinking about new sexual pleasures.

As I think of it now, it was strange how our relationship never changed at work. We would come into school on Monday and act like nothing ever happened. On Monday, Kelly would come dressed as always in some matronly outfit. I stood and wondered if this was the same person who was wearing a black leather corset, with a matching garter belt three days earlier. I still can see and feel the smoothness of her stockings with the black seam that ran up her leg. Was this the same person who was introducing me to some sexual gymnastics that I never dreamed was possible? Hey, I guess it was. It was almost like some dream sequence that would play itself out in slow motion.

Unfortunately, that would all change the next day. After my shift ended, they forced me to bring a box of paper over to Big Lou's office. Taking over the district and keeping little miss Mary satisfied consumed him. Let's not forget that it was a full-time job. His plate was full. I had a funny feeling that both of his jobs, namely running the district and keeping Miss Mary happy, were not simple tasks. She struck me as having the personality of an alligator. You could never feed her enough. Luckily, that was not my problem with Kelly. It seemed like she was as happy as I was having our weekly Friday night rendezvous. Hell, even the motel clerk and I became friends. He and I would secretly high five each other when the time was right. Sorry, I got off the track.

So, here I am toting this box to Big Lou after hours when I see Kelly leaving his office through a side door. What is up with that?

Chapter Eighty-Six
A sleepless Monday Night

You bet it was. My paranoia was running rampant. What the hell was going on? Why was Kelly leaving Big Lou's office after hours? And because Big Lou and Miss Mary were inseparable, I naturally assumed that Kelly was meeting with both of them.

I tossed, and I turned. I paced, and I paced. There would be no sleep for me on that night.

When my alarm went off, I knew that I just dozed. I had to assume that Kelly was over there on some sort of school business. Although I wanted to believe that, I knew that was probably not the case.

I got to work at the same time and quickly went to my favorite napping place to get some shuteye. I did nod off for a bit, but it was purely restless sleep. It was not the type of sleep that I usually would get on a Friday night after my weekly escape with Kelly.

After lunch, I cruised by Kelly's desk and made some small talk. This activity was not unusual because I would frequently visit her. It seemed like the building slowed down after lunch. The school kind of slowed down for the kids and the teachers. You know, there were almost like two schools operating, a morning school and an afternoon school. You could really feel the difference.

Our conversation ended with absolutely no mention of her visit to the "big house." This omission by Kelly was both surprising and telling. I am convinced that on any other given day, her visit to the "big house" would have made the front page of our daily gossip column. Yet there was no talk of this. I let it go.

I went home that night a little more paranoid and a little more depressed. Tomorrow, I would ask her about it and see her response. I think I told you that over the years I have become a bit of a master at reading body language and I could know more about the situation from what is not said than from what they said. If this meeting was innocent and work related, I could tell.

Chapter Eighty-Seven
A lovely day in the neighborhood

I got to work that day at my regular time, but snuck out around Kelly's reporting time and ran to the local donut shop for some hot coffee and donuts. I put on my big smile and delivered these goodies to Mrs. Kelly. This practice was not really strange because I did this periodically and she could step away from her desk and join me in the coffee room. She liked this attention and had a big smile on her face. It is funny though, as I watched her walk into the room. All I could think about was her ass sashaying back and forth in the black leather outfit. I quickly cleared my head.

We made some small talk for a few minutes and then I was quite direct. I told her that her appearance at the office surprised me. She did not see me. I knew I was in trouble within three seconds. Her entire expression changed, including how she held her body. Her shoulders drooped, and she glanced away. She fumbled for some lame ass excuse about a report that needed to be delivered. I knew this was bullshit right away. Kelly would not deliver a report. She probably would have made me do it. And what could be that important that Lou needed her to do it? All indications pointed to the fact that I was in trouble. How much trouble? I did not know. But I am sure I would soon find out.

Of course, my day could only get worse. I saw one of those pink message sheets in my mailbox stating the Beavis and Butthead, our two incompetent detectives, needed to see me. I should call them for an appointment.

You should also know that when the phone rings, 90% of the time it is bad news. I usually run from the phone. I hate talking on it and I only use it when I need it. I state my business and hang up. I have no desire to chit chat or bullshit. When I need information, I use the phone. And always remember, that information is power. Information is king.

I did what I thought was the right thing to do. I crumpled up the message and threw it right away. If those two fools needed me, they knew where to find me.

My life is getting interesting. My life is getting complicated. Shit!

Chapter Eighty-Eight
Knock, Knock—Who is there?

Well, I could weave and bob my way around Beavis and Butthead for several weeks. When I thought I saw their beat up unmarked big old Chrysler pull into the lot, I would run and hide. I had this remarkable ability to become invisible. I knew all the hiding places and I would just turn off my phone. Most times, I would retreat to the old storage room behind the stage of the auditorium. It was a bit of a private place. The play directors at the school were pack rats, and they loaded this room full of old costumes and sets. I could carve out a little roost in there by the window. This perch allowed me to see not only the parking lot but the driveway into the lot. I could easily see who was coming and going and, of course, I could see who was already there. I knew the important cars to look for.

My principal encouraged me, no, it was a bit more than an encouragement, to serve as his lookout and early warning beacon for when the superintendent might make an unannounced visit. Let me just say that at times of stress in the district, this became my most important job. I was the chief look-out. And for my principal, this was a critical task. It allowed him to either hide, act busy or in some other way, prepare for the boss' visit.

All the security officers, Mrs. Kelly, the vice principals and I, had radios. We all knew what to do when visitors arrived. My principal never wanted to get caught with his pants down. Yes, he was a good old boy. We all had a different code name for all the central office administrators. Since Big Lou merely moved up in the chain of command, we kept his code name the same. His name was Prince Charming. Mrs. Kelly could name everyone, and she was a huge Disney fan, so everyone received a Disney character's name. She was quick to name Little Miss Mary, Big Lou's sidekick, Cinderella. Wasn't that quaint? Now it appears I was about to get skewered by Cinderella and Prince Charming. Kelly's codename was Ariel, because she loved The Little Mermaid. She named me Triton, Ariel's father. (They established these codes long before we started screwing. I do not want anyone to make some sort of weird inference. Remember, I have scruples.)

So, I would sit by my perch and lay in wait for Sleepy and Dopey (Beavis and Butthead). We gave each detective a name from the seven dwarfs. You can see what I mean about our strained relationship with the police.

I played this game for a while until one evening, as I was finishing up my dinner, a knock came upon my door at home and when I got to the door, there stood my good friends Beavis and Butthead. They were not too happy that I was making them chase me for the last few weeks. They said they needed to talk with me, and talking at the station was not an option. Nor was talking at the school. I would have to go for a ride with them.

Would this be my last ride as a free man? I hoped not.

Chapter Eighty-Nine
Are we going for ice cream?

I just love an enjoyable ride on a clear spring evening. Maybe we were going to stop for an ice cream cone or a sundae? Nah, I do not think ice cream is on our agenda for this evening.

So, we just rode. We did a tour of the city. They loaded me into the back of the car and they took their proper seats in the front. The car stunk of cigarettes, smoke and trash. There were soda bottles, coffee cups and, of course, donut wrappers littered throughout the car. It embarrassed me for them. The car was a piece of shit and I operated under the philosophy that the quality of a man's car reflected his character. It doesn't have to be new. But it should be fresh. This was anything but fresh.

I sat quietly in the back, wondering what was up. We passed the police station several times and never attempted to turn in. Beavis and Butthead chatted like I was not even in the car. They ignored me and I ignored them. I silently wondered about my destination, both figuratively and literally. The time passed slowly.

We soon headed to the part of town that housed a few warehouses and junkyards. The city yard was there. This is where the city stored the garbage trucks and other maintenance vehicles. It was a real dump. And I am not trying to be funny here. However, there was one bright spot, though, and that was the local topless bar sandwiched between the city yard and junkyards. The bar served as a meeting place for many of the town officials. And I knew what went on there. I had the privilege of being invited there several times with some of the good old boys. Let me just say that a lot more than dancing went on there. When I saw the bar, my heart lightened a bit. Maybe we were going to have this conversation there and enjoy some of the "jigglers." But that did not happen. We pulled in across the street and around several trees where a lone picnic table stood isolated by trees and general debris. This was a secluded location. I immediately thought that I was going to get the shit beaten out of me until I cracked or died. The disposal of my body was easy. The way this whole scenario was playing out struck me as kind of funny as these two cops did not strike me as the rubber hose type of guys. They took this scene from an old Godfather movie. I was living this. It wasn't funny, but yet I chuckled. Was that just some nerves or was this as hilarious as my brain was seeing it? Was I now going to meet a similar fate to Fredo?

The car stopped and their both front doors opened almost simultaneously. Butthead opened my door and pointed to the picnic bench. I saw no other choice, and I seated myself at the table. Now the three of us were sitting here looking at one another. I could smell the stench of the junkyards and I could hear the music of the "jigglers." Normally, I would welcome the sound of that distinct music, but not now. The uncertainty made me nervous, not scared. I put on a big bold front, hoping that they would not see or sense my nerves. I could not let them see me sweat. If I was going down, I was going down with the pride of the Liberator. A hero until the end.

To make a long story short, they outlined every one of my liberations. They knew it involved me in each of them and they told me how impressed they were with my work. Sadly, they told me that Big Lou and Miss Mary had flipped Mrs. Kelly. They threatened to make her an accomplice if she did not help. Even though Kelly was once again fucking me, this time in a way that was not too pleasant, I kind of felt sorry for her. I never thought that it would ever end. I was the Liberator. Big deal. So, now they knew. They could not hurt me.

Chapter Ninety
Once again, the plot thickens

This banter went on for about an hour. We traveled a circuitous route. If I was going to jail, I would have been there already. I sensed, though, that my destination was not jail. But where was I and this conversation headed?

I listened. I kept my big mouth shut. I still didn't know if they had the evidence. However, they told me that last week while I was at work playing hide and go seek with them; they took the time to search my house and yes; they found my collection of key rings and some random notes that I had kept. They found my murder book. Although this book was just that, I did not call it that. I kept the title really simple. On the cover I just wrote in script, Liberations and underscored it several times. I am sure the book resembled the book that police departments keep on each murder investigation and, hence, the name. It was odd, however, because the house looked untouched and my collection of keys looked undisturbed. I never would have thought these fools could do such a good search. They fooled me well. They lulled me to sleep by their perceived incompetence. Shame on me. However, through all of this bullshit, I could only think of one thing, "so where are we going with all of this, boys?"

I could sense that the talking was over. Beavis then said to me, "Mr. Liberator, we've got you. You are through. Unless you do a small job for us."

To say that these words shocked me was an understatement. I wish I had the forethought to record this conversation. But surprise took me and I was unprepared for this proposition. They let this request sit with me for a minute or two before they told me what my assignment was. I kind of felt like Mission Impossible now. You know, the bullshit in the beginning, that my assignment if I choose to accept it is such-and-such. The tape will self-destruct in thirty seconds. What choice did I have? Of course, I had to accept it and they knew this.

We got back into the car quiet as three church mice. We drove around and eventually made it back to my house. Then Butthead said to me, with sarcasm leaking from every word, Mr. Liberator, we need to be liberated from our chief. Take care of it! We will be in touch.

These words stunned me. I stumbled to my porch with my mouth wide open. I looked at both of them as I walked. They never again made eye contact. They sped away.

Yes, the Liberator was still alive and well, with a new mission.

Chapter Ninety-One
Talk about sleepless nights

I know that I have become the master of understatements, but this night was truly sleepless. I now realized sleep would not come my way tonight. I paced and pace. And as I paced, my mind raced. I was wearing tracks on my hardwood floor. I also reached for a package of cigarettes that I had hidden away for a time like this. So, I paced and smoked stale cigarettes. And I thought.

Well, they had me. So, I had to kill the chief. It was really no big deal for me. I hated him anyway. It was my opinion that he was an arrogant jerk who thought his shit did not stink. He hated the schools and hated the kids. He never said this with words, although he said it with every action and with every edict that came from his office. I could never figure this out because what did the kids ever do to him? Oh, I forgot. Most of the kids were black or brown. That said it all. I believed the chief was a racist son of a bitch and every black person in the town knew this. God made the chief from the same mold as Principal Peoples, that racist bastard who floated away into the hereafter. It would not trouble me killing him. However, what did trouble me was for the first time it would not be my decision. I have scruples.

You should know something about the police department. I would probably say that seventy-five percent of the department hated the chief's guts and would have loved to pull the trigger to take him out. The other twenty-five percent were so far up his ass that some of their heads got stuck. When I was around these folks, it sickened me. I know they washed the guy's cars and I would ride by his house and see one of them cutting his lawn. I would not bet against one of them wiping his ass when he took a shit. It was just flat out disgusting to watch them at work.

And as I thought about this, my opinion of the rest of the force changed a bit. He was a dictator and an egomaniac. And perhaps those two words are inseparable. Maybe these guys who I thought were big assholes were just trying to survive. But as I thought more about this, I could not in my mind and heart give these guys a pass just because they were carrying out orders. I have heard this shit before. You know, I think schools, organizations and teams take on the character of their leader. And if their leader is a mean racist, then the team would be mean racists. However, I have to watch that I do not paint everyone with this brush. Perhaps Beavis and Butthead are right. The entire police department needed to be liberated.

Getting back to the chief, he loved every minute of this power and adoration that he received. He both figuratively and literally needed to wear the title CHIEF on his sleeve. So, therefore, over time, he had all of his attire labeled with his name and title. Being the chief was probably more important to him than the job that he actually did. His jackets and golf shirts were hilarious. They emblazoned this apparel with gold badges, stars and deep-set gold braids. The American flag was on his right breast plate besides both sleeves. I get it. You loved America. So do I, yet I did not have to wear it. I had the honor of watching him rip one of his underlings when he did not like what they may have said or done. And it did not take a big mistake to find that if you were a detective in plainclothes, one slip up in his personal protocol would find you back in uniform working nights somewhere. Perhaps watching the jiggle joint I just told you about. Perhaps watching the rats play in the dump. Who knows? If you wanted to find out, just cross him and you would see. The good cops just avoided him. They put their heads down and did their jobs. They put their twenty years in and got the hell out. That is a shame. They trapped the good cops. They all had families and pensions and had made it up the pay scale to prevent them from really leaving. And the chief knew this and used it all the time. If I had a nickel for every time, I heard him tell someone that if they did not like this or that, they should just quit. Yet, where could they go? Their fate was like the rats at the dump; trapped.

Probably the worst thing he did for the kids and schools was to assign the worst deadbeats racists cops to the Juvenile Department. Although I saw some great juvenile officers come and go, the chief, mostly, used this department as a dumping ground. He made sure that these guys hated black people and hated kids. These guys were being punished by being sent there, and they put their time in until retirement. This strategy was a real shame because the force had some good cops, some men and women of color who would have been excellent juvenile officers. But why put your people in the best spots for them and the community? That might make too much sense. Too much sense for even the chief. But I am convinced he knew exactly what he was doing and loved every minute. Being sent to the Juvenile Department was like a death sentence. Now that you know all of this, you can just imagine how he and his people treated the high school kids. Their adult behavior was atrocious. Probably worse than any crime or behavior that the kids were being charged with.

Shit, I knew I was talking myself into relishing the job opportunity that presented itself. Let me put it this way, I wasn't looking for it, but now that it was on my doorstep, I might as well enjoy it.

So, I guess my next step in this process was to wait until I heard from Beavis and Butthead for my next set of instructions. However, first, I had to change my nickname for them because they proved much more competent than my nickname for them inferred. I think I will just call them CSI from now on as a tribute to all the CSI television shows and detectives, who always solve their crimes in miraculous ways within the hour confines of their televised show. They always get their man or woman.

It did not take long for them to pay me a visit. I was out on the school's front lawn blowing leaves when their beat-up piece of shit car pulled up to me. I did not even hear it because of the leaf blower. There was no signal on their part. They just stopped the car by the sidewalk and expected me to walk on over. Once again, they surprised me with their presence. Once again, I was not prepared to tape our conversation. I probably had to lose that idea. They were proving too smart for that. I thought about somehow using my phone, but they were watching me.

I made it to the car window and there was no hello or small talk. The CSI driving just said. "Well?" I told him it would be my pleasure. He was told not to push or rush me. I tried to regain some power and control over this situation. I had to somehow grow my balls back and grow them back quickly. Double crossing them was not on my mind. I didn't really care. To me, it was just another task. But I wanted the task on my terms.

CSI on the passenger side just reminded me not to drag this out too long. They did not want to wait forever.

They pulled away. I went back to blowing my leaves.

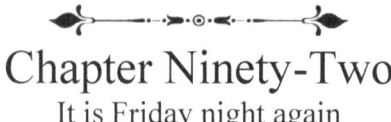

Chapter Ninety-Two
It is Friday night again

Did the time drag or did it fly by? I wasn't sure because one minute it felt like the clock's hand stood still and at other times, I could not slow the hands down. It is funny how time plays tricks on you. It was Friday night. My Kelly night.

Now that I knew Kelly was a double agent, what was I to do? Do I go on our regular date and have some fun? Do I go on our regular date and beat the shit out of her? Well, that was out of the question because I have never struck a woman. I could easily kill a woman, but never smack one. Go figure. Remember my scruples. Do I just cancel? Do I break it off with some half ass reason? Although I tried to avoid Kelly in school, I ran into her several times. She had no clue that I knew. She flirted with me like she always did and promised me a new and adventurous Friday night. And believe me, that promise tantalized me. The statement had its desired impact. Yes, I was horny and yes; I wanted to see what trick she might be up her sleeve. Of course, I was going to keep our date. However, I too had a trick up my sleeve. I had to trickle some fake shit out so she would run back to Big Lou and Miss Mary with some new tales. I might as well have some fun with this.

Believe it or not, this never gets old. We had our dinner and sipped our wine and soon made it to our regular room at the motel. It is funny because I felt I owned this room and the staff treated me like family. To me, it was funny to see all the regulars. In the day of psychobabble bullshit, we could have had a support group of some sort. We could have called ourselves the Friday Night Fuckers (FNF) or some other name like that.

It is also funny that some members of the FNF were prominent members of the community. One time, I ran into the mayor in the hallway when I was grabbing a Coke from the machine. It turns out that he was banging his assistant. And by the way, his assistant was a guy. We said very little, but our eye contact said it all. He knew that his secret would be safe with me and I would use this information at a later date. It could have been my get of jail free card. Hey, to each his own. I respect that. His big mistake was that he was "shitting where he ate." My father always told me that, when he would say, "son, never shit where you eat. If you must, do your business elsewhere." It was certainly expert advice, and I lived by it. Hell, I didn't care about this Kelly shit because I was single. I just wanted my rendezvous to be expedient. I felt no reason to travel. The mayor should have. Maybe he was just too horny and could not wait.

I have digressed enough. Tonight, Kelly carried with her a velvet black bag about the size of a large purse. Was this my surprise? Yes, it was. The velvet satchel contained a variety of adult toys, including some pretty inventive things. However, Kelly remained focused on her S/M stuff, which was all right with me. She liked to be in charge, and I certainly did not mind. I followed her orders pretty well. For this short time, I put out of my mind that she was a rat. I merely just focused on my pleasure.

Now that I was aware of her loyalties, I had to be careful when she pumped me for some more information. And pump, she did. I felt sorry for her. They had her. That pissed me off. Kelly was just Kelly. This shit was getting too complicated for her. So, just to fuck with Big Lou, I told her what I called some good information from the new board president. And the president and the mayor were tight. He said that Big Lou would not get the top job on a full-time basis. He was good in the interim, but the mayor had bigger plans. And now based on my new close relationship with the mayor (remember the motel) I was able to get inside information any time I wanted it. And I let people around me know of my new friendship with the mayor. Couldn't hurt? I also told her that the board was getting sick and tired of Miss Mary. They viewed her as expendable and were ready to clean house.

None of this was true, although it made some sense. It would torture both of them. Big Lou wanted the job and Miss Mary. Miss Mary wanted Big Lou and the power that their relationship brought her. I would have loved to have been a fly on the wall when Kelly told them this information. My prediction is that they would almost shit their pants and then put their heads together for survival. Their gig was too good for both of them, and they wanted it to go on forever.

In the meantime, I bought some time for myself. All of them could get off of me and focus on what was truly important to them. Namely, the status quo. No one wanted to fuck with the status quo, even if it meant losing me. So, maybe there was a way out of this mess for me. We would see.

I had a job to do, and I needed to focus on that. I needed a meeting with the CSI. On my terms.

Chapter Ninety-Three
It's 10:00 o'clock-Do you know where your CSI is?

Well, I did. They were with me. We met at the same place near the dump and the jiggle joint. Hell, after our meeting, I might stop in for a few minutes. It was a beautiful night, and they arrived promptly. They sauntered over to the same picnic table where we first met after that long drive to nowhere and they did a good pat down search of me and the area for any listening devices. And they were not too gentle with me. We were at a new crossroads in our relationship. Who was in charge?

This was a pivotal meeting. I figured I was going directly to jail, or I was going to regain my power in our relationship. I figured I would get a win out of this if we at least left this meeting on equal footing.

It did not take these two long to try to push me around again. I stopped it quickly and told them both to sit down and shut up. I gave them no other option. They could then do what they wanted with me, but at the end of this day, if they fucked with me, they would still have their chief. So, I felt as if I held the upper hand. We yelled back and forth a bit. There was a lot of cursing going on and I think we probably set the world record, if there is one, for using the word "fuck" so many times in a brief conversation. I did not know that there were so many derivations of that simple word.

We got it all off of our chests and agreed that this was not my job, it was "our" job. For me, that was a win.

I then tried to pick their brains a bit about the chief's comings and goings. We bounced around a few ideas, yet nothing seemed to jump out at me. At least they were off of my back.

I also clarified that I needed to take my time on this project. Since I was working alone, this had to be left entirely up to me. Killing the guy did not bother me. Although it was clearly not my idea, I still hated the guy, and I began thinking about seeing his face when he knew his time was up. The look of death always gave me pleasure. I still think back to that fool Ducky Donaldson running around nude in the freezer. He was half nuts before I locked him in. By the time he left as a popsicle, I knew that his freezing process fried his brain. I also thought back to watching that no good prick Singleton, the music teacher, light up like a Christmas tree when he threw the switch for the stage lighting. That was really pleasurable. And I hope his death freed some demons from the girls that he destroyed.

Thinking about my liberations gave me great pleasure. So, being in the neighborhood, why not stop in to see some jigglers? I was working on my second beer, kind of enjoying the moment. You know, I had been around the school district long enough now, where I saw the children of some students that I once had. In some ways, it was quite fulfilling. Some kids were maturing into great adults. I have seen future doctors, lawyers, and politicians walk through my halls. I was feeling good until the next dancer took the stage and it was one of our recent students. She could not have been over 20 years old and now she was up on the stage, for all intents and purposes, naked, shaking her ass at me. Although she had a pretty little ass, I felt as though she was like a child I never had and I threw my money on the bar and left. As I was leaving, I gave the bouncer a twenty-dollar bill and told him to give it to her when she got done. Maybe she could buy some food with it or some diapers for her baby. I hated seeing her up there defiling herself. Seeing this brought me down. I was at a good place emotionally after my meeting with CSI but, now this. Shit.

I drove home sullen and depressed. I prayed for her and prayed for me. I needed to get some sleep.

Chapter Ninety-Four
Game Planning

For years now, I have been hearing about the importance of game planning from my friends in the good old boys club who were our coaches. Some of my friends were great successes. Because of my friendships, I was always like part of the team. I would travel with the teams, be on the sidelines and benches and would provide as much help as possible. Many times, I was an extra security officer. I really enjoyed this facet of my life. I was really part of something. The sense of belonging. Being welcomed as a teammate was important to me because I thought of myself as a loner. I could not coach and had no other skill that would contribute. But yet, I felt my presence on the sidelines contributed. I was a friendly face in many times a hostile environment. And as I told you before, the kids liked me and they confided in me and yes; I believed that in some ways I was a type of surrogate father or old uncle hanging around for them to lean on. They trusted me. And that bond of trust was very important to me.

Nobody really cared about my killings. Just about everyone believed these deaths helped the district. Beavis and Butthead, or CSI, whatever you wanted to call them, did not really care either. However, now they saw me as a means to an end. And that was fine with me. Whatever floated your boat.

That all being said, it was now time for me to get to some serious game planning. I am sure that you have heard all the cliches about preparation and planning, and I would not slip up on what might be my most risky foray into the liberations.

I also knew that my creativity was now a signature. I would think about the easy ways. At first, I thought of just running the chief over in my car. I could kill him easily in that manner and I had enough connections on the dark side that I could have "lost" the car. I had friends down in the junkyard that would have taken the car away and crushed it and sent it out within minutes if I wanted it to end that way. You saw how they helped me with Peoples' car. That could have been easy and clean.

I also thought of just walking up to the man and pulling a gun out of my pocket and shooting him a la Jack Ruby and Lee Harvey Oswald. That would have taken care of him and also taken care of me. Although I wanted to live on, maybe this killing would signal the end of the shelf life for the Liberator. Who knows? I could not go on for forever and maybe it was only right that I go out in this type of blaze.

However, there was one problem with that method. Namely, I wanted to live and get away with it. I was not ready to cross the divide. I was not ready to meet Saint Peter and perhaps some people that I had put there. Although I sincerely doubted if there would be any place in heaven for these guys, I firmly believed that I had my spot reserved. Yes, I was righteous!

So, I had to come up with an appropriate plan that would probably allow me to escape and live for another day and, yes, perhaps more liberations. That is the track that I needed to follow.

I took several weeks of vacation time from the job with the express idea of learning the movements of the chief. I bet he was a man of routines and it would probably not be too hard for me to figure them out.

Chapter Ninety-Five
Operation Surveillance

It did not take me long to settle into the chief's routine, and I was right. He was a man of very simple ways.

He left his house every morning around 9:00 AM and his first stop was at a luncheonette in our sparse downtown region. He would saunter across the street after he got his newspaper from the corner store and then would hold some sort of personal court from 9:00-10:00 every day. It was not uncommon to see the mayor or councilman parade through there at different intervals. It was also easy to see what members of the department were up his ass as they, too, were frequent visitors. I used to chuckle at the younger cops who would pick his car up and return it 45 minutes later, all clean and shiny. He was grooming a new batch of sycophants.

At about 10:00, he would meander to the office, driving his nice shiny car. I wanted to go puke on it. My wait would not be long because he would leave his office again at about noon for his lunch. Lunches were a bit more mysterious because he liked to travel out of town for these lunches. He rotated spots in the neighboring communities. On different days, depending upon the location, I would watch different political leaders from the county and state level join him. Rarely, a fellow chief or mayor from a neighboring town would enter. The son of a bitch was playing all of his cards within both parties and power structures. He was trying to ensure that they would never leave him out in the cold.

I used to sit there watching him, thinking about what deal was going on. And I was sure that in every one of these deals, there were going to be victims. Not nameless, or faceless people, but small-town folk maybe like you or I that got caught up in a game much bigger than they ever could have imagined. And I am sure that in these deals or games, whatever you wanted to call them, destroyed these unknowing fools. He sat back, pulling all the strings. And I am also sure that these deals sat right on the line of being legal. Perhaps what may have given me more satisfaction than killing him would have been to see him taken out in handcuffs. I would want a front seat for that perp walk.

And the more I thought about this, he was probably right. Someone protected him. He was like a Teflon man. When any trouble hit, he could deflect it. When he harassed the black community for some sort of pettiness, the questions about tactics or motivations would all somehow seem to evaporate. After several very public marches and blustery speeches by the so-called enraged neighborhood leader, the discontent all seemed to all disappear. They made some payoff. Not a payoff in cold cash, but in promises to be cashed in down the road by that group leader. Over the years, it happened repeatedly. It was always the same M.O. And let us not kid ourselves. People were getting rich by all of this conniving.

The same proved true when he made a bad arrest. Somehow, it would all go away without him ever getting scarred. I know that in public jobs you get into lots of scrapes and even if you win some minor battle; you ended up getting wounded. Not him. He would always leave a battle clean. To me, this was unprecedented. The guy had survived for years and never got nicked? I wonder why? I know that in the past, a popular upstanding citizen would suddenly get picked up for driving under the influence. And this was on the way home from a local restaurant. I knew the deal here. The upstanding citizen pissed the chief off. A radio car would settle in on the restaurant and then the person would just get pulled over after the guy had a nice dinner with his wife sharing a bottle of wine. The chief had neighboring communities wired into his antics and I am sure that the chiefs had a little "favor doing" network established. Namely, the chief in one town would give the chief a heads up in a neighboring town to take care of this "thing" for him. This so called "pain in the ass." Politicians gave each other the license plate numbers and names of favorite restaurants of their pigeons. It was easy then to make an arrest for a DUI and hence create headlines for the next morning's papers. I certainly don't condone drinking and driving, but this was clearly a "set-up" network. Paybacks were a bitch. The newspapers then destroyed the person. This is how it worked. It was as simple as that. It did not take a newcomer too long to figure this out. You never fucked with the chief!

The chief was also a master at throwing his own department members under the bus. When the shit rolled in his direction, he always had an escape route plan by blaming a subordinate. Here was a man that I believed knew everything about his department and each of its members, but when trouble hit, he knew nothing. He could stand at a podium and plead ignorance when I am sure that any fouled-up operation or bad arrest had his blessing. It always had his blessing, but never his fingerprints.

On the first Friday night of my surveillance, I followed him to a motel in the next community. Very similar to the motel that I would share with Kelly on my Friday night meet-ups. By the way, Kelly still did not know that I was on to her and I used some lame excuse for missing this Friday night. I told her I would make it up to her next week.

It did not surprise me that the chief was screwing around, but it surprised me to see who he was screwing around with. I saw one of the new police hires, who was probably young enough to be his daughter, exiting the car. I say it initially surprised me, but as I considered this, it did not surprise me. His ego, as big as it was, probably needed to be stroked by his bedding down a younger woman. A woman he had power over in the job. It was sad. In a lot of ways, he did not differ from our dear departed music teacher pedophile. However, the woman was of age and that mattered. But she was still young and vulnerable and, yes, naïve to the ways of the world. He was using her. And it was not for the physical sex, I am sure; it was for fulfilling his enormous ego. I watched with disgust for a few hours and then left.

This rendezvous also reminded me of being told many times how this guy was when he was a kid. He was the pudgy kid who got bullied and picked on. The chief possessed few skills or enviable traits. He was not handsome, nor gifted athletically. He was spiteful, knew how to kiss the right ass and possessed a long memory. As he grew, he made his mark by being the biggest suck up in the world. He was fortunate, or perhaps he was smart enough to know this going in. He always knew who was the key person to suck up to. I have to give him this. He picked his winners, and they marched him right up through the command, bypassing many much more skilled and experienced people. He had several key "godfathers" out there and they taught him the game well. Perhaps I should say very well, because he became a master. And now that these guys were dying off, he was on his own. It is funny, throughout my career I have been able to see him stick the knife in the back of some of those that helped him on the way up. It made me sick. I had hoped that even in the world of scumbags, there was a sense of loyalty. This guy proved me wrong.

Saturday night was date night with his wife. They would put some dress-up clothes on and go to dinner. They traveled the county to the finest of restaurants and usually met up with other political figures. This was the night for the adults, not the kiddos. These dinners served as a forum to discuss the secret shit. The wives or dates were probably told to shut up and chat with one another while the men talked shop. I would always wonder when the big cigars came out. Another thought crossed my mind. Who was paying the tab for this bullshit? I am sure that this tab was on the city, just like last night's "sexcapade." Paying for this was the taxpayer's responsibility. And I also bet that he was doing this for so long he knew how to hide all the expenses.

On Sunday morning, the big hypocrisy took place as he and his wife marched their three kids to the church around the corner from their house. He wanted the public to look at this. This happy, secure little family. Our chief was a wonderful family and God-fearing man. What a facade. What a crock of shit.

As I watched this parade, I felt a twinge of sorrow knowing that soon the wife would be a widow and the kids fatherless. That sucked. But perhaps he should have thought of all of that and the repercussions of his behaviors throughout his career in town. And perhaps I was doing the wife and kids a big favor. I am sure that he was a domineering prick at home and probably ruled that house like some sort of dictator. I hope that after the cloud of remorse lifts, the wife would have probably looked to thank me for relieving her of this burden. She would not have to let him lay on her anymore. I hope that would have been a relief enough. Plus, she was still young enough and attractive enough to find herself a nice guy out there. I can't give her a complete pass though because she knew how the chief was and allowed his behavior to continue, if not enabled it. He wreaked havoc, and it was all about to come home to roost. I had no trouble quickly getting over this pang of remorse.

Chapter Ninety-Six
Eeney, meenie, miney mo.

Okay, I set my course. I knew his actions and his habits. That was the simple part. In my sleeplessness, I thought of perhaps making this the end. Maybe I should have just walked up to him and shot him. I would spend the rest of my life in jail, but, oh well, I was getting tired anyway.

Maybe I could just run him over in my car. I could probably make it seem like a genuine accident and maybe get away with it. But that was not good enough. I had to make some sort of statement. I think if you look back on most of my liberations; they had some sort of symbolic value.

What could have been a better demise of that mean old pain in the ass Mr. Solomon than getting poisoned in his own room by the cleaning solutions? Or perhaps, could there have ever been a better ending to Mrs. Westerman, the busybody secretary, than when all of that obsolete school machinery came tumbling down upon her? She was always stirring the soup at work. Constantly upsetting the apple cart and then the apple cart comes a tumbling down. That was a good one. I still enjoy a good laugh when I think of that one.

And I have to keep going back to Singleton, the pedophile music teacher. When he lit up like a Christmas tree, I felt it somehow was a purging of his sins against the school community. Fire was the only way to get rid of his evilness. He went up in flames and yes; he knew what hit him. I can attest to that. And yes, he knew it was because of me and yes; he knew why I had done it. I trust he will in everlasting eternity feel the fire of hell for all the living hell he caused for his sins against the young girls on earth.

Oh well, now what would be a fitting end for the Chief? It was probably during my third night of restlessness and sleeplessness that I came up with the plan. He needed and yes, this community, my community, needed some good old southern justice. But was I good enough to swing it? Of course, I was. For never forget that I am the Liberator!

Chapter Ninety-Seven
What we need is a good old fashion lynching!

He had to die like so many black men had died before him. He was going to be lynched in the town square. I was going to create a spectacle for all to see. I was going to not only liberate a school system; I was going to liberate a community. I hope and I pray that my ancestors, who fell victims to white racism in years past, would smile down on me from heaven. This would be great.

Once I settled on this plan, I fell asleep easily. Now to execute it. Complacency lulled the community to sleep. The chief felt as though he was a Teflon man. Nothing would ever stick to him. He was overconfident and also complacent. He knew it all. He had all of the angles covered. He was an expert at playing everyone against one another and he always came out the other end smelling like a rose. He was immune from all tragedies; or so he thought. For him, awful stuff only happened to the other guys. Well, some nasty stuff was about to happen to him.

Now I just had to figure out the right time to do it. I had the place. There was a beautiful old oak tree that had to be well over a hundred-years-old sitting in the town square right in the middle of city hall, the police station, the fire department and the public library. It was your old-time town center. The high school band would play there at Christmas time and the Farmers' Markets would be there every weekend in the summer. This location was the epicenter of many yearly festivals. It was the perfect place. I got excited thinking about it. Who would be the first person to see this display? How many people would walk by and fake disbelief and remorse while on the inside be happy and laughing about it? How many of his fellow officers, both current and retired, would walk by wishing they had done it? I think this number would surprise most. And how many of the members of the black community, especially the black young men that he loved to abuse, would be joyously celebrating the demise of this evil racist?

I hoped they would not cut his body down too soon. I wanted everyone to see my work. Somehow, I wanted to sign it. I would record for posterity visual evidence of my completed missions and send the gruesome pictures to the media. I also had on speed dial some of the phone numbers of the press.

Lynching was and still is an example of a mob mentality. A mob gets set on some vigilante justice and it becomes unstoppable. It is unstoppable because society allows it. A person who completes a lynching does so with premeditation and organization. Whites usually perpetrated it against blacks. There are thousands of documented lynchings right here in the good old U.S.A. And I must add, lynching is a very sad part of our history. Our society condones both figurative and literal lynching.

I do not want to get caught up in a history lesson on lynching. It is enough to say that they were examples of a mob mentality filled with hate with a need to be a public spectacle. And I swore I would make the lynching of the chief a public display. This was going to be about power; the power of the Liberator.

Hatred is just hatred. It is that simple. This community hates the chief. He was just a mean old racist bastard. A racist bastard with power. Could anything be worse?

It will probably be my most difficult and risky undertaking.

I set the course. I must do what I must do. The Liberator is alive and well.

Chapter Ninety-Eight
Game Planning, again

Game planning energized me. I was now in the game planning mode. The game of my lifetime is near. I can't be in a hurry, though. Although I want to get this done, I cannot sacrifice efficiency for speed.

I really wanted to lynch the son of a bitch. The hard part of this mission was to incapacitate the chief. Once I rendered him helpless, the rest of the job could be easy. Believe it or not, I trained and work out a little for this job. I watched what I ate; I exercised a bit more; I gave up the grape (except for my nights with Mrs. Kelly) and I made sure I was getting enough sleep.

OK, you heard me right. Yes, my nights with Mrs. Kelly. Why should I give up on a good thing? Even though I knew she was a rat, I kept my Friday night encounters. I said when I missed several Fridays watching the chief, I would make it up to her and make it up to her I did. We did things I never even thought you could do. We rolled around like two horny teenagers. You had to laugh, but the energy and excitement that these Friday nights would generate for both of us were unimaginable.

After this lynching, I wanted my sexual encounters with Kelly to continue. I needed them and wanted them. After I completed this liberation, I wondered if these encounters would continue. Who knows, but I hope so. I did not care that she was now "state's evidence" against me. I believed that Beavis and Butthead, I mean CSI, would keep their end of the bargain. And I had hopes that Big Lou would not want to see his sexual adventure with Miss Mary end. Somewhere in the dark recesses of my mind, I believed that after this event was over, after a few hectic weeks, all would return to normal. It always did. We had our share of scandals and somehow, after a brief period of chaos, everything would return to the way it was before. We would then wait as a community for the next scandal to hit, which, although unknown, was right around the corner.

Sorry for the digression. After conducting my share of research, I felt that the best way to incapacitate the chief was to shock him into submission with a stun gun. I researched this topic fairly thoroughly, and I was sure that this was the way to go. First, owning a stun gun for self-defense and protection was legal. Legal all the way. So, I could legally own one. And I could legally carry it. That made it easy. I really did not want to or have to skulk around hiding a weapon to knock him out. Plus, I did not want to kill him. He needed to be aware of the lynching. I wanted him to really enjoy the experience. I knew I would.

As I conducted a bit more research, I found I did not want a stun gun; I wanted a Taser. They are similar, but mostly, Tasers will work from a distance. I could shoot him from fifteen feet away and deliver a good thirty seconds of shock. If I had two, I could operate with a back-up if needed. When one uses a stun gun, you have to be close enough to your intended target to press it directly to the skin. They are smaller and perhaps easier to conceal. I needed something I could use from a distance.

So, I went down to the local "big box" sporting goods store and did some shopping. I couldn't believe that these things are legal and anyone can buy one without a permit or any sort of background check. This is true in almost every state. I purchased two of them. The clerk was more than happy to sell them to me and was kind enough to give me a comprehensive demonstration about how to use them.

I was also confident that the Taser would not kill the chief. Of course, there was a remote chance of a heart attack, but I will take my chances. This liberation could be easy for me if I just shot the chief with a real gun. I was pretty good with a pistol from my military background, but a shooting death would not have had the same effect as a lynching in the town square. I was ready to act. The drama was necessary for me. I almost felt the need to sign my work. And maybe I would. Who knows?

Chapter Ninety-Nine
It is kick-off time

I set the game plan. I thought I practiced enough. I was ready to go. I had some contingency plans, and I knew when I would abort if needed. I checked the long-range weather report. The weekend looked clear. Saturday morning would be bright and sunny. Enough of this. It is game time.

I would spring into action on Friday night. No sense ruining a good Friday night's action for both of us. I would take care of Mrs. Kelly and scoot on over to the motel where I knew the chief would be, probably banging the young pretty cop and wait. I was totally heartless. One last time, I let him go on a power trip.

The time dragged during the day. Nightfall finally came and Kelly and I had dinner at our usual spot and then quickly headed over to our little love nest. I mentally sped up my internal clock, and I wanted to finish a bit early so I would not be late for my meet-up with the chief. I stayed away from the grape because I wanted to have a logical mind so I could spring into action. All was going according to plan. It is amazing that both Kelly and I were not becoming bored. Each Friday night brought a fresh experience. Could I be falling in love?

We said our usual goodbyes and left, each one going our separate ways with a brief fantasy thought for the week. A little anticipation of what would occur next weekend. We made this anticipation a regular part of our evening. You would not believe how one could become excited on a Wednesday afternoon thinking about what would occur on Friday night. It is amazing how the human mind works. I wonder if the chief would do the same thing?

I knew that there would be a next weekend. I never thought about getting caught. Come to think of it, the thought of an apprehension never entered my mind in any of my previous liberations. Perhaps I was becoming arrogant. I knew I was not becoming careless. I had this act thoroughly planned. What could go wrong?

My biggest concern for the evening was not efficiently subduing the chief. I then had to get him into my pickup truck to tote him on over to the big oak tree. He was a fat, lead ass son of a bitch. That would be my major hurdle.

I laid in wait at the chief's motel and watched as he exited his room and kissed his young princess goodbye. She went her way, and he went his way. I tucked in behind him far enough back that he could not see or sense my tail. He was a man of routines, and I knew he would stop at headquarters to annoy his night shift crew before heading home. I had heard through the rumor mill that the entire night shift knew of his antics and would all have a good laugh at his expense behind his back. The chief was a vindictive prick. This revenge factor scared the rank and file. Yet, they still enjoyed any type of locker room humor about the chief. However, he was too good of a target to let it go. He was easy to spoof, and it was easy to make fun of him.

I watched him leave headquarters and walk to his car. The chief's status allowed him to park closest to the building. This made it difficult for me because he parked his car closest to the building. Of course, they emblazoned his name and rank on his spot with white paint besides a sign reserving his spot directly in front of the place. As I had already told you, a lack of ego was not his problem. I had taken the precaution of knocking out the light that was near his car. It was nice and dark. It disappointed me because it was such a beautiful night, and the stars provided some background lighting for this event.

As he was about to enter his car, I pulled over to him. He recognized me and greeted me with a big hello. We were not strangers. He probably did not like me and I had no good feelings about him. I knew in my heart that my black skin probably made his milky white skin crawl. I got out; we shook hands and made some small talk.

I was standing about five feet away from him. I had the Tasers, both of them, in my waistband in the small of my back, hidden by my light coat. As he walked back to his car, I pulled the right Taser out and, with his back turned, made a direct hit to the flesh of his neck. He went down like an old sack of potatoes. Both of our vehicles shielded us. When he hit the ground, I went right for his handcuffs. I slid them off of his belt and easily secured his hands behind his back.

As he gathered his senses, I pulled the other Taser out with my left hand and gave him another shot to his bare back where his shirt had risen up. He flapped around on the pavement like a big old fish once hooked and reeled in, laying on the pier. I caught him.

I scurried around him and dragged him to where my pickup tailgate was down. With one good heave ho, I could get him in the truck's bed. He was a real sight, flopping around stunned, snot, tears and spit rolling down his face. I think that he may have wet himself. I was not sure at this point. I duct taped his feet together, and I also used some duct tape to secure him at the knees. Finally, I dried his face and secured a good wrap of duct tape around his mouth. Once again, duct tape to the rescue. It's good for most any repair and I always kept a roll in my car and at home. I would also always bring a roll with me on vacation for those minor mishaps. All I thought was duct tape, please don't fail me now!

Chapter One Hundred
Half time

There was no marching band and no big-time half-time speech. It was about 2:30 in the morning and I wanted to wait until about 5:00 in the morning to string him up. I drove around a bit and finally settled on one of my favorite spots down by the strip joint and the city dump.

I parked close enough to the bar so we both could hear the sounds of the last sets of the strippers. The chief was floating in and out of it. Part of it was the double dose of shocks, and part of it was probably fright and anger. No one ever got the better of him. This would be both the first time and the last time.

I got out of the car and strolled around to the pickup bed. I poked him and got his attention. He struggled against his restraints. I used the remaining part of my time telling him about all of my liberations. I think the biggest thing that was running through his mind right now was him not getting to solve my crimes and reap all the accolades and good press. He would have probably been on television. He lived for tragedies. I remember seeing him interviewed several times on the boob tube, and you could tell that he loved every minute. The more horrific the tragedy or accident, the more he liked it. Too bad he will miss the press coverage of this one.

I also used the time to lecture him about his ways. I started by blasting him about banging the young cop. I had no beef with him if he was keeping something on the side. Shit, most men did that, but it pissed me off he was using his power and position to conquer this new cop. I also read the litany of wrongs that he committed against his police force. I tried to remember all the stories that I heard about him running rough-shod over them. He led by fear and intimidation, which was no way to lead. I also felt compelled to tell him that Beavis and Butthead put me up to this. His eyes almost bulged out of his head. A collective police department decided to frag the chief. Beavis and Butthead were just the lucky ones who drew the short straws to make this happen. They were just using me. I was an easy mark for them. The time really flew by. At about 4:45 AM, I drove back over to the town square and parked as close to the tree as possible.

I had about a one-hundred-foot length of rope in the truck's front. It was a good strong rope. Thick enough to hold the dangling chief and thick enough to make an impressive noose. I prepared the noose and left it in the bed of my truck.

I got out of my car and walked on back to the bed of the truck. I carried the rope in my hand. But before I did anything else, I stood on the front of my truck and threw the one end of the rope up and around a thick branch that was about twenty-five feet off of the ground. It was quite thick and perfect for this hanging. I had added a big knot on the end of the rope, which made it easier to toss over the branch. I had watched this location on late Friday nights, so I knew that no one ever drove by. They would not see me.

After I did this, I slipped the noose over the chief's head and tightened it down nicely. I then grabbed the other end and kept pulling with all of my strength. Stringing him up was not too difficult as the branch served as a fulcrum for my pulley. Within minutes, he was about ten feet off of the ground and I quickly tied the other end securely to the trunk of the tree. He was not going anywhere.

I moved around where I had a splendid view of him swinging in the breeze, kicking his legs. His eyes were bulging out of his head as he took his last breath. It did not take too long. I stood and watched and felt absolutely no remorse. I went back to the cab of my truck and took out a can of green spray paint and painted a big scripted L on the tree trunk. I also used that as a moment to pay respect to all of my black brothers that died similarly, swinging from the end of the rope on some tree. But unlike the chief, society convicted my brothers of non-existent crimes. They suffered the ultimate penalty; death. The chief was guilty of many crimes. I just took it upon myself to serve as judge, jury and executioner. I did not mutilate the body as the white mobs did to my forefathers. Plus, I believed in my heart that no one would want a souvenir of this bastard.

I got back into my car and drove back to my initial hiding place by the bar. I wanted to wait until daybreak and try to watch someone find him.

His wife never called to report him missing. I also knew that this call would never take place. It was not uncommon for the chief to stay out all night with many women. Everyone knew this. Everyone knows everything in a small town. You may not want to believe it, but it is true. It is very true and if you do not believe me, go out and do something stupid and you will be on page one of this informal news service within 24 hours (at the latest).

Chapter One Hundred One
A beautiful Saturday morning

Dawn broke a little after six on that morning and it did not take me long to hear the sirens blare. It was then that I cruised on over and see what was happening. Of course, I knew what was happening and could not wait to see the reaction.

I took my time and stopped for an extra-large coffee and a donut. It was going to be a long and entertaining morning. When I got back to the old oak tree, the chief was swinging in the breeze. He looked taller because gravity was stretching his neck. His skin was a bluish green color, and it was now clear that he went to the bathroom in his pants. There was a pained, anguished looked upon his face. He looked almost cartoonish in a morbid sense. He was clearly dead.

The police were helplessly milling around. Some cried. Yet, others I could see smirking and laughing. I am sure that within these groups, there were pockets of officers who had wished that they had done the job. As time passed, the body still rhythmically swung in the breeze. Time was now working against the police as the city was awakening and a crowd of onlookers was forming. Many were snapping pictures of the swinging corpse for posterity. I have to admit it, that I took several pictures for myself. And guess what? I got his keys!

I am sure that the police were waiting for the county or the state to come by before they disturbed any evidence. The fools that drove their police cars all over the place had already destroyed any trace evidence. Their incompetence shined again. As some people arrived, I both saw and heard many people retching and losing their breakfast. It was a pretty grotesque sight.

Finally, some genius had a good idea. Perhaps the first good idea some moron had his or her entire life. The police summoned the fire department and with their two big ladder trucks could string up some tarpaulins stretched across the ladders of the trucks to block out the sight of the body from the crowd. Mostly, it worked. However, that did not curtail the crowds from assembling. Some of our industrious high school kids went to the grocery store and got some cases of water and starting selling them. Young entrepreneurs, good to see. I was waiting for some hot dog carts to appear and believe it or not, soon a soft serve ice cream truck arrived. There was money to be made from this spectacle. I never thought about that. It was becoming a good old fashion lynching. Exactly what I had hoped for. Only this time, a white man was swinging from the end of the rope. Boy, that was a change.

This festival probably lasted about three hours. After about the first hour, all the news trucks arrived and their telescoping satellite dishes made a bit of a skyline. Several news copters crisscrossed the sky. For one small minute, our small community was making the big time. I felt pretty good about that.

The fire department, with the help of the County Coroner finally cut him down, preserving as much evidence as they could. Out of the corner of my eye, I saw Beavis and Butthead. We made some subtle eye contact. We all knew what had happened.

It would be an interesting next couple of days.

Chapter One Hundred Two
Showtime

Let the festivities begin. It was now showtime. The city would do a fine job of mourning someone that most people hated.

Police Headquarters now became a beehive of activity. Something that I did not count on was the FBI in addition to the State Police investigators. Everyone was viewing this crime as a hate crime. Although I never really processed this, they were right. Most everyone hated the guy. I was eager to see how the press would spin the racial factor. A white man lynched? What type of headlines would that generate?

It did not take long to see those headlines. The Sunday papers did a great job. Big bold headlines explained what had happened. They used a distant picture of the chief swinging. I don't think that they wanted to shock all of their readers. That being said, I was a bit surprised how the story read.

The big papers interviewed several members of the police department and the Town Council President. Listening to these fools made it seem like the chief was a combination of John F. Kennedy and Martin Luther King Jr. Both the white members of the community and the African Americans were eulogizing this racist chief as if they were talking about Kennedy and King. I was astounded. The paper printed pictures of his wife and kids. This was a sad vision. I wish I could extend my apologies to these folks. However, I hope that after the shock and their initial grief, they would like to thank me. He was not a good husband, and I doubt he was a good father.

I visited some bars in the town. Unlike the papers and the public rhetoric, the men and women at the barstools, both black and white, were laughing and joking and, most of all, talking the truth. There was a genuine feeling of exhilaration. I visited the bar that the local cops hung out at and it was like they just won the Super Bowl. A real celebration was going on. I was more observant of who was missing than who was present at this festival. That told me quite a bit.

I saw where this was going. We were going to put that solemn face on for all the outsiders and paint an actual picture of remorse. Losing a great man was going to be shown to the community. We were going to lie, lie, and lie. I almost threw up at the thought.

And the city fathers did not disappoint me. They made the decision that the local funeral parlors would not be large enough for this man and his grieving friends, so they moved his viewing and services to the high school gymnasium. Believe it or not, they put me in charge of the facilities and I was told to make sure that the event was sacred. What a joke. Ironically, the political bosses placed me in charge of preparing the site for his viewing. Shit, I put him there.

But I knew how to play the game and play I did. We built a nice stage at one end of the gymnasium and lined the walls with photos of the chief in action. They placed large floral arrangements throughout the gym and I made a sort of chute out of flowers for the mourners to pass through as they made their way to the raised casket. It actually looked nice.

Several things ran through my head. This guy never visited the gym unless he was looking to pull one student out in handcuffs. He loved making a big spectacle out of the arrest. I am convinced in my heart that he hoped for a little resistance so he could beat the shit out of the kid and send that terror message to all that witnessed it.

The second thing that I found ironic were the signatures on the floral sprays. The NAACP sent a beauty. What a joke. They hated him and he hated them. The PBA was not to be outdone either. What a bunch of hypocrites. There were several bundles and arrangements made like red rose hearts which were unsigned. You know, the hearts a wife would send to her late husband. I could only assume that these hearts were from his secret lovers. I would keep my eye out for them. It could be an entertaining scene if they all showed up together. At my last count, there were seven of them. The old chief was some sort of busy stud which, if you ever set eyes on him, was laughable.

They commandeered the school personnel to take part. The Junior ROTC cadets were all decked out in their dress uniforms and the PBA sent their honor guards.

A group of students from the orchestra played chamber music while the select chorus at different times sang.

This viewing lasted for two days. They also held there the last service, and they gave him the sendoff of some sort of hero. They portrayed him as a doer of good deeds. Just like the "Wizard of Oz." He loved his "munchkins" and they loved him. What a crock of shit. Hollywood could not have written a better script.

When it was over, they loaded him on top of a fire engine for a parade through town. I am not sure if he went to every street, but I am told he hit most of them. One question came to mind. Did he visit his favorite motel? I wonder who will get his weekly reservation? Perhaps some other big politico.

Okay. I now thought I could relax. One captain replaced the chief in the interim. He was a placeholder, and both the town council and the community knew this. Could the city return to normal now? Time will tell.

Let me give you a quick summary of my recent works. The police chief, school board president and school superintendent were all gone now because of my work. Yes, I felt pretty good. It was now time to relax.

Chapter One Hundred Three
A return to normal, once again.

As I told you before, we returned to normal really well. It did not take us long. We were used to it. Something big would happen in the school or community and we would pop back in a pretty short while. And within days or weeks, depending on the significance of the issue, we would go right back to normalcy. Nothing would ever change for the better. And that normalcy was not good or bad. For us, it was just normal.

The city and the schools were all back to work with new leadership. I had hopes that this would be better than before. But they let me down many times in the past. The cops hated the kids, and the kids hated the cops. And sometimes it was hard to tell who the children were.

The FBI and the State PD were still snooping around and the local detectives did their best. And believe me, if we were relying on their best, the crime, like all the others, would not get solved.

The schools were back to normal, yes; I mean, the normal before the old bitch was here and Big Lou returned the calm of the good old boys. Little Miss Mary was still here now as a district employee and continued to follow Big Lou around like a puppy dog. It was kind of cute. Whenever he spoke, she was at his side with her big green eyes staring at him and shaking her head in affirmation of anything he said. From afar, it looked funny. Years ago, they would call them "goo-goo eyes." I used to think that no one ever made "goo goo" eyes toward me. I would chuckle to myself and decide it did not really matter. I would survive. Come to think of it, maybe the closest I may have gotten to this was with Mrs. Kelly. However, I had to be in our motel room to see into her baby blues. I never let her down on my end. I now thought about Big Lou and wondered if he ever let Miss Mary down in the bedroom. If you based it upon the way she looked at him, you would doubt it.

Chapter One Hundred Four
All things can change in a minute

It was almost two months after the passing of our dear chief, when I was walking away from the school to grab a cup of coffee, when I saw Beavis and Butthead roll up to me in their same old, beat-up unmarked car. Once again, I had to laugh because probably everyone in the city if not the state recognized this car. It did not sneak up on anyone. They asked me to join them and I readily slid into the backseat. I figured we were going to go for a bit of a celebratory ride to discuss the liberation. I figured maybe they were going to buy me a cup of coffee.

However, I detected something was odd by the tone of the chatter on this ride. It was absent. And when they spoke, it was almost businesslike. I could tell we would not visit the junkyard or the go-go bar. Nor were we going to visit at our favorite picnic table in town. Coffee was off the list as they both were sipping big cups of coffee as we drove. I was getting a little worried. What could be up?

We pulled into the police station and pulled around the back. They both jumped out to open the door and escort me in the back door. This is the door that was used by police officers and suspects or arrested individuals. I knew I wasn't a cop. Was I a suspect or was I being arrested?

They hustled me into the first open room. This wasn't like television, with interview rooms designated by numbers. They put you into one of two rooms. They dropped me in and left. I was told they would return. I was not in a hurry. I could see that I was not going anywhere.

Little did I realize that when I went out for that afternoon coffee, I was probably seeing my last day of freedom. It would have been a delicious coffee.

Chapter One Hundred Five
Mind games

It will be hard for me to describe to you what was going through my mind. It felt as though my life was now in some sort of suspended animation. I am not really sure that I know what that phrase means, but I could best describe it like my mind was really out of my body looking at what was going on. My mind comprehended what was going on and yet was not willing to accept it.

I thought of all of things that I would miss. A good cup of coffee is what I started with. I loved my coffee, and I was at a genuine loss thinking about never tasting it again. I would miss work. I enjoyed it. The people made me feel good. I liked the job. I liked my status. Yes, I had status. I had that enormous set of keys. And remember what I said. In schools, keys equate to power. That was going to be gone. But most of all, I would miss Kelly. Sure, I would miss the sex, who wouldn't? But I was old and that would surely diminish soon. I think I would miss her companionship. We were coworkers and friends. We were lovers. But perhaps now, for the first time, I realized I had fallen in love with her. Probably the first time I had fallen in love in my life. And yet I knew she turned on me. Finding love took a lifetime. Losing it took seconds.

I guess about an hour later, Beavis stuck his head into the room and interrupted my nap by asking me if I wanted a Coke. I usually drank Diet Coke, but I figured in my life, at this point, a little sugar would not hurt me. That was the least of my problems. It amazed me I could doze off. I had read that a guilty party when caught and questioned, slept. The innocent ones were the ones wired and wide awake. Who knows if this was true? I napped.

Beavis and Butthead returned, bringing in my Coke and wheeling a portable television with them. They asked if I wanted to see something. Shit, we all knew that I was going to see it whether I wanted to. I remember just shrugging my shoulders.

They flipped on the TV and fiddled with the computer that was hooked on it. The TV sprung to life and on the screen was a lovely color shot of me using the Taser on the chief. Although it was dark out, the picture was as bright as day. They both laughed. At that moment, I knew they set me up. I was the fall guy. They had me. I was staring right into the camera. My face looked focused and yet somehow, I was pleased with myself when the chief hit the ground. The chief's face was twisted and tortured. I wondered if he knew what awaited.

Beavis and Butthead's mouths kept moving, but I am not sure if I heard what they were saying. They saw me abducting the chief. There it was in living color. There was no doubt about it. My face and my truck. Unmistakable. I should have autographed it.

Beavis and Butthead used me. I am a dumb son of a bitch!

When I could shake the cobwebs out, I had to listen to them tell me they recently installed a new series of cameras. I knew nothing about these cameras. They did. And they never told me about them. The set up was smooth as a baby's ass. They wanted me to do this job. They could have told me about the new cameras. Instead, they sat idly by and I am sure that they were laughing and enjoying every minute. But they wanted to catch me. And catch me they did.

I also came to find out that in my truck, they planted a GPS device that would show my every step. They could do this through a court order, as they now identified me as their number one suspect in the series of "accidental" school deaths. Suspect? Shit, they knew I did them. I basically told them that. They also had my key collection.

They punched up the GPS record for the night of the murder and I saw my car monitored by a big red light on the screen. A red line followed my car through town. It paused when I paused. It paused when I toyed with the chief by the jiggle joint, and it paused by the big old oak tree when I lynched the bastard. What more evidence could they have?

Chapter One Hundred Six
The next play

I sat and thought about my next step. I sat in this small, dirty, and smelly cell in the station house for a few days. My court-appointed lawyer turned out to be a former student of ours. I recognized him immediately. We had spent a great deal of time together in the high school. His name was Raymond Garcia. He was an outstanding athlete, and I watched many of his football and basketball games. We spent a great deal of time talking in the cafeteria and I would critique his games. We had a strong bond. The only problem that I saw was that he probably only had a handful of trials behind him. I would be his first big case. We both liked and respected one another. Even though we were friends, what the hell was he going to do for me? Probably not much. However, he knew the town well and probably knew each of my liberations.

I sat back and watched as the state and federal prosecutors got into some pissing match who was going to try the case. I had heard that the federal facilities were nicer, but really did I care? I didn't. I wondered if I could find a jury that would be sympathetic to my cause. In my heart, I really still believed what I did was right. The people that I took out needed taking out.

One day, a van pulled up and Beavis and Butthead manacled me and walked me to the van. There was no conversation. When I found out my destination, I knew who won the battle. I was being moved to the capital city, where the federal prosecutors would have their way with me. Any advantage that my rookie lawyer had just went right out of the window.

When I arrived, they escorted me into my new home for the next unknown number of weeks or months. It was nicer. They placed me in a segregated cell that had a small window which allowed me the benefit of some sunshine. The food also was better. I was sleeping and eating well. I cannot say that I disliked my surroundings. However, a "cot and three hots" are not enough. I missed my freedom. I enjoyed having the ability to come and go as I pleased. I missed the good old boys and shooting the shit about sports or some new lady that was in town. We always gave the new women in the district a good once over. We rarely changed our initial opinions. And yes, I missed Kelly.

I had lost track of time and before long they escorted me into a new interview room where some new guy in a suit sat waiting for me. He introduced himself and I recognized his name. He was ready to be my new lawyer. It appears a citizen's advocacy group had raised the money to hire him. It turns out that this group liked what I did. They liked the Liberator and all his liberations.

I thought long and hard to determine if I needed this suit or really if I wanted this suit. I actually liked Raymond. He was open and honest. I trusted him and I believed that although he would be short on resources, they would not outwork him. This would be his big break. I knew deep in my heart that he or the suit would not win my case. But if I selected the kid, would that piss off the citizens that raised the money for me? It most surely would. I wanted their support. I thought long and hard if I could somehow get a win-win out of this. I needed to think about it.

The major newspapers ran stories about me. One newspaper published a chronology of my actions dating back to the mysterious disappearance of Mr. Peoples. They now had pieced all the accidents together and knew that the accidents were no accidents. Big Lou and Miss Mary were getting a great deal of air time on this. I did not care about this because Big Lou was one of the good old boys and he might as well get something out of this. I liked him. He was a young guy who I thought was good for the district. I could give a shit about Miss Mary (although she always looked fine). Thinking about Big Lou having his way with Miss Mary filled my mind at night in this lonely place.

Well, it turns out that I was going to be prosecuted in the federal court system for the murder of the chief. Besides the murder, they attached several hate crimes against me that basically assured the death penalty if convicted. It would be the case of the year, maybe the decade.

I met with my pastor, and we talked about many subjects. We talked about the case, the other murders, my relationship with Kelly and my relationship with God. I enjoyed our conversations and looked forward to them. We also talked about my lawyer. I kept the kid and let the $5000.00 suit go. I did not really like him. He really could not care less about me. By retaining the kid, I would give something back to the community. I forgot to mention that Raymond looked just liked me, which made my decision much easier. Raymond would never get an opportunity like this again. I wanted to see him get some good press and recognition out of this case. I never thought that he was going to get me off.

Chapter One Hundred Seven
Me and the kid

He was three years out of law school and in his second year of working with the public defender's office. The PD assigned cases rotationally. You got whatever case you got because of your spot on the line. If it was a good case, you were lucky, otherwise it was just a slow tortuous process of poor defendants with basically unwinnable cases who were most likely guilty. And they were most likely black. Most Public Defenders stayed in their job for a few years and then they left burned out and disillusioned. The old ones that never left, with that rare exception, were useless.

Well, I showed the $5000.00 suit the door, and I began my journey to freedom, or death, with this young black warrior. We met a bunch, and I gave him very little. He never asked if I was guilty or not. For him, it did not matter. After several meetings, I knew I had made the right choice. I knew he possessed that personal quality that I was looking for. I knew he was bright, and he was going to be relentless.

I also adopted the philosophy that no matter what evidence the police may have against me, I would never admit it. It really did not matter if they had my misgivings on film, which they did. I would admit nothing.

The Feds protected my rights to a speedy trial. They paved the way for a quick conviction. They were charging me with a capital murder offense for killing the chief and a variety of hate crime statutes along with a violation of the civil rights of Peoples, Donaldson, Singleton, Westerman and Solomon. There was nothing on me for the deaths of the board president and the superintendent. In the end, it was going to be one big happy federal trial, all rolled up into one theatrical courtroom drama. A drama in which I was going to be the very silent main character.

Raymond had several psychiatrists talk to me. This proved useless because I basically just sat there and smiled. I think he was trying to prove some sort of insanity claim for me. Shit, I was saner than most people. I knew for a fact that I was saner than those that I killed.

Motions to the court came and went. The press coverage was great. One of the big metropolitan papers had me on the front page dressed like Superman, with a big "L" on my chest. The press loves to create nicknames, especially for serial killers. They did not have to create one for me because I already had one. And the more I think about it, I was a serial killer. I think we talked about that before. However, I liked the Superman comparison. The cover photo had created many copycats. I had heard that the major social media forums already had emojis created in my likeness. People were loving every minute. I was loving every minute.

The trial was going to start soon. My life could come down to a very few critical days. I think that the waiting is the worst part. The death penalty did not scare me. I was always ready to meet my maker. I think the worst part of the death sentence was waiting for the execution. Counting the days until death. I already made my mind up. There would be no appeal of a guilty verdict. There was no sense in dragging it out. I one time heard that in Russia, when they intend to execute someone, a chosen assassin just sneaks into your cell at night and while you are sleeping just blows your brains out. I don't know if that is true or not, but for me, I wish that could be the case. I do not want to take part in any countdown to the gallows. Who needs that?

The kid wanted to push for a change of venue. I wanted to keep the trial as close to home as I could. I was hoping it would be a tainted jury pool. How could you not love me? I remain convinced that everyone loved the Liberator. Although the kid pushed for a change in venue, they denied it. The trial was soon to begin. I couldn't wait.

Chapter One Hundred Eight
Kickoff

The big day had finally arrived. My trial would start in the Federal Court House. They drove me to the court in a nice new comfortable and clean black SUV with all the windows blacked out. However, I could see out easily. My chariot arrived two hours early to beat any expected crowd, but they missed the mark. Hundreds of people were already in line, waiting for a chance to get in as a spectator. Potential jurors were already upstairs preparing for jury selection. Others were there just to protest on my behalf. They were showing me an enormous amount of support. As I rode through this friendly gauntlet, I could feel the love. They boosted my spirits.

Jury selection started right on time. They wanted me to wear a suit, but I refused. I looked fine in my nice, casual outfit. They did not let me wear one of my hats. They knew me for my hat collection. Any hat I put on looked good. I would not put on a tie for the masses. I wanted just to be me.

There was little pre game conversation between Raymond and me. We had gone over a rough game plan the day before. He was the coach and quarterback. The game was on his shoulders. My life was in his hands. I would sit and wonder how this kid was going to pull this game out. With all the direct evidence that they had against me, it was like being down by three touchdowns, with two minutes left on the clock. But this kid was a competitor. Raymond's eyes revealed his intense focus. His demeanor told me he was ready. Before he uttered a word, he looked at me with fire in his eyes and said, "let's go, this game is not over."

The judge seemed like a fair arbitrator of justice. He had handled big trials in the past, and everyone knew and respected his experience. He was tough on the media and spectators and assured me he would go by the book and let the evidence speak for itself. The prosecutor was equally experienced and came with a bevy of support. He had three junior assistants carry his lawyer cases and other boxes. I would laugh at this vision because all he needed to do was to put on the videotape. That video really cooked my goose.

The kid had an idea up his sleeve and he was showing some of his cards in his juror questions and ultimate selections.

I knew he would somehow play the race card. Someone once told me it was always about race. I felt kind of bad for the kid. He was busting his ass, and I was not being of much help. I was basically just working on keeping my mouth shut, even to him. We were cordial, if not friendly, but I certainly was not helpful.

This was going to be a spectacle no matter how you sliced it. And I was enjoying it.

Raymond drilled down his questions to prospective jurors. It became apparent quickly that he was looking for primarily poorly educated black or brown people. For the kid, a college degree was a disqualifier. The perfect juror for my lawyer was a not too smart, hardworking black guy. This perfect juror was going to be a renter. Home ownership was another of the kid's disqualifiers.

Some of his questions surprised me. He really wanted a person who read the New York Post or Daily News. He wanted the person who would grab several of the weekly tabloids at the check-out counter before purchasing his or her scratch off lottery tickets.

The kid also wanted someone who would be okay with a little physical force in his family. It would be fine if the juror took his or her kid to the "woodshed" now and then. The kid would love it if the juror would get into a bit of a barroom scrape for whatever reason. They used the same criteria when he was questioning women. It was okay with the kid if the wife gave the husband a crack now and then.

Juror selection was slow. However, at times, it became interesting. Some of the back-and-forth commentary with the potential jurors was comical. I saw the judge several times hide a chuckle. Likewise, the prosecutor chuckled some but there was a point in the process where everything seemed to turn serious for him.

The first day of jury selection concluded with only a few jurors seated. The judge was searching for twelve jurors and three alternates. Before they whisked me back to the jail for the night, the kid and I met in an anteroom near the courtroom.

In the few quick moments, the kid explained to me his strategy. He was trying to seat a jury that would not convict me if even if they saw me actually committing the crime. He told me about jury nullification. Jury nullification would usually occur when the jurors found the defendant not guilty, despite all the damning evidence against him. Sometimes the jurors may have felt that the law may have been unjust or perhaps the punishments did not fit the crime. He could not find any examples of jury nullification where the charges were as intense as mine. I asked him about OJ and he told me he really did not think of that as nullification and we could discuss that case when mine was over. I did not really care. He also assured me that jurors were allowed to make poor decisions. Ray explained the judge could ultimately overrule the jury. He could do that, but I do not think it would bode well for him. The citizens would kill him. Well, maybe not kill him, but kill his career. He asked me to trust him. What choice did I have?

Chapter One Hundred Nine
An interesting night

The guards took me back to the jail the same way that I arrived in that new SUV. As I was leaving the courthouse, there was a bigger crowd out in front of the courthouse. Now I saw people holding signs in my support. I also noticed several of the news trucks parked nearby with their satellite dishes extended high into the air.

I had established a pretty good relationship with the guards at the jail. They liked me. They found me funny, and they seemed to cut me some breaks during my stay with them. For the trial, I was in a special cell that allowed easy access in and out of the jail. In this solitude, I saw no other prisoners or cells. That was all right with me because it allowed me to get a good night's sleep.

That night, the guards plugged in a small television in the hallway where I could hear the news. I was the star of the night, both on the local shows and the national program. I was watching myself become a bit of a folk hero. That was okay with me. Maybe it would be harder to stick a needle in the arm of a folk hero.

At sunup, the guards brought me my breakfast, along with a clean shirt and a clean pair of drawers for the day. Today on my breakfast tray they included the tabloids from the city. There I was again, on the cover. Each one carrying a similar picture along with a catchy headline. I was lucky that there was not much happening in the country to push me from the headlines. The spotlight remained on me. And yes, I was enjoying it.

Chapter One Hundred Ten
The draft continues

I looked at the jury selection like the NFL football draft. Over the last several years, the draft had become a media circus. Now the circus had arrived in the Federal Court House under the guise of my trial.

However, I need to share with you about the ride in today. It was better than yesterday. Today, I had a police SUV along with two motorcycle cops pave the way. I did not understand why until we got closer to the building. It was a crazy scene. Now, instead of several hundred people waiting for me, there may have been at least one thousand. There were too many signs to recall any of them specifically. People surrounded the outside of the courthouse dressed in white shirts with a big green scripted L on their chest. Others had green capes to adorn their costumes and still others had created a green matching mask. My motorcade proceeded through this throng at a snail's pace. Cheers and applause serenaded me. At one point, one fool with an electronic megaphone asked the crowd to spell out LIBERATOR. You could hear him call out, give me an "L" and the crowd would respond. Each letter's response generated thunderous applause.

I also noticed several circling news helicopters overhead. Yes, it was a circus, and maybe that was an understatement.

When I arrived at the courthouse, they allowed me to relieve myself with my personal guard watching. Then I went to my assigned seat in the courtroom. It was humiliating. Perhaps another day, I will tell you about all the humiliation and degradation that takes place in the justice department holding pens. And I have not even done hard time yet. Throughout this trial, personal humiliation will reach a new level for both me and others.

Raymond arrived, ready to go. He showed so much energy that I am sure that he drank a few Red Bulls prior to the start of today's theatrics. The effects showed. I was glad he was on my side. His eyes always told me his story. I liked the kid's focus. His eyes never lied. I hoped that laser beam focus would tear up the prosecutor.

The prosecutor and his entourage arrived not long after they seated me. They entered, with the boss leading the parade. His flunkies were behind him the requisite number of feet for his highness. Old Mr. Prosecutor did not look well today. He was already off his game.

The kid explained to me he liked where we were with the jury selection. It appeared the prosecutor was guilty of a little over confidence yesterday and burned some of his peremptory challenges. He only had six in total and he already used four of them. We had ten to use, and we only used three yesterday, so that left us with seven to go. I found out that these peremptory challenges are like gold and you never want to burn them because you will never know when you are going to need one. I likened it to time outs in a basketball or football game. You never want to burn any of those on stupid things early in the game. You need to save them for the end of the half or the end of the game. Court proceedings were easy for me to understand when I could put a sports analogy with them.

The judge started as warmly as yesterday, however quickly showed his teeth when the attorneys started bickering over some procedural nonsense. He assured both lawyers that they would complete jury selection on this day and the meat of the trial would begin tomorrow. Hell, that was fine with me. I wanted to get this damn thing over with quickly. If it all ended now, would the jury favor me?

The day was slow. However, some responses from the prospective jurors were hilarious. It appeared there was a preponderance of white folks sitting in the potential jury pool. Years ago, the only potential jurors were black or brown. The white folks knew how to play the system to get out of doing their duty to the community. That changed several years ago and now watching the good old white folks squirm and lie was comical.

Well, the judge was right. They completed jury selection concluded promptly at 6:00 P.M. in the evening. The kid had one of his challenges left and the Prosecutor was out of his. I thought that this was good.

The final jury comprised eight men and four women. The alternates were two women and one man. Of the fifteen people chosen as jurors and alternates, only four of them were white. Only one had a college degree. The kid was happy.

The return trip was a mirror of the trip in. The crowd was perhaps bigger. I saw some tents take shape. They were making a little tent city. Isn't that nice? I am sure the white mayor and council were happy about that. Let me also tell you that the crowd assembling was not all black. I would say 50% of the crowd was white. The Liberator was building a multiracial coalition. This would all be over soon. I had to enjoy it while I could. It might be my last enjoyment in quite a while.

The guards allowed me a shower that night and when I got back to my cell; they had a bag full of Chinese food waiting for me. If only we had a couple of beers, we could have had a little party.

Chapter One Hundred Eleven
First up, Dr. Death

Batting lead-off was the coroner. He was a morbid son of a bitch. How could he not be doing his daily work? He was an old timer and I would bet that he liked a taste of some Irish whiskey now and then (more now than then I am sure). He assured the crowd that the Chief died of strangulation from the hanging. It pleased me it was a slow death rather than a broken neck. For the right effect, the prosecutor had large poster size pictures made up to show the jury. I took a moment to study the jury. It did not bother them. That was a good sign. So, we all knew how the chief died and now we were going to hear about who helped him take his journey to the great beyond.

Batting second was my old friend Beavis. He was all decked out, including a new haircut. Frankly, I had never seen him look as good. He shared how he and his partner had completed a security audit for several months, on their own initiative, and then convinced the chief to upgrade the surveillance system. He was so full of shit I thought I had seen it coming out of his ears. Yes, he and Butthead had the system installed after they had set me up. Only somehow, they forget to tell me about the new system. Remember, they had the energy comparable to two sloths. They never had an original idea in their lives, let alone the wherewithal to complete it. You know, I have to take that back. I am sitting here getting ready for the lethal injection because of their initiative. Selfish motivation made men capable of moving mountains.

They ran the videotape and there I was, clear as day, in a posed picture in the bright sunlight taking care of the chief. I don't need to run through the entire thing. It was painful to watch. I have to say it was painful, not because of my actions, but because of the embarrassment. I wanted to run and hide. I know if I could blush; I was blushing. This went on most of the day. If I was to grade myself, I would have given myself an A. But that A quickly would get turned to an F because I got caught. How could I let those two fools, Beavis and Butthead, trick me like they did? Shit, forget about the lethal injection. I wanted to kill myself right there. And it did not trigger this response out of regret or remorse, because I had none. It was all about how foolish I felt getting used by them.

Upon the prosecutor's completion, the kid stood up once again and said, "no questions." What the hell was going on? Ask anything for Christ's sake.

Raymond told me to relax. He had it under control.

Chapter One Hundred Twelve
Next up, Big Lou and Little Miss Mary

I can assure you the ride back to the jail was not fun nor interesting on this night. Although the guards were nice again, I did not really feel like eating or showering. I was plunging into a depression. I slept little and was a bit surprised when they came to get me at about five in the morning. They hurried me out of the door and we were on the road by six. Court did not begin until 10:00. What the fuck was up? Well, it turned out that they did not want me to have the little bit of a thrill or exhilaration that the crowd provided. The prosecutor was running scared. At least, that is what I told myself. I only hoped that it was true. They dropped me in a holding cell next to the courtroom and the wait was tedious and tortuous. However, because I did not sleep well last night, I could doze a bit. They had to actually wake me to go into the courtroom.

Big Lou looked good, as did Miss Mary. She looked mighty fine. I smiled at Big Lou and he returned the smile. I liked him and he liked me. It was odd. I also gave him a look to show him I knew about him and Miss Mary, and he chuckled. I wanted to high five him, but I had to remember he was here to hang me. Shit, he was here because he had to be here. He knew in his heart that every killing was righteous. Remember, these civil right charges were add-ons. How many times could they kill me? All the evidence was just circumstantial, except my key collection that they now had, plus my personal notes. I blew it there. One should keep no notes or souvenirs. That stuff will do you in every time. But I thought it was circumstantial. I kept telling myself that.

Miss Mary took the stand and basically supported Lou's testimony and shared the financial costs that her old insurance company had to incur because of these deaths. It all fell on deaf ears because everyone was too busy flirting with Mary. She was showing the right cleavage, her skirt showed every curve and her shoes were knockouts. When she came within five feet of you, she just smelled wonderful. It was intoxicating. It was flat out hilarious watching the prosecutor and the judge playing to her. They were actually tripping over each other to impress her. I felt like telling both of them to put their tongues back in their mouths and put their eyeballs back into their sockets. She was all Big Lou's, and he seemed to do a good job of satisfying her.

The day closed with Mrs. Kelly taking the stand. I felt bad for her. She cried through most of her testimony, and the prosecutor did not keep her up there too long. We made eye contact, and I knew that even though she betrayed me, she loved me and I knew I loved her.

The day was almost over, and the kid still had not asked a question. I am glad that I was not paying him. I asked him a bit more sternly, what the fuck was up?

He once again put his hand on my shoulder and told me to relax. He assured me we were in a solid position. He shared he believed the prosecutor was way too arrogant and over-confident. Raymond believed he did not prepare his case.

We got the ball to start the second half. I am glad that he felt that way because by now I was just picturing myself on that gurney and wondering if I would be a man about it or would I be a crying like a little bitch. Time would tell.

Chapter One Hundred Thirteen
The second half kick-off

The judge was punctual and just like the NFL, if he said kick off was at 1:08, it occurred at 1:08, not a minute later or earlier. It was 10:00 o'clock, and the judge was bringing the courtroom to order. After the traditional morning pleasantries, Raymond got to play quarterback. But this was not a game. This was a fight for my life.

The jury had to like me. I tried everything that I could to make pleasant eye contact with them. I would nod good morning and show that I was paying close attention. I tried not to let my body language be any kind of "tell" that would work against me.

The first witness that the kid put on the stand was the local NAACP president. He walked her through a series of questions that painted the chief as a real bigot. She told the courtroom of situations where the chief not only served as an obstacle to any request from the black community; he undermined any activity that was ultimately planned. The chief thwarted any sort of community celebration. Yet the white community had carte blanche with him. Where was the equity?

She also provided data that showed that 80% of all the arrests during the chief's tenure were of black individuals. When one really thought about that, it was unbelievable because the black population of the town was only about 25% of the total population. Raymond could also drill down deeper and presented a series of poster sized prints showing the photos of those arrested. These individuals had any combination of their eyes swollen shut, lips bloodied and swollen, and an assortment of broken and disfigured noses. The overall picture that the kid presented was one of a police department being out of control and clearly a department that operated with a pervasive bigotry. The chief vehemently opposed the use of body cameras. If used correctly, these body cameras could help reduce the police brutality. But the chief never really wanted that to occur. He was OK with the young black men getting the shit beat out of them for some simple alleged offense.

I was surprised that the judge let all of this in. I was more surprised that the prosecutor did not object. He allowed Raymond to continue to kill the chief even though he was already cold, dead and buried.

Next up was the chairperson of one of the many block associations. The block associations were very important in the black community because they provided a sense of keeping the community and neighborhoods together. They usually centered on one of the black churches in town. The neighborhoods reflected the church. If asked, you identified yourself as being from a church area, not a street name. That said everything.

The churches and associations raised a little money for this and that, and they would always provide a little scholarship for several of the graduating seniors from the neighborhood. The chairperson's sole purpose was to show how the police, under the chief's direction, would harass the neighborhood children as they walked home from schools. One cannot argue that walking in the streets was a problem, but the solution that the chief instituted was to arrest as many black kids as possible and charge each juvenile with some sort of disorderly person offense. And now and then, one kid would resist and then all hell would break loose. Raymond could close with this witness, painting the picture of the chief's desire for every black juvenile to end up with some sort of police record. And once a kid had a record, charges would somehow just snowball. Her testimony became credible when she provided the real numbers of kids with records during his tenure. The chief's data was bullshit. It was unbelievable. The data did not lie. It showed basically no white juveniles being arrested. And believe me, if you did not see the data presented in that manner, you would never have believed it. We can chalk up a small win for my team.

The kid threw everyone a curve ball when he called Big Lou to the stand as a defense witness. I think this move surprised Big Lou as much as anyone. The kid wanted Big Lou to explain his role as a school administrator with the chief's frequent round-ups of stray street walkers. Big Lou did not disappoint me. He was both a prosecutor's witness and a witness for the defense. He told the truth and did not let me down. The chief ordered the arrests and encouraged the school to impose severe discipline on the students. That meant suspending more kids from school. That is exactly what the students did not need. They needed to be in school every day. Nothing good ever came from suspensions, except perhaps giving the school and teachers a rest from some of the terrible kids. Please, do not misinterpret what I am saying. Some kids had to go, but certainly not most of these students. When I look back, I think that maybe I should have liberated the school from some of these students. Oh well, you can't look back.

I now saw Raymond's direction. He was trying to make the chief look racist and evil. It had nothing to do with me. The chief's character was being assassinated by him. He was putting the victim on trial. He really could not dispute the videotape because there I was, this smiling fool, Tasing the chief and hauling him away in the back of my pickup truck.

We closed the afternoon when Raymond put on the stand the motel clerk where the chief conducted his extracurricular, extramarital business. I had a hard time not laughing. The prosecutor did not raise any objection. I know Raymond would have never let this happen. He was right. The prosecutor was ill prepared. However, I felt bad for the chief's wife sitting there. At about the midpoint of his testimony, I saw her leave the courtroom out of the corner of my eye. The clerk could provide video footage of the chief entering the motel on a variety of different Friday nights with a variety of different women. And in this footage, although not named directly, it was easy to recognize some of the young police women that the chief was bedding down. I also recognized one of our teachers joining him arm in arm on one night. One thing I will say for the old chief, he still had it going on at his age.

Raymond was successful in proving that the chief was without scruples or values. He was a bad guy. The inference was obvious. The chief had to go for the sake of the community.

As they hauled me back to jail for the night, I was feeling pretty good. I got back, and the guards were nice again and they allowed some television for me. I even got to take a shower. The demons were quiet in my head when I went to bed that night. Yes, it was a good day.

Chapter One Hundred Fourteen
Heading into the fourth quarter

We used the same procedure as the previous day to get me into the courtroom. I would say that the crowds were getting bigger and more television trucks were present. Once again, I took a little snooze in the anteroom. Although the kid never told me anything, I sensed that this trial was ending.

When I looked around the courtroom on this day, it looked different. I saw a fairly large group of middle-aged black men and a large group of middle-aged white women.

When I first saw Raymond, it looked as though they fired him out of a cannon. Man, something amped him up. He looked good, and he had the energy of a thousand men ready for battle. There was absolutely no worry or trepidation on his face. Once again, his eyes showed his intensity.

He called each one of the black guys to the stand and they all testified about how Principal Peoples treated them. The picture revealed that calling all of them niggers was only a part of it. It was easy to see. He treated them like slaves and second-class citizens. He continually gave the black kids the worst teachers. Suspension and retention rates of black students far exceeded those of white students. It was as though I could hear Peoples whistling Dixie from far away waving the Stars and Bars.

Everyone in the courtroom now knew that Peoples was an awful racist who somehow forget that slavery was over. Any black student that was in a school with Peoples never had a chance.

Raymond could also link the police chief with Peoples. Each of them acted in the same manner. The chief was a bit more subtle, but he was also from a different generation. Different generations or not, they were both similar racists.

This took us to the lunch break. I ate in the anteroom with a guard and the kid ate at the courtroom table with his associates, if he ate at all. I had a feeling we were going to be in for one hell of an afternoon because I now knew why all the women were there.

The afternoon session started promptly as usual, and then Raymond put each of the ladies on the witness stand. We then heard a long-drawn-out description from each one of them of the heinous acts perpetrated on them by Mr. Singleton. The stories were right out of some dark and dirty porno movie. I understood little of the psychological talk used by the doctors that Raymond put on the stand, but it clearly did not sound too good. Each girl was ready to tell her story about the sexual abuse perpetrated by this teacher. Their graphic stories made everyone sick. This all occurred on school property. Sex acts took place in offices, behind the stage, closets, in his car and on the catwalk high above the auditorium. I sat there and almost cried for these girls. Believe me, most people in the courtroom on this day were crying. The judge adjourned a bit early for the weekend. I don't know if anyone else could have taken any more of these horrible tales of abuse.

How could other adults not know? They knew and did nothing. Right now, sitting alone in the courtroom, I only wish that they could release the Liberator on some people who were as complicit in the Singleton's acts by ignoring them as the evil bastard committed them. And you know what, I almost got the feeling that if the Liberator could work, the judge might very well pin a medal on him.

The kid told me we would meet on Saturday to figure out how we were going to close this thing out.

For me, it was a very somber ride back to the jail. I did not eat on this night, nor did I sleep. I laid on my simple cot crying my eyes out for these girls. I was feeling good that I prevented more victims, but was kicking myself in the butt for not acting soon enough.

Chapter One Hundred Fifteen
The last drive?

Raymond and I met early on Saturday morning. I do not think that the kid slept any better than I did. For me, it was grief. For him, I think he was just sharpening his sword for the kill. The kid readied himself to call in a host of people prepared to assassinate the character of Ducky Donaldson, the custodian that got himself frozen, Mrs. Westerman, the big mouth, pushy, nosy do-nothing secretary that had the old equipment fall on her, and finally all the students that Mr. Solomon, the math teacher, tortured because of his cleaning and smell disabilities. They would have been excellent witnesses and maybe they would have been helpful if we put them on the stand before the women talked about Singleton, the deviant music teacher. We were now at a high. Putting these folks on would not help now and might only take away from the powerful testimony of the women. We decided our game plan was just about executed. All that was needed now was a powerful closing argument.

I did not even wonder if the kid would be ready. He was already raring to go. I told him to go home and relax, which I knew he would never do. He spent the rest of Saturday and Sunday polishing and practicing what might be the best speech of his life. I would spend the same time leafing through old magazines on my flimsy cot. Raymond was told that there would be no appeals if we lost. I was mentally, physically, and emotionally drained. I prepared myself to go meet my maker if that was the will of the people. I was going to walk out a free man, or I was going to walk right into the execution chamber to get the needle. He did not argue with me. Yet, he told me the game is never over until it is over. I knew that I have heard that one before. I am glad that he did not talk to me about some fat lady singing.

Chapter One Hundred Sixteen
The last play of the game

Monday morning came quickly. Believe me, time drags on in jail, but this weekend time just flew by. The guards once again got me out of bed early and allowed me a shower. I also could put a clean shirt on and once again a clean pair of drawers.

The crowd on the drive in was still large and perhaps growing. I saw people holding up the newspaper tabloids with my picture on the full page. I could not see the headlines, but I knew it was big and bold. Once again, local and national television trucks, with their satellite disks raised, lined the streets. I think everyone knew in their hearts that this circus was coming to a close.

I took my usual nap in the anteroom before the judge was ready for us, but this time, Raymond came in for an early morning visit. I have to say he looked good. He spent some time at the barbershop and was wearing a new suit. His shoes shined so brightly that the sun's reflection off of them could have blinded you. Before he ever opened his mouth, I knew he was ready. He told me of his final strategy, which I had already guessed.

Namely, he was going to rest our case and get right into the closing arguments. For this argument, we were like the visiting baseball team and batted first. I know I am mixing my sports up here, but it is my only frame of reference. Now, if we were playing football, we would be on the five-yard line ready to score with just one play left.

Just like on television, during that final desperation Hail Mary play, time seemed to stand still. The day for me was like watching myself on television going in slow motion.

The kid was high tech and used some vivid pictures of the victims of the chief's abuse. He hit heavy on the uncontrolled, if not encouraged, racism of the police department under the chief's direction and leadership. He called the chief corrupt and evil, and the crowd in the audience was nodding in affirmation. Also, Raymond had blown up some of the still pictures of the videotape of the chief heading into the hotel for his weekly Friday night sexual interlude. I looked around and did not see the chief's wife in the gallery. I thought that maybe she finally jumped off of his bandwagon.

The chief's morality in this trial took an enormous blow. And when Raymond put pictures of the chief walking to church hand in hand with his family right next to the chief entering the motel with one of his young cuties, the picture was powerful.

The kid pounded on this lack of ethics and morality and finally asked everyone to think about how many lives it ruined because of the chief's blatant racism and his tremendous ego. And his department followed his lead. He wanted to be king of the community and nothing was going to stand in his way. He was a power-hungry ego maniac.

His last attack on the chief came when he posted a picture of a good young black kid hanging from the swings by the neck after he committed suicide. The youngster's suicide note told of his disappointment because he shamed his family when he got caught up in one of the chief's round-ups for walking in the streets. A really nothing offense. Yet the youngster could not get over the guilt that he felt and the embarrassment that he caused his family. The youngster was on the fast track to a good college to help him get out of this town and now the only image that one could see was the young man hanging from the swings, with his neck stretched out and his eyes and tongue bulging out of his face. Raymond left that image on the screen for a while.

The kid then quickly attacked Singleton, the music teacher. Raymond had a split screen picture of every one of the victims that testified showing the student as a twelve or thirteen-year-old next to the person as an adult. Each victim had an individual slide and while they displayed the slide on the screen, he reviewed the sexual acts committed. He skillfully showed where in the building this monster perpetrated these crimes. No space in the school proved safe. As I looked to the audience, there was not enough Kleenex to go around. Several times, the judge had to warn the audience about outbursts.

Finally, Raymond listed the issues that the adult victims of his sexual abuse had to face. This rampant sexual abuse significantly altered lives. He enumerated the number of estimated counseling hours and costs to these ladies. He enumerated the number of divorces and failed relationships and then he finally spoke of the number of hospitalizations and the number of drug and alcohol abuse cases. The kid attached all the issues to the sexual abuse at the hands of this one teacher.

Raymond never mentioned the liberations. He thought he did not have to mention them. I am not sure if that was a good idea or not. Only time would tell. However, going in another direction now would have minimized the effects of the closing argument.

In closing, the kid emphatically stated that these were righteous kills. Left unchecked, each person would never stop doing harm to citizens of this community. They had to be eliminated. There was no other way. These murders were not the result of some evil person or some madman. These deaths resulted as an act of a savior, the Liberator. Gotham City had Batman. Metropolis had Superman, and this community had the Liberator. Instead of looking to convict him, they should look to pin a medal on him. Raymond let his words hang and then walked back to the defendant's table. Win or lose, I felt good. I was proud of the kid. I was glad that I had never switched to that big-time attorney. For me, it was over. Now the only question would be if my life, like my trial, would now be over.

Chapter One Hundred Seventeen
The final whistle

The judge ended the day on that note, which I think was good for me. They unceremoniously transported me back to the jail, and I ate a quiet dinner. Yeah, I felt good. I don't know if I felt good because I was optimistic about a good verdict, or I felt good because this nonsensical circus was about to end.

I ate a quiet meal and fell quickly asleep. It was perhaps the first good night's sleep that I have had in quite a while.

We were up bright and early again for the trip into the courthouse, and the mob scene had not changed. However, this time I saw some people wearing Batman outfits and many in Superman capes. I was probably most proud when I saw many with green capes adorning the big script capital L. Step aside; the Liberator is on his way into the courtroom.

There was no nap for me in the anteroom today because I slept well the previous night. The guards found some old automotive magazines that I happily thumbed through. It was hard to explain how I felt. I could not get a handle on my emotions. They were all over the place. I was flip flopping from periods of great happiness and anticipation to lows of depression and hopelessness. My stomach was jumping all over the place and I had to ask to go to the bathroom a bunch.

Soon, I walked with my escort into the courtroom, where I still viewed the crowd as pro Liberator. The judge was right on time, like always, and court began as soon as his gavel pounded the desk. Today, the sound of the gavel sounded like an explosion in my ears. It was now showtime, ladies and gentlemen.

Now it was the Prosecutor's turn. He, too, was going to use the television monitors like the kid did. He immediately put up on the screen the freeze frame of me, Tasing the chief. The picture stayed on the screen. One could see the distorted expression of the chief on the televisions in the courtroom. A shit-eating grin somehow adorned my face. This was not good. I wanted to throw up.

Next, he slowly and methodically showed pictures of each one of my liberations. Although he was evil, seeing Singleton's burned body was effective. Likewise, seeing Ducky frozen stiff with a pained look of anguish on his face was equally effective. The prosecutor then followed with pictures of Mrs. Westerman crushed and bloody by the old copy machines in the stockroom. For a final effect he put the picture of Mr. Solomon, the crazy math teacher turned blue, who crawled up against the door with his fingernails broken and bloody and ripped apart with the scratch marks on the oak door as he tried to claw his way out of the storeroom. To be honest, I had to turn my head away because it was gruesome. And yes, it was highly effective.

The prosecutor just turned to the jury and said, "The evidence speaks for itself. This man who calls himself the Liberator is nothing more than an evil killer who saw himself as the jury and executioner for this community. He is responsible for at least eight deaths. Eight deaths that we know about. Eight deaths that had this Liberator's signature all over them. Now I ask you, who elected him as God?" Then he marched to the jury box and pointed at each individual juror and asked each one specifically, "Did you?" No one answered him directly, but it was theatrical. It had an effect.

He returned to the Prosecutor's table and loudly and powerful declared, "your Honor, the prosecution rests!"

And like that, it was over. It probably took about fifteen minutes in total. Did it have the same impact as the kid's closing? Who knows? But remember, in this land of ours, the prosecution gets the last word.

Then, for the next several hours, the judge explained the rules to the jury. The rules seemed complicated and bored me. I almost dozed off. My ears came alive when he talked about the options if they could not reach a verdict. The jury went to have lunch and then went straight to the deliberation room at about one o'clock.

But how in the hell could the jury not reach a guilty verdict? After all, I was guilty as hell.

Chapter One Hundred Eighteen
Do I get the big box or the curtain?

Raymond joined me in the anteroom, where they brought me my usual bologna sandwich and an apple. It was the same lunch that I have had every day since the trial started. It was OK, but inside me I was hoping for a little something else. One thing that I have learned since they have incarcerated me was that everything and everyone operated with a set of routines and practices and they never, ever deviated from them. Was it just easier doing things that way? No, everything here is about control and power. You learn that quickly.

We briefly hashed over the trial and the kid did his best to keep my hopes alive. Yet inside, I knew I was a goner. How could I not be?

When the verdict came in, I would go directly back into the courtroom. That was it. It was kind of anticlimactic. My feelings were all over the place. This spot was new to me.

On the way back, I noticed the crowds were thinning out and several of the television trucks were packing up. When this was over, I knew I would be yesterday's news until they executed me. Then I would be back on the front page.

I arrived back at the jail at about 3:30. It was going to be a long night.

Tonight, during the meal, the guards explained to me that a quick verdict would most likely ensure guilt. They told me I should hope that the jury would be out for a long while. They were sure it would be days, if not weeks. And during this time period, I would be their guest. I might as well enjoy it.

The guards hung around with me while I ate. At about 7:00 P.M., they locked everything down. I felt myself slowly nodding off, fully dressed, into what would be a deep sleep.

Chapter One Hundred Nineteen
The last knock

Well, there was really no knock. There was just the clanging of the cell bars. In walked Raymond and with him my minister. Raymond looked like crap. He hasn't slept and I doubt if he shaved in the last week. Like always, he carried his briefcase in. But I did not recognize this stooped over person who looked like a little old man. I knew that regardless of the outcome of my trial, Raymond's career would benefit from it. However, today it looked like he would never practice law again.

Soon, the guards brought in the food that I had requested. Yes, folks, this would be my last meal.

I had told you that there would be no appeals and there were not any pleas for mercy. Shit, I did not want to spend the rest of my natural life in any six by eight-foot cage like some animal. That was not for me. We were also in an era now where states could not execute you fast enough. I know that in society, the death penalty is a fiercely debated issue. I was just unlucky enough to be caught on the upside of the pendulum that swings back and forth. A swift death penalty and execution awaited me.

The guards brought me a new set of prison garb to wear for the day. It was nice of them to ask me my sizes the night before. They wanted to make sure that my clothes fit just right, so I looked good as I died. Mission accomplished. The clothes fit perfectly. However, the sizes of my new clothes told me I was withering away. Stress is a good weight loss program.

Raymond and I shared a case of White Castle hamburgers and chocolate shakes. My minister just sat there reading from the good book. If he was reading aloud, I did not hear him. I also enjoyed one last cup of Dunkin' Donuts coffee. Raymond pleaded with me to allow him to appeal. But I declined. I had no other visitors. It was nice of my preacher to join me for my last journey.

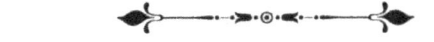

Chapter One Hundred Twenty
What's the buzz?

Yes, there has been a buzz going on in my head since the trial ended. I think that my biggest fear would be that I would not walk to the death chamber like a man. And I am a man and would go to my last destination with my head held high, moving under my own power.

I was proud of what I had done. I had no remorse. Let me rephrase that. I only had remorse for the chief's wife and his kids. They were innocent victims. But I learned in the army that in any war, you would have some collateral damage. And yes, I was waging war on what I perceived as the evil in this community. I hoped they would forgive me and perhaps years from now would thank me.

I know that many of the folks on death row ask for some sort of forgiveness or apologize for their actions. Not me. I was not sorry, and I felt I did not have to apologize to anyone, with the exception that I just mentioned.

Raymond and I made some small talk and tried to tell some funny stories. Mostly, we were unsuccessful. There is nothing funny about putting a man to death. I can attest to that.

We were ready for that long walk. My accommodations were now right next to the death chamber. I knew that this short walk would seem like miles. Thankfully, they gave me a strong sedative to take my edge off.

The last thing they made me do was to put on an adult sized diaper. That was the most humiliating thing in my life. They did not want me to soil their clean and sterile death chamber. People told them that on upon death, I would lose any sort of control over my bowels and bladder. All I could think of was, "let's get this thing over with." That is the actual torture. The genuine pain. The actual effect of the death penalty. I tried to fight them on this, but the effects of the sedative had already kicked in.

I was proud of myself that I walked down the hallway like a man. I was ready. I was not kicking and screaming. Not one of the five guards that served as my escorts had to hold me up. All I heard was the preacher. (And I wish he would just shut up already.)

Chapter One Hundred Twenty-One
Inside the death chamber

The five guards that helped me into the room lifted me onto the gurney and strapped me down. My knees were wobbly. The straps held me tight. Some medical technician had already put a stent into my arm for the intravenous line, which would transport the chemicals into my system used to kill me. The warden stood next to me. After about ten minutes, time no longer meant too much for me. They tilted me up to about a 45-degree angle and the curtains opened before me.

I quickly made eye contact with Raymond. The kid did one hell of a job defending me. I hope this case would catapult his career.

Next, my eyes then shifted to Big Lou and Mary Magdela, the new power couple in town. Lou smiled at me and gave me a thumbs up sign and Mary just sat there looking pretty. Even as I awaited death by the state, I had to check out Miss Mary. She looked as fine as ever and I am sure that she bought a new execution outfit for this day. Big Lou and Mary never disappointed me. I wished them the best.

Also in the crowd, I spied Beavis and Butthead sitting there now with shit-eating grins on their faces. I am sure that they were enjoying this. They were just pawns. One day they could sit where I am now. I used to think that they were harmless fools. Now, their guile and wit proved me wrong.

Th chief's widow sat nearby and my quick assessment of her told me it did not overly upset her and was really only here for the show.

Finally, as I panned the crowd of about 15 people, I saw Mrs. Kelly sitting in the back, crying. She looked awful. She was hurting. Her eyes somehow pleaded with me to just get up. This was not possible. I could not take my eyes off of her. Perhaps I was sorry after all. Sorry for the pain that I caused her. Sorry for her disappointment and, yes, grief. Maybe we were in love. It just pissed me off. Why did it take me so long to find love? Why did I have to be on death's doorstep to feel what love was really all about?

When asked by the warden if I had any last words, I passed. My work spoke for itself. He then read the death warrant aloud. This gave him the state's permission to kill me. I hope he can live with it. I certainly can't.

The last sounds I heard was the push and pull of some machinery from the closet behind me. My eyes never left Mrs. Kelly. It is over.

Epilogue
There was no song from the fat lady.

It is not over until that fat lady sings. And for me, the fat lady would have to wait for another day to sing for me.

After about three or four hours, two guards awakened me, shaking me. I blinked my eyes hard and fast. Was I dead? It was hard to awaken from such a deep sleep. A deep sleep brought on by my emotional exhaustion. I struggled with the guards while they assured me I was not dead, but the jury had returned with a verdict. One way or the other, it would be my last trip over to the courthouse.

My execution was just a damn dream. I surely hoped that it was not a predictor of what was to come. It is funny that for months now; I did not think that I cared if I lived or died. Who was I kidding? I wanted to live, and I wanted to live badly. I hoped for a future.

They unceremoniously marched me over to the courthouse and took my assigned seat at the defense table, where I shortly stood to hear my **NOT GUILTY** verdict.

My knees buckled, and I almost went down. The kid held me up. The prosecutor was as astonished as me. He took a fit. The judge, acting on the prosecutor's demand, individually polled each juror. Each juror stood tall and proud and looked right at me and said, "Not guilty."

It was short and sweet. I was a free man. Afterwards, some jurors came up to me and thanked me for my service. I was speechless. Everyone in the courtroom was speechless.

Raymond won the big one. I could no longer call him "the kid." He played for jury nullification and got it. He made me the sympathetic figure looking to save a community. Yes, this community was looking to save itself from itself. Does that make any sense? It would if you lived there. The evil had to be removed, never to return. None of my liberations would ever return. They existed no more. They were righteous kills. I think I told you that before. I killed no one that did not need killing.

I was a free man. Down the road, could they bring some other charges against me? Who knows and right now who cares? I was walking out of this. And I was walking out of this community.

At the bottom of the stairs, I saw the person I was looking for. We made eye contact from far away and by the time I got to the curb, Kelly leaped into my arms. We embraced for a few moments and jumped into her car. I escaped the press. As we were speeding away, I saw Big Lou and Miss Mary arm in arm, headed to his car. He gave me a big smile and two thumbs up. After all, Big Lou and I were still members of the "good old boys" club.

I let the Raymond handle all the publicity. He was going to be on every news network and television talk show. How he could craft out this verdict was amazing. He deserved all the attention and hopefully winning this case would catapult his career to some fame and the big bucks. I would forever be indebted to him.

Well, Kelly had already left her dead-beat husband, and we just got into the car and drove. Our destination pointed south. We both liked the warm climates and the beach. I liked to fish and Kelly just liked to hang out in the sun.

We found a small town, I won't tell you where, but it was nice and peaceful. The Liberator was going to retire. Then one Sunday, Kelly and I saw an advertisement in the local paper that the local school district had several openings for secretaries and custodians. Another district needed us. They accepted our application and our new work life began. Maybe the Liberator lived on after all. Time will only tell.

About the Author

This is Louis Edwards' first fictional work. He used his almost 4o years of school administrative experiences to help guide him as he created this novel. Edwards has published two works of non-fiction about school life and school leadership written from an administrator's perspective. He has presented on the national level and has served on several school improvement national committees. Edwards continues to mentor new principals and continues to write about school leadership. If one looks closely, many of the themes presented in **Cleansed** can be used as school leadership lessons.

CPSIA information can be obtained
at www.ICGtesting.com
Printed in the USA
BVHW071058300922
648138BV00001B/85